TALES FROM THE LAUNDRY PILE

TALES FROM THE LAUNDRY PILE

Kathleen Kole

This is a work of fiction. Names, characters, places and incidents are either the product of the author's imagination or are used fictitiously, and any resemblance to actual persons, living or dead, business establishments, events or locales is entirely coincidental.

TALES FROM THE LAUNDRY PILE

Copyright © 2013 by Kathleen Kole

ISBN-13: 978-09868956-9-2
ISBN-10: 0-9868956-9-5

This book is published by Sublime Coyote Media. For more information please visit sublimecoyote.com.

For Peter.
My Heart.

CHAPTER 1

Claire pushed her sandy blonde bangs from her forehead and regarded the chaos masquerading as her kitchen. God, moving was a nightmare. Boxes everywhere, cupboard doors ajar, dusty tile floors and a pile of clothes growing at an alarming rate in the adjacent laundry room. How was it possible to have that many clothes already awaiting the washing machine, when she'd worked her tail off before they'd left the city making sure everything came to the new house clean and fresh? It was a mystery.

She lifted the damp hair sticking to the back of her neck. Man, it was hot. She'd forgotten just how steamy it could get in Boxwood Hills in the summertime. She stepped around a box labeled *Kitchen Dishes* and padded on bare feet toward the thermostat in the hallway, keen to fire up the air conditioning. Halfway there, she was stopped in her tracks by a loudly shouted, "Mommy!" from the backyard.

"Oh, hell." Claire spun on her heel and rapidly retraced her steps back to the kitchen. "What new emergency is this?"

She didn't have long to find out. Before she'd taken her last step back onto the dusty kitchen tiles, Claire's identical twin sons came charging through her wooden framed screen door, swinging it so hard she winced.

"Slow down!" she blurted, hands clenched by her sides. They never seemed to do anything gently. They were like two reckless sheep, bouncing off of everything in their path. "We need to keep that door *on* its hinges, at least for the summer. Okay?"

"Look what we found!"

Claire's voice clogged in her throat as she looked down at the delighted grin on her son's round face. Noah's hazel eyes sparkled as he clutched an armful of something grey and clearly living.

"It's a cat!" His voice was even higher and squeakier than normal in his excitement.

Claire smoothed her hands down the front of her jean shorts and took a steadying breath. If it wasn't one thing, it was another.

"Isn't it cool?" Evan, his voice an echo of his brother's, piped up.

"Now listen," Claire began, preparing to inform them they'd probably cat-napped someone's pet, when the animal turned its face toward her and fixed her with its large, orange eyes. "Holy Dina," she exhaled, reflexively taking a step back.

"I don't know, Mommy." Noah's dark brown eyebrows pulled together, his tone heavy with skepticism. "It doesn't look like a Dina to me."

Evan shook his head, his face equally serious. "No. Not Dina. More like an Elmo, or Arthur."

Noah's face lit up. "Arthur!"

"Wait!" Claire raised her hands in front of her imploringly, trying to get her bearings. Four and a half years later and she still found herself struggling to keep up with them. And the older they got, the worse it seemed to get. "Before you go naming it, remember it probably belongs to someone nearby, making it someone's pet."

Noah shrugged his narrow shoulders beneath his blue and red striped t-shirt while the cat lounged, dead weight, half hanging from his embrace. "It was on the street."

"Then it probably, or rather *definitely*, belongs to one of our neighbors." Claire folded her arms across her chest and tried to look firm.

"But not on *our* street," Evan finished, while picking grass from his green and yellow striped t-shirt.

"Pardon me?" Claire's eyebrows shot up on her forehead to be hidden behind her shaggy bangs.

Evan placed his small hands on his hips and said, matter of fact, "We found it on the street over there." He proceeded to point toward the back door, as though that would make his directions more clear.

Claire was sure she felt a twitch beginning in her left eye. "Boys!" she said, tugging the bottom of her baggy, beige t-shirt in frustration. "How many times have I told you, you must stay in your own yard, never mind on your own street?"

"Lots?"

Claire frowned at Evan's reply, or rather question. "Yes, *lots*. And, even before we left the city, Daddy and I specifically said you had to stay in your *own* yard, remember? *Specifically*."

Claire clenched her teeth so hard she thought she might give herself lockjaw. Good God, was it a sign of her being an utterly crap parent that her sons seemed to take her directions as nothing more than mere suggestions? If they were like this at four and a half, what in the hell did that say about the future? Was she going to have to resort to drinking, just to survive their teen years?

"It looked lost." Noah's eyes grew round and pleading. "When we found it under the bush—"

"Which explains the grass stains on your knees and the leaves in your hair," Claire said, cutting him off. They'd been so clean and non-smudged when they'd left the house a mere half hour ago. And now.... Well, the less said the better.

"No, Mommy." Evan stretched his arms wide and did a small spin on the spot as he swiftly came to his brother's defense. "The grass stains aren't from the bush at all. They're from playing tag."

Claire released her t-shirt from her grasp and tried to smooth the wrinkles she'd created. "What, on your knees?"

"Yup!" Evan grinned. "Animal tag. It was fun!"

"Okay, fine." Claire took a breath and focused on the present. "Priorities. Stains are the least of our worries at the moment. First thing we have to do is get this cat back to where you found it."

"Awww," Noah began to whine as his arms sagged and the cat dangled more loosely in his grasp.

"No." Claire wagged her finger at him. "No *awwwing* at me. We're not stealing someone's cat and that's final. For goodness sake, we've only been here a day and a half and there's no way we're acquiring a reputation for thieving our neighbor's pets! At the very least, we need to pace ourselves."

"What's reputation?" Evan scratched his cheek with a dirty hand.

Claire suppressed a groan. What she really wanted to do was toss the pair of them in the tub. But, no. Instead, she had to deal with a stolen cat and a dictionary lesson. "Umm, well, it means people could think you're one way, even when you're not that way."

"Like what?"

"Like...." Claire fished around in her brain for an example. She snapped her fingers. Found it. "Like they could mistakenly think you're a meanie, when you're really very nice."

Evan nodded while, beside him, Noah's fingers started to unlace; allowing the cat to slowly ooze from his embrace.

"Whoa," Claire said, quickly stepping forward to catch the animal before it hit the floor. It was so relaxed when it dropped into her hands, she felt a stab of worry it might be more dead than alive. However, the moment she had it in her grasp and it twisted its neck around to give her its full attention with its large orange eyes, Claire knew her worries were unfounded. Score one point for their side.

"Good catch, Mommy," Evan said, sounding just like his father.

"Thank you," she replied, before a shudder ran up her spine. Against her better judgement, she was going to have to hug the cat closer to her body. It was that or dangling it in front of her, which felt wrong. She really didn't want to, who knew where it had been, but basic decency won out. Damned decency.

"Now what?" Noah cocked his head of messy brown hair as he gazed up at her.

"Now, you show me where you found it."

The boys' were at once all smiles and excitement at the idea of leading their mother on an adventure. Claire couldn't help but grin at their enthusiasm. She turned her back on the disarray of her kitchen, maneuvered around the jumble of boxes on the floor, slipped on her blue sandals and followed them out of the house.

* * * *

Claire's sandals slapped sharply against the pavement as she walked stiffly behind Noah and Evan, the cat still in her grasp. The two of them chatted back and forth to one another, oblivious to the fact that their mother was becoming more and more vexed the further they walked. Under normal circumstances, she might have been admiring the thick foliage in her neighbor's yards and appreciating the way the warm yellow sunshine dappled across the green leaves. Or, she might have been savoring the sweet smell of blooming lavender on the breeze. Possibly, she'd even be enjoying the melodic song being sung by the robins in the treetops. But, she wasn't. Instead, tension pulled across Claire's shoulders as Evan and Noah led her not down their own street, but around the corner and into the neighboring, skeleton key shaped crescent that backed on their own.

My God! They were so far from home! Claire was becoming increasingly concerned she might start to hyperventilate if they didn't soon stop walking. They were in so much trouble for wandering off. She wanted to jump up and down and stamp her feet in agitation. However, first things first. The cat, or *evidence* as she'd been starting to think of it, needed to be dumped.

"Over there." Noah pointed ahead of himself, while skipping along the hot sidewalk in his red and black Velcro sneakers.

"The cool looking one," Evan added, his legs moving at speed as he gave it his all to match Noah step for step.

Claire glanced at the homes on the street. In her opinion, they all were pretty 'cool' looking. Much like the houses on her block, the residences were cottage style with brightly painted, shutter framed windows, deep front porches, cobblestone paths, lots of green grass and flowers....

Well, all except for that one up ahead on the right.

She grimaced as they traipsed closer to the house. With its weathered grey paint, dirty windows and peeling white frames, it had definitely seen better days. And the yard? Whew. Branches from overgrown oak trees swept across the front sidewalk, weeds were growing between the path stones, gnarly looking bushes sat in unkempt clumps, the lawn hadn't seen a mower in a good long while; the entire property appeared to have been left to do as it pleased.

Evan and Noah halted on the sidewalk and turned around to face Claire.

"Whoops!" She was unprepared for their abrupt stop and swiftly stepped to the left so as not to run right smack into them and send them tumbling down onto the pavement. She squinted into the sunshine as she read the expectant expressions on their identical faces and sighed. Of course. She took one more glance at the derelict house and asked, "*This* is the cool one, right?"

"Yes!" Evan punched his small fist into the air above his head and Claire raised an eyebrow. Where on Earth had he learned that trick?

"Fine. Perfect." She shrugged, then turned to face the edge of the yard, hesitant to cross into it and be caught on the property. Who knew what sort of person was lurking inside? Or, for that matter, what was lying in wait in the overgrown grass? "Let's hurry and put the cat back and get out of here before we're spotted."

"Maybe it doesn't live here," Noah said, shrugging his shoulders in a perfect imitation of his mother.

"Maybe it was just visiting." Evan's face was thoughtful.

Oh, boy. That's all she needed. A debate. No thanks. Claire leaned forward from her waist and prepared to drop the cat into the yard. "Well, if that's the case, then it can make the choice to leave from here and go back to wherever it—"

The front door to the neighboring house opened - a well-kept, slate blue house with pristine white frames it needed to be said - and a tall, curvaceous redhead stepped out onto the porch.

Claire froze, her voice caught in her throat.

"Wherever it *what*, Mommy?" Noah cocked his head.

Claire barely registered his question. She was too busy feeling like a child caught with her hand in the cookie jar. Oh, crap, she thought, desperately. Please don't look this way, please don't look this way.

The woman locked her door, flipped her long auburn curls behind her shoulders and turned around; an expectant expression on her pretty face. Claire cringed when it occurred to her she'd probably been watching them the entire time from inside her house. Who knew what conclusions she'd already drawn? Or authorities she'd already called?

"Hello!" The woman waved broadly and smiled in a friendly manner as she walked down her wooden porch steps, her ankle length, sunshine yellow skirt flowing behind her as she crossed the lush green lawn.

Claire eased herself back upright and gave a weak smile in return, desperately wracking her brain for a reasonable explanation for their presence.

"Hi!" Noah blurted, giving her an extra moment to think.

"Hi!" Evan echoed, adding yet another.

The woman grinned at the boys. "Well, hello!" She looked into Claire's blue eyes. "I'm Jessica. I live next door. Can I help you with something?"

Claire tried not to gape. It was just she'd lived so long in the city, she couldn't remember the last time a stranger had voluntarily offered her help.

"Are you looking for an address?"

Claire cleared her throat, then attempted a small, casual laugh. She hoped she wasn't as disheveled as her sons, but had a strong suspicion she was. "Oh, well, that's very surprising."

"Pardon?" Jessica raised her eyebrows and blinked.

"Sorry, I just wasn't expecting...." Claire smiled and skipped over her thoughts. No need to expound about her surprise.

Jessica waited.

"Anyway! Yes, please. I think you just might be the perfect person to assist us." She swallowed and hoped it wasn't noticeable that sweat was starting to form under her arms.

"We found that cat," Noah offered, helpfully, and pointed at the grey cat still lounging languidly in Claire's embrace. It was nearly asleep and had started to purr.

"*And*, even more importantly, we're trying to return it," Claire added, making sure there were no questions about what they were doing lurking around on the sidewalk. She looked at Jessica and asked, "Is it yours?"

"Oh, okay, now I see," Jessica began, but was silenced as Claire pressed on.

"Or, does it maybe live around here?" she glanced at the peaceful, picture perfect crescent. The street sign had said *Sunrise Place*, how fitting.

"Actually," Jessica attempted to start again.

"Because the boys said they found it here. And since I was inside unpacking in the kitchen, I didn't actually get to *see* them find it. Not that they wander around alone as a rule, of course. No, no. They don't." Claire shook her head to emphasis her words and her bangs swept forward into her eyes. She peered between them.

Jessica nodded. "Okay."

"It's just that I said they could go outside for a moment or two for some fresh air, with the stipulation they had to stay in the yard of course, but did they listen? Nope. Granted, they're only four, so...." Claire shrugged her shoulders.

"And a half, Mommy," Noah threw in.

"Right." She nodded at him. "And a half. So, anyway, they sometimes get caught up in their games and forget what I've told them."

Claire stopped prattling and caught her breath. Jessica's green eyes had grown steadily wider the longer she'd chattered and she wanted to smack herself. She was doing it again. Rambling at top speed. She always did that when she was flustered; began talking and talking. And the boys seemed to give her many reasons to get flustered. Well, it was a vicious circle.

"Actually," Jessica offered, again, taking advantage of Claire's need for oxygen. "I do know this cat. He belongs to my neighbor." She pointed at the overgrown yard the boys had labeled 'cool'. "His name is

Corkscrew. He prowls around this yard and the neighborhood; harmless."

"Corkscrew?" Claire repeated, taken aback. "Your neighbor's name is Corkscrew?"

"Oh, no!" Jessica laughed a pretty trill, displaying straight, white teeth. "Not my neighbor. I meant the cat. The cat's name is Corkscrew."

Corkscrew raised his head at the sound of his name.

Jessica shrugged. "My best guess is it must have something to do with his kinked tail."

"You smell nice." Evan smiled at Jessica, his hazel eyes shining up at her.

"Thank you." She grinned in return, charmed to her core.

Claire nodded, processing what Jessica had said, then promptly extended the smoke colored animal away from her body. Now that she knew it belonged there, she was thrilled to get rid of it. She placed Corkscrew gently into the overgrown grass on the property, even though what she really wanted was to toss him and run. But that would have looked odd.

"Well, now that we have that sorted, perhaps we can start again." Jessica smiled widely and extended a slim, manicured hand. "I'm Jessica and it's lovely to meet you."

Claire was slightly dazzled by her open friendliness. She quickly wiped her palms on the front of her shorts and brushed her bangs away from her eyes. "I'm Claire and these are my sons, Noah and Evan," she said, while reaching out to shake the hand being offered. "They're usually less weathered looking. We all are."

Jessica laughed and shook both boys' hands as she had done Claire, making them grin from ear to ear. "Nice to meet you," she told them, while Claire watched and marveled at how much she looked like a cartoon princess come to life.

"I like your shoes." Noah pointed at one of Jessica's purple strappy sandals, adorned with yellow flowers and rhinestones that traveled across the arch of her foot.

"Thank you!" Jessica looked at Noah's sneakers. "I like yours and your brother's, too. Very cool."

"Alrighty, then." Claire, eager to move things along, interrupted the compliment fest. "Thanks so much for your help. I can't tell you how relieved I am this turned out okay."

"No problem at all." Jessica smiled at the boys.

"Anyway, it's getting hot," she added, nudging Noah and Evan with her knee. "And we really shouldn't take up any more of your time."

"Right." Jessica nodded. "You probably want to get some cool drinks going."

"We live over there," Evan said, pointing to his right. Claire raised an eyebrow at his 'directions'. Oh yeah, he was on a direct path straight into manhood alright.

"We're on the street behind you," she elaborated. "*Mountainview Terrace*. We just moved in yesterday, in fact."

"That's what I said." Evan shrugged his shoulders at Noah as if to say Claire was the one who was a bit clueless.

Jessica, putting the pieces together, nodded. "Oh, okay. That explains why we haven't crossed paths before. I know the house. I saw the sign on the lawn when I was out for a walk. Nice place."

Claire smiled. She liked this woman. "Thanks, we like it."

"You can come and visit us," Evan informed her, nodding his head up and down.

"*Evan*," Claire said, her voice full of warning. "Remember what we talked about? About putting people on the spot?" She smiled apologetically at Jessica. "Sorry. We're just learning this one."

Jessica opened her mouth, then shut it again as she looked off into the distance behind Claire's head. Claire twisted around, followed her gaze and blinked. Holy Dina.

* * * *

A middle aged man loped around the side of the dilapidated house and Claire froze like a doe in headlights. He was a vision.

"There's Thomas." Jessica's face broke into a sunny smile as the man raised a hand in greeting.

Claire was speechless. Sporting creased tartan-patterned cargo pants and a faded grey t-shirt, his unkempt salt and pepper colored hair waving in the light breeze, Thomas began to saunter toward them, smoke trailing behind him from a cigarette dangling loosely between his lips above his greying van dyke beard. If she hadn't know better she'd have thought Billy Connolly, or at least his brother, had shown up in Boxwood Hills.

"Is that cat his?" Noah asked, his eyes wide as he watched Thomas wade through the overgrown grass and weeds.

"Uh-huh," Jessica answered.

"Oh, boy." Claire found her voice and turned to face Jessica. "Listen, we don't want any trouble. When the boys found the cat, they didn't realize it could be seen as stealing if they took it."

"Claire," Jessica said, attempting to stop her in her verbal tracks.

"And, if your neighbor was missing it," she didn't miss a beat. "I don't want them to get into trouble because of their innocence."

"*Claire.*" Jessica placed a gentle, calming hand on Claire's forearm. "Relax. If there's one thing I'm sure of, it's that Thomas did not notice Corkscrew's absence." She saw the skepticism on her face and added, "Honestly. I'm not stretching the truth whatsoever."

"*Still,*" Claire began, before Jessica stopped her a second time.

"*And,* even if by some miracle he did happen to notice - which I'm sure he didn't," she repeated, patting Claire's arm soothingly as Thomas took his final steps through the yard and met them at the sidewalk. "I'd be willing to bet big money he made the assumption Corkscrew was off on an adventure. Trust me, *nothing* fazes this man."

"Guid efternuin, thar!" Thomas nodded congenially, completely unaware of the fretting going on.

Claire gaped at the Scottish brogue that came out of the man's mouth. Seriously? What were the odds? She snapped her jaw shut, then darted her eyes back and forth, wondering for a brief moment if she was being recorded for some type of pranking program.

"Hey, Thomas." Jessica let her hand drop from Claire's arm. "Meet some new neighbors from the street next door." She gestured to Claire. "Thomas MacLeod, please meet Claire—"

"Jamieson," Claire supplied, politely. "Nice to meet you, Sir," she said, extending her hand.

Thomas released a bark of laughter, making his cigarette bob up and down between his lips and the ash at its tip break loose to drift lazily toward the ground. "Aye, lass, I donna give any tuck to formalities. *Sir* is for me Da. Call me Thomas." He turned his focus to Noah and Evan. "And who might yea lads be?"

Noah was the first to speak up. "I'm Noah."

"I'm Evan." Evan furrowed his brow as he stared intently at Thomas. "Why do you smoke?"

"Evan!" Claire said, aghast. "Be polite!"

Thomas laughed again, sending more smoke and ash fluttering around them. "Nay a worry," he said, before addressing Evan. "Guid question, lad. And guid name ya 'ave there. Smokin' is a part o' me heritage. The MacLeod family is riddled with a long line o' smokers."

Evan nodded and turned to Claire. "Is smoking a part of our family's hair tidge?"

"No!" Claire's eyebrows shot up in alarm. She blushed and tried to cover her hasty reply with a short laugh.

Noah scratched his knee. "What's a tidge?"

"Like a bridge," Evan said, matter of fact.

Claire left them to it and turned to Thomas. "Please excuse them." She pressed her hands to her pink cheeks as she apologized. "They're, umm, usually much more, umm...."

"Nay a worry." Thomas shrugged his shoulders.

She paused to catch her breath and slow down her speech. "Well, we've only just moved in. And they're getting used to being in a new house and a new neighborhood."

"Juist lads being lads. Reminds me of another bairn, well grown now, who badgered me somethin' fierce ta build one o'them small carts with wheels. Long time ago mind, but juist the same—"

"*You* made a go-kart?" Noah spun on his heel and stared up at Thomas, his eyes bright with excitement.

"Aye." Thomas pointed a finger at him. "That's exactly what he called it."

Evan jumped up and down on the spot. "What color? Was it fast? Did it have a steering wheel?"

"Boys!" Claire blurted, then smiled apologetically at Jessica when she jumped in response. "Stop badgering Mister, umm, Mister Thomas."

Thomas exhaled a stream of smoke and grinned at Noah and Evan. "You lads like cars then, aye?"

Noah nodded enthusiastically. "Yes! Daddy said we could build one, but he needs someone to draw it first."

"Instructions," Claire explained. "He needs a kit to work from."

"Ach!" Thomas shook his head. "*Dinnae fash yersel.* Tis a straight forward task."

"Pardon me?" Claire was at a loss as to what he'd said.

"Dinnae," he paused, cleared his throat and tried again. "Ya dinnae have ta go stressin' yourself over kits and such."

"Oh." Claire nodded, finally understanding. "Right."

"Well, now *that's* an interesting thought." Jessica cocked her hip to the side and wagged her finger back and forth between the boys and Thomas. "Maybe *you* could work with Noah and Evan to build a go-kart, Thomas."

Oh, no." Claire grimaced and extended her hands to pat the air in front of her in an attempt to slow things down. "Really, Mister, I mean *Thomas*, there's no need–—"

"Pleeeease, Mommy," Evan begged, his small hands clutched together as though praying.

Claire let her hands fall to her sides and raised an eyebrow. Where had he learned that move? Clearly children's programming was teaching a new set of skills that hadn't been around in her day.

Jessica grinned. These boys were good. "Maybe Mommy wants to have a think on it, and Mister Thomas as well." She looked at Claire, hoping she'd said the right thing.

"Yes!" Claire snatched up the life preserver offered. "That's exactly right. I have to talk to Daddy first and, of course, Mister Thomas might be very busy and not have the time."

Thomas took a last drag on his cigarette, then dropped it to the pavement and ground it out with the heel of his boot. "All guid for me. Juist say the wurd and we'll wurk it oot."

Jessica threw a virtual life raft Claire's way and changed the subject. "So," she asked, while Thomas bent down to retrieve the stamped cigarette butt from the sidewalk and stuff it into his pocket. "Whereabouts did you say you all were moving from?"

"Oh." Claire was taken off guard by the question. Of course, it was a reasonable inquiry. She just hadn't yet wrapped her mind around having to start telling their background. "We're moving back from the city."

"And that's why we don't have a go-kart yet," Evan piped up as he sat down and made himself comfortable on the pavement.

Noah nodded sagely, backing him up. "It's hard to have fun stuff in the city."

Jessica bit her lip, trying to suppress a grin at their tenacity.

Claire shot a narrow-eyed glare at the pair of them.

"So, by 'back' do you mean you're originally from Boxwood Hills, then?"

"Uh-huh." Claire tucked her hair behind her ears. "My husband and I both grew up here. Not this neighborhood, his family was in the Lake District and we moved around, so...." She shrugged and wrapped it up. "Now we're back."

Jessica thought she detected hesitancy, or maybe self-consciousness, in Claire's voice. "Isn't that nice," she said, skirting it and pretending not to notice. "So, do you still have family here?"

Claire suppressed the desire to roll her eyes and said simply, "Both of our parents."

"Wonderful." Jessica smiled at the boys. "Great for the kids to have some family around."

"You'd hope so." Claire gave a small laugh in an attempt to soften her words. They sounded rather cryptic, even to her ears.

"Will they go ta the local schuil, then?" Thomas rocked back and forth on his heels as he spoke.

Claire blinked. "Schuil?"

"Aye. The primary."

"Oh! Right!" She flushed. "You mean Sunrise Elementary?"

"Aye."

"We get to go to the big kid school in one more year after play school, right Mommy?" Noah asked, now sitting on the sidewalk beside Evan.

She nodded. "That's right."

"Kevin's a teacher there," Thomas said. "Not the heidmaister mind, but still a guid lad."

"Oh, umm," Claire stammered. She was clueless. Thankfully, Jessica came to her rescue.

"Thomas is referring to my husband, Kevin. He teaches fourth grade at the school, so odds are good Evan and Noah could end up in his class one day."

Claire shifted from one foot to the other. She was suddenly overcome by both exhaustion and restlessness. "He'll be kept on his toes when that happens, that's for sure," she offered, while wracking her brain for a polite way to wrap things up.

She didn't have to think for very long.

"A dog!" Evan shrieked, practically vibrating in his excitement as he pointed and gestured toward the house on the other side of Jessica's property.

Claire snapped to attention as both boys scrambled to their feet. "Wait," she said, trying to capture their attention.

"Over there, Noah!" Evan tugged sharply on his brother's shirt. "It's in the flowers over there!"

Before Claire could even begin to form words to stop them, the two boys shot off across Jessica's lawn toward her neighbor's flower beds.

"Oh, nuts," Claire muttered, then turned to Jessica. "Sorry! I just have to grab them." She didn't wait for her reply and took off at speed after her sons. "Evan! Noah! Stop right now!"

Oh yeah. No question about it. They were making one hell of a first impression.

* * * *

"Hey," Jake's deep voice rang out as he opened the kitchen door and stepped inside the house. "I'm home!"

Claire grinned. It was one of her favorite times of the day.

"Hey, you," she said, before being drowned out by a chorus of "Daddy!" from upstairs. She winced at the sound of Noah and Evan thundering down the staircase; rattling the glasses in the cupboards above her head.

"There they are!" Jake laughed joyfully as his sons bounded into the room. "The dynamic duo," he added, while crouching down to lift them up into his arms.

Peace welled up inside of Claire at the sight of them and her face softened with affection. Her boys. And the icing on the cake was the twins looked like mini versions of their father; all dark tousled hair and wide smiles.

"Oof," Jake exhaled, before giving in and easing himself back down to his knees. "You guys are getting way too big to hold for very long anymore."

He released his hold on them and they promptly sat on his feet and wrapped their bodies around the calves of his tan dress pants. Claire giggled as he shuffled straight legged, like a rusty Tin Man, across the tile floor toward her.

"Hey there, *you*," she repeated, while simultaneously draining a pot of spaghetti noodles into a strainer in the sink and leaning back for a quick kiss. "Welcome back to the funny farm."

"I'm a lion!" Evan, dressed in blue plaid pajamas, firmed up his grip around Jake's pant leg.

Noah, in green plaid pajamas and tucked snuggly against his father's other calf, remarked, "Lions aren't on farms."

Evan frowned, then his face cleared. "A horse!"

Noah nodded his approval. "I'll be a donkey."

"Funny farm, or not," Jake said, looking around the nearly immaculate kitchen in appreciation. "You managed to get a lot organized in here."

Claire picked up the colander by its handles and gave it a firm shake. "Oh, well, it's a start."

"Some *start*," he said, giving her shoulder an affectionate squeeze. "You're a force of nature."

Claire smiled, warmed by his praise, and poured the spaghetti into a white ceramic bowl on the countertop. "One room down."

"Oh, please," he said, over his shoulder, as he turned and shuffled across the floor toward the table. "By the end of the week, this place will look like we've lived here for ages."

Claire shrugged. He was right. She just couldn't leave things alone and would only rest when the house felt like home.

"We helped." Noah looked upward at Jake as he spoke.

"You did?" He paused in front of a chair.

"Uh-huh. We stayed out of the way."

Jake snickered, then tried to sit down with both boys still plastered to his legs.

"Once we're done with the rest of the unpacking, I'll be able to start thinking about paint colors." Claire grimaced at the kitchen walls before covering her bowl of pasta with a plate to keep it warm. "For the life of me, I can't understand how a person could willingly pick navy blue for a kitchen. White cabinets or not, it's too dark and gloomy."

Jake attempted, and failed, a second time to position himself close enough to sit down. "This isn't going to work guys," he said, affectionately, looking at his sons. "Time for the monkeys to take flight."

"Horse and donkey, Daddy."

"Right."

Evan unwound his arms and legs from around Jake's calf and pulled himself upright.

"Don't go too far," Claire called after him as he sprinted from the room, Noah just a step behind. "Only a few more minutes and then we're going to eat."

Jake sat down and unfastened the top two buttons on his burgundy dress shirt. He sighed and stretched his neck. "So, can I assume you had an interesting day?"

Claire smoothed the bottom of her white peasant blouse over the top of her black capri pants. She'd managed to grab a moment amidst her sorting to shower and change from her grubby t-shirt and shorts. "I don't even know where to start," she told him, inwardly cringing at the memory from that afternoon.

"Something with the boys?" He was pretty sure he already knew the answer. His lovely wife was a person of schedules, routines and efficiency; thus, she was often flustered by Noah and Evan's unbridled enthusiasm.

"Well, let's see." She turned off the burner on the stove that was keeping her pot of pasta sauce warm and walked over to the fridge. "It started with them taking off out of the yard."

Jake braced himself.

"They know they're not supposed to," she said, crossly, while pulling open the fridge door to retrieve the containers of lettuce and veggies she'd prepared for salad. "And, still, they did."

Jake stood up and walked over to take them from her.

Claire handed him the Tupperware and closed the door sharply with her hip. "I mean, seriously, I don't think I'm being out of line here. They're only four years old. They can't be wandering around all over the place without supervision!"

Jake put the containers on the countertop and started pulling off the lids. "But they were fine, right?"

"That's not the point," she insisted, her voice tight. "Not even close."

"I know, I know," he appeased, while he grabbed a large green bowl from beside the sink. "This one?"

Claire nodded.

He poured the salad contents into the bowl. "Anyway, what's done is done."

"It's too dangerous!" Claire blurted, on a roll. "What if someone had come along—"

"But no one did." Jake stacked the empty plastic bowls in the sink and reached out to wrap her in his arms. "And we're not in the city anymore, Hon. This is Boxwood Hills. We grew up here."

"That's so not the point."

He stroked her hair. "*And*, even though it's grown, it's still pretty much the same."

Claire let him soothe her and spoke into his shoulder. "This isn't Mayberry, Jake. Admittedly, it's better than the city, but *still*."

Jake pulled her away from him and held her gently by her shoulders. "I'll have a talk with them, okay?" He looked directly into her blue eyes, his expression earnest.

Claire softened under both his gaze and his touch. "Okay. If you talk to them, I'll feel a bit better."

"I will. I promise."

She sighed. "And you're probably right. They are fine. But, I still don't like them doing stuff like that. It freaks me out. Boxwood Hills or not, you have to impress upon them they can't leave the yard without supervision."

He nodded and picked up the green bowl.

"Oh, and for interest sake," she said. "They didn't just leave the yard. No. They went into the crescent next door and brought back an animal with them. A cat they insisted was lost."

"Was it?" Jake carried the salad to the table.

"No, not even close." Claire grimaced at the memory of the cat. "The two of them came waltzing into the house with the darned thing and then we had no choice but to return it to the scene of the crime. Which, of course, did not go unnoticed by the neighbors."

Jake paused, his face concerned. "It didn't cause a problem?"

"No." She shrugged. "Just more of a case of my dignity being stomped on as I tried and failed to return that freaky looking thing back where they'd found it, only to get caught in the act."

"Freaky looking?" He crossed over to the cupboards and started opening doors.

Claire picked up the bowl of spaghetti and brought it to the table. "Oh yeah. Grey and skinny, with a kinked tail and huge orange eyes." A small shiver worked its way up her spine as she remembered. *Corkscrew.*

Jake found glasses and pulled two from the cabinet. He put them on the table and went to the fridge for a bottle of white wine.

Claire sighed and pulled out her chair at the table. "And, I gotta say, it probably wasn't the best way to introduce ourselves to the neighborhood."

He brought the wine to the table. "It was an honest mistake," he said, pouring two generous measures. "Anyone would forgive a four year old for it. In fact, my sister was forever bringing home so-called strays when we were kids and people were always really nice about it."

"Oh?" Claire rested her elbows on the table and raised her eyebrows at him. "This is the first I've heard of it. So you're telling me this klepto problem runs in the family?"

He chuckled and offered her a glass.

"Okay, enough about that." She took the glass. "It's bad enough I had to live it the first time. Tell me about your day. Did it go well?"

"It did." He pulled out his chair and sat down. "Rob, the other dentist, is a good guy. The front end staff and the assistants are all friendly and competent. I think I was spot on in this one."

Claire raised her wine in a toast. "Excellent. I look forward to meeting them," she said, genuinely pleased. He was such a great dentist, he deserved all of the good he received.

"Hey, boys," Jake called out. "Time for dinner." He lifted the plate from the pasta bowl as the sound of Noah and Evan's feet hitting the stairs met their ears. "Anything else I should know before we're interrupted?"

Claire flashed back to the boys tearing off toward Jessica's neighbor's dog; her attempt to catch up to them, then the stumble that sent her gracelessly face down into the dirt, and shook her head. It just wasn't worth rehashing.

Noah and Evan burst through the doorway, their faces eager.

"Noodles, yay!" Noah cheered as Evan squeezed past him and climbed up into his chair.

Claire placed her wine glass on the table, reached for the serving spoon and smiled. Yes, they were a handful, but they certainly were a happy handful. Silver lining.

* * * *

CHAPTER 2

"There it is *again*, Mommy!"

Claire jerked on her step ladder. She was standing in front of to her soon-to-be-painted kitchen wall, paintbrush at the ready, when a metallic ratta-tat-tat on their furnace vent hammered through the house.

Damned woodpecker, she thought. She'd banished from her memory all the wildlife moments that had occurred throughout her formative years in Boxwood Hills. However, as the woodpecker used her house for its drum solo, those memories were coming back at speed.

Noah came charging into the room, Evan hot on his heels, the two of them brandishing matching orange and yellow water pistols. More like water cannons, truth be told.

"We're going to scare him away!" Evan declared.

"Boys, hang on," Claire said, trying to keep her balance on the ladder and parent at the same time. It was like trying to keep up with a tornado.

Evan didn't even glance in her direction, his focus solely on following his brother outside through the porch screen door, water pistol resting on his shoulder like a machine gun.

"Oh, Jake," she muttered, as her sons disappeared from sight into the backyard. "This is your fault."

It had been Jake's inspired idea to use the water pistols, stating that he, his brother and their sister had done the same thing when they were kids to humanely deter the woodpeckers. Claire debated, did she throw caution to the wind and continue with her edging on the wall, or follow behind them?

"Don't shoot!" a woman's voice rang out from the backyard. "I come in peace!"

Claire's eyebrows shot upward on her forehead. Decision made. She rapidly descended the steel step ladder, turned on her heel and nearly wiped out when her foot tangled in the drop cloth.

"Nuts!" she blurted, only just managing to keep herself upright by clutching at the kitchen table for balance.

"Boys!" she yelled, shaking off the drop cloth and regaining her footing to take off at speed through the door. She thundered down the back steps in her bare feet, paintbrush still held aloft. "Do not shoot those things at anyone! Do you hear me—"

Claire's voice dropped off and she ground to a halt when she saw Jessica, the neighbor from the other crescent, sitting cross-legged on the back lawn.

"They shoot far." Evan, seated next to Jessica, was wearing a proud-as-punch expression on his face while she admired his water pistol.

"Very cool." She nodded, then looked up as Claire approached.

Claire smiled, gave a small wave with her free hand, then tugged on the hem of her faded pink t-shirt in an attempt to smooth it. She was sure she looked a sight. And, after taking in Jessica's perfect outfit of mint green capri pants and yellow and white flowered blouse, she was all that much more certain.

"Hey," Jessica said, her face as open and friendly as it had been the first time they'd met the previous week. "Thought I'd stop in and see how things are coming along."

"And she brought us cookies." Noah was sitting on the grass beside Evan, his eyes practically dancing at the promise of an unexpected treat.

"Which, I have to confess right from the start, I didn't make." Jessica shook her head and held her hands up as though in surrender. "I fully admit to buying them from the bake shop next door to my salon. They're far superior to anything I could create in my oven. My sister took all of the baking genetics in the family, I'm afraid."

"Wow." Claire cleared her throat and fumbled for words to express her gratitude. It was so unexpected and so kind. Maybe she'd been wrong and they had moved to Mayberry. "I mean, thank you. It's just so unexpected, I don't quite know what to say. Usually we're the ones bringing cookies, to apologize for something."

Jessica laughed. "I find that hard to believe."

"Oh, believe it." Claire swept her bangs out of her eyes with her free hand and imperceptibly tilted her head toward her sons. "We've had a few things in our past that needed smoothing over, if you get my drift."

"Well, then, I guess today's your lucky day," Jessica said. "Free cookies and no apologies necessary."

"Yay!" Noah enthused, scrambling to his feet. "Can we have some, Mommy?"

Evan stood up and danced around Claire's legs like an excited puppy. "Please?" he added to his brother's request.

She raised an eyebrow at her son. Smooth. "As long as it's okay with Jessica."

"Of course it is." Jessica lifted the white plastic container in her lap, stood up and brushed the back of her pants with her free hand. She extended the container to Claire and smiled at the boys. "I think these cookies are one of the shop's best batches yet."

"Wonderful." Claire gestured toward the house. "Come on in and I'll make some coffee."

Evan reached out and slipped his small hand into Jessica's. She looked down at him with genuine affection. "I'd love to."

* * * *

"Uh-huh," Claire said, into the phone. She nodded, even though the person on the other end couldn't see her, then shrugged apologetically at Jessica. "Right. Okay. Sure."

Jessica, seated on a cushy, tan colored sectional sofa in Claire's family room, smiled in return. She was patient. While she waited she glanced at the room, taking in the freshly painted, wheat colored walls; the precisely organized bookshelves, the carefully placed artwork, dust free knick-knacks and well-tended plants. It was seriously impressive. In such a short period of time, Claire had pulled the room together impeccably.

"Okay, then," Claire said, trying to wrap things up. "It's just, I've got company, *so*...." She waited a beat, then exhaled in relief. "Okay. Yes. See you soon."

Jessica raised her eyebrows as Claire pressed the *End* button on the phone. "Let me guess," she said, playfully. "Relative?"

Claire rolled her eyes as she placed the phone on the maple coffee table in front of the sofa. "Mother-in-law. She's in a state over being on vacation while we're moving in. It's nothing."

"Ah," Jessica offered, leaving it at that. From the expression on Claire's face, it was obvious she had no desire to talk further about the woman. "So, I've gotta say, you've really settled in nicely."

Claire smiled, pleased by the compliment. "Thanks," she said, reaching for a cookie from a pile she'd transferred from Jessica's container to a plate.

"Seriously, I'm impressed. A person would never know you'd just moved in a week ago."

"Well, I debated over doing this one or the kitchen and even though there's no question the kitchen needs the attention, the family room won. We spend a lot of time in here and I wanted it to feel welcoming and ready to be lived in, you know? Especially for the boys. It was important for them to feel at home as soon as possible and not like we're living in a state of flux."

Jessica raised an eyebrow and nodded. From what she'd witnessed, it didn't appear either of Claire's sons were fazed by much. They seemed very balanced and easygoing. She had a hunch it was Claire, herself, that needed the sense of being settled.

Claire took a bite of her cookie. "Mmm, these are so good," she said, before beckoning her sons. "Boys, if you're thirsty, I have juice boxes in the fridge."

"Grape?" Noah asked, as he and Evan stood up from where they were seated on the cinnamon colored carpet.

She shook her head. "Apple."

"Apple's good, too," Evan offered, before stepping around the many, many *Hot Wheels* cars and accompanying play sets on the floor and darting out of the family room behind Noah.

Jessica leaned back into the plump, burgundy colored pillows scattered on the sofa. "So, have you guys moved around a lot then?"

"No." Claire finished her cookie and dusted crumbs from her fingertips onto a napkin on the coffee table. "This is our first move, actually, as a family."

"Oh," Jessica said, taken aback.

"Something wrong?" Claire cocked her head. "You look surprised."

"No. I guess I just thought—" Jessica paused and picked up a yellow coffee mug from a tray on the table. She wanted to choose her words carefully. "I just thought, since you said you didn't want Evan and Noah to feel in flux, you had moved a few times. Silly to make assumptions, I know."

"Not at all. I understand," Claire assured her. "I can see why what I said would make you think that. And I guess I feel that way because we - my Mom and I - did move around a fair bit when I was a kid, after she and my Dad divorced."

"Oh, sorry." Jessica was contrite. "It's none of my business. I wasn't meaning to pry—"

Claire cut her off. "No, no, don't worry about it. Really. It's not such an uncommon story, anyway."

That's true," Jessica acknowledged. "My Mom and Dad split up as well, when we were young."

"See?" Claire nodded. "Common. I just found it a bit difficult because it was tough going from one school to the next, making friends and leaving them, that sort of thing. I guess those memories have stuck with me and now I want to make sure the boys don't have the same sort of experience, you know? I want them to feel their home is stable. Reliable."

"Absolutely," Jessica agreed. "Makes perfect sense."

Noah and Evan came back into the room, allowing for a distraction, and Jessica sipped her coffee as she let Claire's words sink in. Poor thing. Seemed like what she really needed was a friend.

"So." Jessica placed her mug back on the table and pointed to a large, ornately framed photo sitting on an adjacent bookshelf. "Is that your husband?"

Claire visibly softened as she looked at the photo of she and Jake, dressed in their wedding finery. "Yes, that's Jake."

Jessica stood up and leaned in for a closer look. "He looks like someone, doesn't he?" She wracked her brain, then it hit her and she snapped her fingers. "Oh, I know. Ryan Reynolds. That's who he reminds me of."

Claire smiled. "Yeah, he's been told that a number of times and it cracks him up. He doesn't see it, but...." She shrugged.

Jessica sat back down on the sofa. "Yeah, Kevin was told a while back that he looks like Nathan Fillion. We both drew a blank; we had no idea who that was until we looked him up."

"He's that actor from Castle, right?" Claire reached for her coffee mug, a perfect yellow twin to Jessica's cup.

"Uh-huh."

"So, does he?"

"Yes." Jessica snickered and added, "I had fun teasing him about it."

Claire laughed.

"Can we have another cookie?" Noah asked, his eyes bright and hopeful.

"Yes," Claire told him. "Then you have to take a break until after dinner, okay?"

He and Evan vaulted themselves toward the plate on the coffee table. "Deal," he said, making Jessica grin. The pair of them were a riot.

As the boys resettled themselves back on the rug with their toys, Jessica looked at Claire's wedding photo a second time. "So, how long have you and Jake been married?"

"Seven years." Claire picked out another cookie for herself and took a large bite, relishing the sweet, yet slightly nutty flavor of chocolate and oatmeal. She'd have to get the name of the bakery.

Jessica nodded appreciatively. "Where did you meet?"

Claire swallowed her mouthful. "Through a friend, actually."

Jessica waited. It sounded like there was more story to tell.

"Well, truth be told, she was more than a friend at the time." Claire coughed and reached for her coffee cup. "She was my roommate."

Jessica nodded.

Claire squirmed in her seat, ate the rest of her cookie and shrugged. "Okay, fine, I'll fess up. Paula decided we should have a party."

"Paula was your roommate?"

"Uh-huh. And I wasn't very keen on the idea because I thought we were getting a bit old to be throwing house parties. But, she was in the dentistry program at the university and knew a lot of people, so in no time she got the word out and, go figure, this really great guy turned up—"

"Jake?"

"Yup." Claire placed her mug on the table, then wrung her hands together. "We bumped into each other - literally; it was wall to wall people at one point - and started talking and...." she took a breath.

Jessica found herself sitting on the edge of her seat, waiting.

"Just as I was about to be bold and suggest we get together at another time, Paula found us and got all excited that I'd met the guy she'd been going on and on about for a couple of weeks."

Jessica grimaced. "Oh, dear."

"Yeah. Turned out Jake was also studying dentistry, so they spent a lot of time in class together and she was under the impression it had potential." Claire shook her head, remembering.

"Daddy says we have good teeth, right Mommy?" Evan paused in pulling out a play mat for their cars from a toy box in the corner, waiting for an answer.

"Yes, that's right, he does."

That was all the encouragement they needed. Both boys charged at them, grinning like fools to show off their small, straight white teeth.

Jessica giggled and nodded. "Very nice. Both of you."

"Okay," Claire said, putting a stop to things before they began opening their mouths for further inspection. "You both have lovely teeth, thanks for sharing."

Satisfied, they returned to spreading out their city embossed play mat on the carpet.

Claire smoothed her hair from her face. "Sorry about that."

"No worries." Jessica laughed. "I always enjoy a good show of teeth."

It was Claire's turn to laugh. "Excellent. So, what was I saying?"

"That Paula and Jake were classmates and she'd been swanning on about him and was all excited that you'd met him at the party."

"Right." Claire nodded.

"So," Jessica prompted, eager to hear the rest. "What did you do when you found out he was the guy she'd been going on about?"

Claire cast an appraising eye at Noah and Evan to gauge how much they were listening to her tale. It appeared they'd returned to their make-believe world, zooming their cars around the two dimensional city, but looks could be deceiving. She chose her words carefully and continued.

"The only thing I could do. I was polite and extracted myself from the two of them as fast I was able to, without seeming obvious. They were *friends*, after all, and I didn't want to mess up their *friendship*."

Jessica looked at the boys, then back at Claire and nodded. "Right. So, how did you and he finally become *friends*?"

Claire grinned. "He showed up at the art gallery I was working at. He'd seen some of my work at our place and asked Paula about it—"

"Wait. You're an artist?"

Claire's eyes widened and she shook her head. "Me? No. Not really. I used to dabble before we had the boys."

Jessica looked around the room with renewed interest. "Do you have anything you've made? I'd love to see it. What was your medium?"

Claire blushed. "It's no big deal," she said, before getting up and crossing the room to a tall, built-in bookshelf on the opposite wall. "I used to work with glass."

Jessica watched her slide a blown glass vase from the depths of a shelf and her jaw went slack. She wasn't for real, was she?

Claire carried the vase over to the couch, sat down and placed it gently onto the coffee table.

Jessica looked from the vase to Claire, then back again, stunned and silent. Fluted and standing approximately twelve inches tall, it was blown from glass in a riot of passionate colors. Rich chocolate brown blended with hues of deep, cobalt blue and earthy forest green, while delicate wisps of scarlet, orange, amber and plum dashed across the glass as though it was at risk of becoming engulfed in flames. It was exquisite.

Claire watched Jessica's face, saw confusion and swallowed. "It's okay," she said, beginning to wish she'd left the vase hidden. "You don't have to like it."

"Oh, no." Jessica shook her head while she leaned in for a closer look. "Don't misunderstand my silence." She took a deep breath and exhaled. "It's absolutely beautiful. I just can't believe you said this is no big deal. Because it is. It's a very big deal."

Claire's cheeks flushed. She was both flattered and slightly embarrassed. "Thank you," she said, shyly. "I made it a long time ago."

"May I?" Jessica asked, gesturing to the piece.

"Of course. Go ahead." Claire watched her carefully pick up the vase, then run her index finger around the rippled rim, tracing the seamless smooth wave.

"Wow," Jessica breathed as she found herself repeating her earlier pattern of looking at the vase, then at Claire, then back again. She was finding it a challenge to reconcile the passionately vibrant piece of art in her hands with her seemingly vanilla colored, new friend. Granted, she'd only had a couple of interactions with her, but never once had Claire demonstrated even a hint of an uninhibited side to her nature. Quite the opposite.

Jessica held the glass up to the light and wondered where on earth had this fire come from and, even more importantly, where was it now being hidden?

"I have a couple more pieces," Claire offered, with a small shrug. "Do you want to see them?"

"More?" With exaggerated care, Jessica placed the vase back on the table. "Seriously?"

Claire nodded and returned to the book shelves. "These ones are smaller and make nice paperweights." She carefully retrieved two near perfect spheres, there bottoms slightly flattened to allow them to sit without rolling.

Jessica blinked as Claire carried one in each hand, each about the size of an apple, then extended one for her to hold.

"Wow," she repeated herself, receiving the delicately blown orb and marveling at the life that was captured within its depths. "It reminds me of when I was a child and we'd see a rainbow of colors in the oil that had leaked from someone's car, remember?"

Claire smiled and nodded.

"Not the greatest thing for the environment, I'll admit," Jessica said, with a wry grin. "But we didn't know any better and thought it was beautiful."

Noah paused in his play and got up to stand beside Jessica.

"Pretty nice, huh?" She held the paperweight out for him to see.

Noah stared at the glass. "I like the bubbles."

"They almost look like Mommy added drops of soap in there, don't they?"

Noah grinned. "Soap bubbles that will never burst."

Evan got up from the mat and leaned into his mother. "I like the swirls in yours, Mommy. They look like candy canes."

"Do we have any candy canes?" Noah quickly shifted gears. The paperweights were known entities.

Claire placed her glass orb back on the bookshelf. "No, we don't. But I do have fruit snacks."

"This is exquisite, Claire. Truly." Jessica let her fingers glide along the smooth cool surface, her face entranced. "You have a gift. I'm surprised you didn't have people lining up to create for them. Did they sell well at the gallery?"

"Oh, I never actually sold any of my work," she said, over her shoulder as she walked into the kitchen. "It was a hobby."

"Well, be that as it may, you could have easily created a following." Jessica gently placed the glass ball on the table beside the vase.

Claire chuckled as she returned from the kitchen, fruit snacks in hand. "I gave a few as gifts," she admitted, while handing Evan and Noah their snacks. "And then, after Jake entered the picture—"

"Oh, right!" Jessica said, enthusiastically. "You said he tracked you down at your work? Nice. I love a man who's willing to go after what he wants."

Claire blushed, then shrugged. "Actually, at the time it was a bit awkward. I mean, don't get me wrong, clearly there was no denying we both wanted to be better *friends*, but there was Paula and all that."

"Ahh." Jessica raised her eyebrows, getting her drift.

"Anyway, it did get resolved, *obviously*." Claire laughed and waved her hand in the air to indicate the house and the kids. "He and Paula's relationship was still just a friendship and hadn't been taken to any serious levels, so I wasn't actually stepping on any toes. We managed to smooth things out amicably in the end, when she saw Jake and I were serious about being together."

Jessica nodded. She understood. Very well. "So, if I remember correctly, you said both you and Jake grew up here, right?"

Claire picked up her vase from the coffee table and tucked it back into its place on the bookshelf, almost hidden from view. "Uh-huh."

"And you never once crossed paths during your growing up years?"

"No." Claire reached for the glass paperweight of swirling colors still on the table. She sat it next to its candy cane mate on the shelf.

"Wow." Jessica shook her head. "That's amazing."

"Yeah. I'd imagine it was because my Mom and I lived in and around the Pine View area mostly, whereas Jake's family was in the Lake District." Claire turned away from the shelf and walked back over to the couch. "And then, once I'd finished high school I took off to the city; while Jake went off to work and then into university."

"That's really something then, that fate crossed your paths regardless of circumstance. A great story for the grandchildren."

"Yeah." Claire smiled as she sat down. "That's what I like to think."

Jessica watched Evan and Noah acting out a mini traffic jam on their mat. "So, does that mean you don't have any siblings?"

"No." Claire shook her head, then brushed her bangs off her forehead. "Just me. And you? You mentioned you have a sister?"

"Yes." A happy grin spread across Jessica's face. "April. We pretty much grew up the opposite of you, in the city. She's still there, actually, working for the Tribune newspaper. She has her own column."

Jessica's pride in her sister was so obvious, Claire felt warm in the presence of it. It was the sort of thing she hoped Evan and Noah would feel for each other one day. "Wow. Good for her. What's her last name?"

"Patterson."

"Oh!" Claire pointed at her, excited. "I know her column! She does city beat sort of stuff, right?"

"Yes," Jessica said, delighted she knew of April's work. She'd have to pass it along the next time they talked. It would make her day.

"I loved her column," Claire gushed, before sighing and slumping heavily into the sofa cushions. "I'm going to miss my routine of going out to grab a coffee and the paper."

Jessica reached over and patted Claire's hand affectionately. "You can still do that, you know. It'll just have to be a different coffee and paper."

"Maybe we can get cookies again, too," Noah offered, while keeping his eyes focused on his cars.

Surprised by the comment, Jessica laughed. "Sounds like a plan, buddy."

Claire shot her son a wry smile. Little pitchers and all that. "Anyway, it won't be the same," she told Jessica, pointedly. "But I'm sure I'll survive and adapt."

"First world problems?"

"Exactly," Claire agreed, then added, "Now you know about us, how did you and your husband—"

"Kevin," Jessica supplied when Claire's voice rose in question.

"Right. Kevin. How did you and Kevin meet?"

"Through my sister, actually." Jessica dropped eye contact and shifted in her seat to watch the boys.

Oh, dear, Claire thought, calculating her obvious body language. Clearly she'd stumbled onto a touchy subject.

"Well, that's nice to meet through family," she offered, keeping things neutral, while mentally scrambling to regain their easy footing. "How long have you been married?"

"Just a little over a year." Jessica swept her hair back behind her shoulders and Claire was relieved to hear the edge in her voice soften. "We've known each other longer than that, but...."

Evan abandoned his cars, stood up and walked over to Jessica. "Do you want to see my room?" he asked, gazing at her adoringly.

Sometimes, Claire thought with affection, their timing was perfect.

Noah jumped up and joined his brother. "Mine, too."

Claire exchanged a look with Jessica. Clearly her boys were smitten with the beautiful new woman in their life. "That sounds like a great idea, if Jessica wants to."

"I'd love to," she told them. "Do you each have your own room?"

"Yes." Evan slipped his hand in hers.

"It's our first time having our own rooms," Noah added, reaching for her other hand.

Jessica allowed them to pull her off the sofa and lead her toward the stairs. "Lucky," she said, grinning from ear to ear.

Claire watched them go upstairs and hugged herself. She had a friend.

* * * *

"So, tell me more about this Jessica woman."

Claire paused, toothbrush clamped between her teeth, and poked her head out from the ensuite bathroom. She hadn't had a chance to mention Jessica's visit in the chaos that was dinner, clean-up, bath time and so on.

"How did you know about Jessica?" she asked, around a mouthful of toothpaste.

Jake, lounging on the king-sized bed, smiled. "The boys mentioned her and her visit."

"Ah," Claire said, before disappearing back into the bathroom to spit and rinse. She wiped her face and turned off the light.

"Between every throw of the ball," he said, referring to the spirited game of catch he, Noah and Evan had played after dinner, "it was *Jessica* this and *Jessica* that. Sounds like she made quite the impression."

"I'm sure," Claire agreed, walking into the bedroom.

"Apparently cookies were involved?"

She laughed as she climbed into bed and settled herself beside him under the soft, goose down comforter. "Go figure, they'd mention that."

"Oh, they did," Jake affirmed, placing his iPhone on the bedside table. "A lot. As well, they were pretty clear they want to visit the bakery where she bought them."

Claire giggled and shook her head. "Honestly, those two. We have a lovely visit from a new friend and they're all about the cookies."

"It was a good visit, then?" Jake plumped his pillow and laid back into the sheets.

Claire nodded. "Absolutely. She's really nice and looks like a tall, curvy *Jessica Rabbit*."

"So, does that make her husband *Roger Rabbit*?" Jake was swift on the uptake, his voice filled with humor.

Claire lightly punched his shoulder, before snuggling up close to his side. "I highly doubt it, but since I've never seen him I can't say for sure."

"Ah," Jake said, raising a finger in the air. "So, there's a possibility—"

"Anyway," she interrupted, rolling her eyes. "She came in and we had a great visit."

Jake turned on his side and wrapped an arm loosely around her torso. "Excellent."

Claire ran her fingers through her hair, thoughtful. "In fact, I showed her my pieces and she really liked them."

"Not surprising. They're brilliant."

Claire smiled and turned to kiss his cheek. "She seemed really surprised by them at first, but then she was adamant I could sell my work."

Jake said nothing when she sighed. He'd learned the hard way it could be a touchy subject.

"Of course," she finally said. "I told her they were a part of my past, but still, it was nice to hear."

Jake cleared his throat, choosing his words carefully. "But does that mean it will always be a part of the past?"

Claire stiffened and pulled away slightly. "What do you mean?"

"Nothing," he said, casually adjusting the covers. "I'm just asking if you think it *might* be possible you might go back to it. Not immediately, obviously; you have a lot on your plate. But, maybe when the boys are older...." He tapered off, treading carefully.

Claire relaxed and considered his words, while her thoughts drifted back to the hot shop where she'd developed her skills. The heat, dry and intense, often raising the mercury within the walls to a stifling, sweat inducing one hundred and ten degrees. The furnace and glory hole; molten glass the consistency of thick honey and amber fire so bright she'd worn sunglasses to shield her eyes. Then there were the tools. Blowpipes, shears, tweezers, paddles, paper - each one giving her the ability to transform the molten glass into something... magic. Claire's heartbeat began to slow as her body remembered the soothing rhythm that overtook her when she immersed herself into a piece. It was like a dance flowing between her, the glass, the fire and her imagination.

"Claire?"

She startled when Jake said her name and took a deep breath, centering herself. "I don't know." She fidgeted with the sheets. "I'm different now. I'm a Mom. I can't very well go off and ditch the boys."

"Of course not." He rubbed her shoulder, placating. "I was just saying, once they're at a different stage—"

"Which won't be for a while," she finished.

Jake nodded. He knew the tone. "Right." He gently pulled her closer, changing the subject. "But that doesn't mean we can't pretend you've just finished a piece, right?"

Claire felt her body respond to his touch and a slow grin spread across her face. She remembered very well the energy that had built up inside of her when she'd finished a piece. Working in the heat with the fire and glass has stirred something in her, something deep and passionate, and Jake had been her physical outlet for all of that energy.

"One with lots of color and movement," she agreed, slipping deeper under the covers and molding herself into his embrace.

"Lots of red and purple," he breathed, sliding his hands beneath her pajama shirt and letting his fingers trail along her skin until he found the swell of her breasts.

Claire gasped and reached for the switch on the bedside lamp.

* * * *

CHAPTER 3

The low rumble of voices emanated from a Panasonic RF-1090 portable radio in Thomas' kitchen. He'd purchased the radio new in nineteen eighty and it still worked like a charm. Still matched the decor, too.

Listening with half an ear to the topic of conversation, Thomas poured thick cream into his black, water stained coffee cup and nodded in agreement to something the host was saying. He chuckled when the discussion switched gears - he'd figured the host wouldn't stand a chance in the long run of winning his point - then reached out to switch it off. He had other matters to focus upon; namely the arrival of Claire Jamieson's boys, Noah and Evan, to the neighborhood.

Such nice lads. Energetic, engaged in their surroundings, sharp as tacks; they brought back memories of Thomas' own childhood with his younger brother, Angus. Barely more than a year apart, he and Angus had grown up as near to twins as was possible without actually being so. And, like Noah and Evan, he and his brother had been up for anything and interested in everything - much to the delight, and sometimes chagrin, of their favorite grownup, Uncle Albert. Kind and patient, Albert had indulged them at every chance and Thomas still felt deep gratitude toward his uncle for helping cultivate his love of inventing; thus, giving him a path to travel for life.

He leaned against his hunter green colored countertop, his thoughts drifting to the plans he'd drawn up for a go-kart stylized to imitate a vintage soap-box car. They were sitting on the bench top in his workshop and he had to admit he was keen on the idea of getting down to the work of it with the lads. It went against his better judgement - he usually did his best to stay well out of the daily neighborhood flow - but nostalgia for days past was a strong force and he was certain he was going to enjoy the process as much as those boys.

Thomas picked up his mug and chuckled under his breath when he recalled the blatant, wide-eyed panic on the face of their Mum when Jessica had suggested the joining of forces. Poor lass. She seemed a bit skittish. He hoped she'd been mulling Jessica's suggestion over since then and had grown fond of its appeal. If that was so, he gambled he'd soon be receiving a knock on his door, asking if he was still keen on the idea.

"Time will tell," he told his silent kitchen, before grabbing a package of cigarettes from the table and exiting the house via the back door.

* * * *

"Excuse me, Thomas?"

Thomas slowed the shuffle of his tartan patterned slippers across his concrete patio and braced himself.

Deborah. Uptight, skeletal thin, every hair on her brunette bob in perfect order; she rarely spoke to him directly. She lived two yards over with her husband and Thomas never knew what to expect next from his eagle-eyed neighbor.

"Mornin'," he replied, turning to his left to better assess the woman from beneath his bushy eyebrows.

"Ah, yes. Good morning." She smoothed her hands down the black yoga pants covering her bony hips and stood rigidly, almost as though she was at attention. "A quick question, if I may?"

Thomas lifted his cup to his lips, took a sip of coffee, then nodded. "Gae on."

Deborah stiffened, if that was possible. "Pardon me? Gay? I'm afraid I don't follow."

"No, no." Thomas shook his shaggy head and sighed. The woman was a serious piece of work. "I meant 'ave yur say. Wots on yur mind, then?"

"Oh." Deborah cleared her throat and flattened imaginary wrinkles from her purple, long sleeved t-shirt. It wasn't her fault the man was such a challenge to understand. If he'd just learn to enunciate, there would be no problem. She pulled her shoulders back and took a breath. "I just wanted to inquire about a rumor I've been privy to, regarding some children in the neighborhood. I'm not sure what exactly is going on, some sort of large craft project perhaps, but I trust you'll be respectful of the serenity of our lovely block, yes?"

Thomas bent forward and placed his cup on the concrete beneath his feet, straightened up and tapped a cigarette from the package in his hand. "Aye," he offered as he tucked the cigarette between his lips, fished his lighter from a pocket on his beige fisherman's vest and lit the tip, inhaling with a flourish.

"Is that a yes?" Deborah waved her hand reflexively in front of her face, even though she was so far away there was no possible chance the smoke could reach her.

Thomas let smoke plume from his nostrils and raised an eyebrow. "Perhaps it is, lass," he said, while Corkscrew slunk out from the low, overgrown bushes on either side of his workshop, making a direct line for his cup on the patio.

"Oh!" Deborah visibly startled at the grey cat's sudden appearance, then pointed when he arrived at Thomas' mug and began to lap neatly at the coffee within. "Your cat," she began, before swallowing against the bile that rose into her throat.

Thomas stepped around the cat and meandered toward his workshop; his original destination before being interrupted.

Deborah gaped at him as he stepped inside the shop, closed the door smartly behind him and left only a wisp of cigarette smoke in his wake. Had they finished talking? Had he said yes? Had he even understood her question? And, finally, should she march over, rap on his door and demand a more definite response? She gave one last short glance at Corkscrew still drinking steadily from the cup, grimaced, and turned her back. Maybe another time.

* * * *

CHAPTER 4

"Yoo-hoo! Claire! Claire Rose Jamieson! Anybody home?"

Claire pulled herself upright from the jumble of clothes she was attempting to sort on her laundry room table and smoothed her hair back from her face. "Deep breath, stay easy," she quietly counseled herself before straightening the hem of her blue t-shirt, plastering a smile across her face and walking into the kitchen.

"Mom! What a surprise!"

Josephine, or 'Mom', laughed and charged across the room toward her daughter. "Surprise? Come *on*," she said, pulling Claire into a tight embrace.

Claire hugged her back, her vision obscured in the jumble of vibrant red curls around her mother's shoulders, and inhaled her familiar scent of cinnamon and vanilla.

"It's so good to see you!" Josephine squeezed her tighter for emphasis. "It's been too long."

Claire raised an eyebrow. It had been a couple of months, tops, since her mother had visited them in the city.

"Sorry I haven't been around sooner, but I thought you'd need some time to settle in. I left a message on your machine that I'd pop in today. Didn't you get it?"

"I got it," Claire said, while disentangling herself from Josephine's surprisingly strong embrace. "I just wasn't sure what time you were coming."

"Oh, *well*." Josephine shrugged and looked around the kitchen with eyes the exact same shade of hazel - and filled with as much mischief - as the twins. "I wasn't exactly sure when my class would end, so I didn't want to commit to a specific time."

Claire pressed her lips together and kept quiet. Her mother never set anything in stone. Ever. She'd learned from previous experience it wasn't worth mentioning. Instead she lifted her eyebrows and asked, "Class?"

"Oh! It's so much fun!" Josephine's slim hands flitted through the air as rapidly as her words flowed from her mouth, the sleeves of her loose fitting, white peasant blouse sliding up and down her arms as she gestured. Claire took a step back to avoid the commotion. "You should join me."

Claire hesitated. Did she ask her next question, or not? If she went by past interactions, she'd keep quiet. But, it was a new day and a new house, why not. She braced herself and dove in. "What's it about?"

"Pottery." Josephine fingered the cotton fabric of her long, purple skirt, the sequined flower pattern twinkling as she moved, and grinned at Claire. It made her look at least ten years younger than her current sixty one.

"Oh." Claire folded her arms across her chest and nodded, pleasantly surprised. "That sounds interesting."

"We're allowed pretty much free rein, so a few of the girls and I are competing to see how accurate we can be in sculpting anatomically correct pieces." She arched an eyebrow suggestively, grinned and let her hands form visually intimate shapes in the air. "If you get my drift."

And *there* it is, Claire thought, rolling her eyes as the other proverbial shoe dropped. She turned away and walked over to a Cookie Monster shaped container on the countertop while her mother chortled.

"It's a hoot, I'm telling you."

Claire pulled a blue plate from the cupboard above her head and set it on the counter. "I can imagine," she said, while lifting the lid from the container and reaching inside.

Josephine took a couple steps forward and trailed her fingers along one of the newly painted kitchen walls. "A great creative outlet. Might be just your thing."

Claire began piling oatmeal raisin cookies on the plate and sidestepped. "The boys are playing in the yard. Did you see them on your way in, or were they in the tree house?"

"Uh-huh. They've grown." Josephine turned away from the wall, covered her mouth with her hand and yawned behind it. "I was surprised they were out there on their own."

Claire stiffened. She knew her mother thought her overprotective. She took a breath, determined not to be baited. "We have an understanding," she said, casually.

"Understanding?"

"Uh-huh." She brushed cookie crumbs from her fingers into the sink. "They know to stay in their own yard."

Josephine nodded, her face admiring. "I'm proud of you, dear. And getting them a cat, that was a great idea."

"Pardon?"

"Quite the unique looking creature, I must say. Startling eyes. But, good for you, opening your home to an animal in need. Did the boys choose it?"

Claire frowned and turned to face her mother. "Wait. *What?*"

"I was a bit worried Bear might frighten it off, but it seemed just fine." Josephine tilted her head from side to side, gently stretching her neck. "What do you call it?"

"Jesus," Claire muttered under her breath as she walked briskly to the back door.

Josephine's eyebrows shot up. "Seriously?"

"What? No!" She paused, her hand on the doorknob, as her mother's words sunk in. "Did you say bear? What's a bear?"

"Oh." Josephine snapped her fingers. "Didn't I mention I adopted a rescue dog? Huh. I could have sworn I had." She shrugged her shoulders.

Claire stared at her.

Josephine, oblivious to her daughter's incredulous expression, cocked her head and pointed at the kitchen wall. "I must say, I really like this color. Reminds me of smooth butter. Did you choose it, or was it already here when you moved in?"

Claire yanked open the back door. First the boys. Then her mother. Then the dog. "I chose it," she said, over her shoulder, as she rapidly descended the stairs into the yard.

* * * *

Josephine sat at Claire's kitchen table, Bear laying contentedly at her feet on the pale tile floor, and watched her daughter. Good God, the poor thing ran herself unnecessarily ragged. Her concentrated activity gave the impression she was auditioning for a game show where her mothering skills would be compared against other mothers and she was fighting to win. From the moment Evan and Noah had stepped into the house, she hadn't stopped *attending*. It was exhausting to watch.

Josephine rubbed her hand across the distressed wood table top and took a sip from a glass of iced tea Claire had poured for her before she'd began scouring the twins. She sighed, knowing she had no choice. She couldn't just sit and watch. She had to jump into the fray.

"I think they'll be fine, Claire."

Claire continued to assist Noah and Evan, each of them standing on a sturdy white step stool in front of the kitchen sink, washing between each of their fingers. "Of course they will," she replied, while lathering on more soap. "But the only way they'll learn how to do it properly is by example."

Josephine rolled her eyes and leaned over to give Bear an affectionate pat on his small, shaggy head. Judging by Claire's reaction to discovering the boys hanging out with that neighborhood cat, a person would think the damned thing was carrying the plague.

"Animals are cleaner than we are," she offered, flexing her feet in front of herself and admiring her purple painted toenails. "It's a scientific fact."

Noah twisted his body in her direction, his face a picture of surprise. "Really, Gramma? Cats and dogs are cleaner than us?"

Josephine grinned at her grandson. She could understand his incredulity at the statement. Especially as his mother appeared to have cornered the marked on cleaning products. "Yup. And even if they're not more clean, they're *just as* clean."

"That's cool," Evan offered, nodding his head thoughtfully.

Claire rolled her eyes. Another one of her mother's *scientific facts.* Oy. She turned on the faucet and gestured to the boys to rinse their hands. "Well, either way," she said, pulling fresh hand towels from a drawer. "It's just good sense to wash your hands after playing with a stray animal."

"Corkscrew isn't a stray, Mommy." Evan shot her a pitying look as he took one of the towels she was holding out and began drying his small hands.

"Corkscrew?" Josephine laughed delightedly and picked up a cookie from the blue plate Claire had set on the table.

"Uh-huh." Evan nodded. "And he belongs to Mister Thomas. Which means he has a home."

"Mister Thomas?" Josephine brightened, while she took a bite of cookie.

"Uh-huh," Noah replied, taking the other towel. "He's our friend."

"Really?" Josephine swallowed and picked up her glass.

"*Anyway*," Claire said, swiftly nipping the bud of the conversation she knew was to follow. "Whatever Corkscrew's living status, he's an outside cat and you don't know where he's been."

Josephine snorted and took a sip from her glass. Claire shot her a warning look, before shifting the twins' focus. "So, I think you're okay in those shorts and t-shirts, they still look relatively clean. Do you boys want iced tea with your cookies like Gramma, or some juice?"

"Iced tea," they said in unison, dropping their towels on the countertop and jumping down from their step stools.

"Coming up." Claire tucked her hair behind her ears and reached into the cupboard for two spill proof cups.

"Can we pet Bear?" Noah crouched down in front of the small dog, making him wag his long tail furiously back and forth across the floor.

"Of course you can." Josephine grinned as Bear scrambled upright, then sat politely waiting for attention.

"You're so cute," Noah said, before he and Evan began to lavish the small dog with affection.

"So, when did you get him?" Claire asked, even though she really wanted to ask what had possessed her to adopt a dog in the first place. To her knowledge, her Mother had never indicated she was a 'dog person'.

"About a month ago. Not long after my last visit to see you." Josephine put her tea back on the table and ate the rest of her cookie. She knew there was more.

Claire finished pouring iced tea. "Here guys," she said, holding out the cups and suppressing the desire to make them wash their hands all over again. "And you got him from *where*, exactly?"

"The SPCA." Josephine regarded Bear with eyes full of affection as he resettled himself at her feet. "He was so sweet and soft and gentle and just plain didn't belong there." She sighed and shook her head. "Well, none of them do, do they?"

"I like him," Noah said, firmly, clutching his cup.

Evan nodded and set his cup on the table. "He's a keeper."

Josephine laughed and shifted her adoring gaze to her grandsons. They were fantastic. "I have to agree. That's why he's our new family dog."

Evan and Noah's faces lit up and Claire clenched her teeth. "Wait, wait," she said, raising her hands out in front of herself as though she was slowing traffic. "That doesn't mean Bear gets to stay here." She pointed at the dog, then at Josephine. "Even though Gramma said he's now part of the family, he still lives with her at her house. Right, Gramma?"

Josephine smirked. Her daughter was making it very difficult to not say the very thing that would drive her around the bend. *However....* She cleared her throat. "Yes. Mommy's right. Bear is our new family member, and he does live with me, but we all get to give him affection when he's around." She raised a questioning eyebrow at Claire to make sure she'd said the right thing.

"Exactly." Claire gave her a sharp nod, answering her silent inquiry.

The twins deflated slightly and reached for cookies from the plate on the table.

Claire pulled out two chairs and gestured for them to sit. "So, what breed is he?"

"The people at the shelter said he looks to be a Maltese and Silky Terrier mix." She cocked her head at the shaggy, cream colored dog. "He looks a lot like that dog from that TV show, remember? Benji?"

"Benji?" Evan echoed around a mouthful of cookie. "I thought he was a Bear, Gramma."

"Mouth closed when chewing," Claire interrupted.

Evan pressed his lips together.

"Can I offer you anything else?" Claire looked around the kitchen. "Some fruit, maybe?"

"No, no." Josephine waved her hand dismissively. "Don't worry about me. I'm just fine and dandy."

"Fine and dandy," Noah repeated as he munched happily on a cookie. "Like dandelions."

"Exactly like that," Josephine agreed, chuckling.

"Noah, mouth," Claire said as Josephine snapped her finger.

"Hey!" she said. "That gives me an idea."

Evan and Noah turned toward her, eager to hear whatever she had to say. In their experience, when Gramma said 'that gives me an idea', fun was just around the corner.

"Why don't you boys go and check in the grass in the backyard for some fine and dandy dandelions. You can give them to Mommy to decorate the table."

Jackpot.

Noah and Evan simultaneously stuffed the last of their cookies into their mouths. They were in such perfect unison, Claire was slightly startled. She quickly regrouped.

"Hey, hey. Slow down. No choking."

"Sorry, Mommy," Noah said, swallowing his mouthful, then chasing it with a gulp of iced tea.

Claire cringed. She hated when either one of them did that. It was a choking episode waiting to happen. Not to mention, terrible table manners.

"Can we go?" Evan rubbed his fingers on his shirt, his eyes wide and hopeful.

Claire could have told them to use napkins, but what was the point? To keep the dandelions clean? She nodded, releasing them.

With eager energy, he and Noah leaped from their chairs and shot out of the kitchen on their quest. Bear stood up, alert, and Josephine patted his head soothingly. "They'll be right back," she told him.

Claire cut her eyes at her mother. "Thanks a lot, by the way."

"What?" Josephine's eyebrows knotted together in confusion. Bear turned in circles a couple of times, then resettled himself with a sigh on the floor. "What'd I do?"

Exasperated, Claire waved her hand in the direction of the back door. "I just got them cleaned up and now they're going to go slithering through the grass, getting covered in more stains, which will mean more—"

"Oh, *Claire*." Josephine pinched the bridge of her nose and sighed. "For goodness sake! They're four year old boys. Let them be children while they have the chance."

"Easy for *you* to say," Claire muttered under her breath, while she finally poured herself a glass of iced tea and pulled out a chair to sit down. Honestly, it was like her mother was still the twenty two year old woman she'd been when she'd started mothering. Not that she'd worked all that hard at it. Claire had had to learn pretty early on to get things handled herself, or they didn't get done.

"Pardon?" Josephine fixed her with a knowing eye. "Something you need to say, daughter of mine?"

Claire settled into her chair. "I was just *saying*, it's easy to offer comments when you're not doing the work."

Josephine laughed out loud and looked at her with affection. "Well, of course it is! I do remember, you know. But, instead of worrying so much about everything being just so, I chose to spend at least some of my time enjoying you while I could. I knew it would go by in a shot and your childhood would be over."

Claire held her tongue and took a sip of her tea, refusing to be baited. Her mother had raised a girl, not twin boys who seemed to be carbon copies of each other. Wasn't it supposed to be that, with twins, they had opposite temperaments? Almost as though they had divided up the personality traits, making one more cautious and the other more adventurous, or some such thing. Clearly, her boys smashed that theory.

Josephine leaned her elbows on the table, making her silver bracelets glitter in the sunshine streaming through the large kitchen window. "All I can say, dear daughter, is just please try to remember that the only *work* you have is what you make for yourself."

"What's that supposed to mean?" Claire frowned at Josephine's code and placed her glass on the table.

"It means exactly that. There are things in the *have to do* pile." She held her left hand aloft, palm up. "And things in the *get to it* pile." She put her right hand out to match her left. "And most of the things we put in the *have to do* pile, don't need to be there at all." She mimed tossing the imaginary things in her left hand over to her right.

"Oh, please." Claire pursed her lips in annoyance. "Are you suggesting I take all of the things, like laundry for instance, that need to be done and just dump them in your *get to it* pile? Because, trust me, with two four year olds in the house, laundry needs to get done!"

"Well, of course it does!" Josephine sat back in her seat and folded her arms loosely over her chest. "But, every darn toy doesn't need to be put away and every surface freshly dusted." She cocked her head and asked, "My God, who's looking over your shoulder anyway? Is it Jake?"

"Of course not!" Claire shifted her glass of tea further back on the table, concerned that in her vehemence she'd slop it all over her clean kitchen floor. "Jake never says boo about anything I do, or *don't* do. He's well aware I work hard taking care of the boys and our life and he's nothing but supportive."

When Claire stopped to take a breath, Josephine interjected, "Okay, so we've determined Jake is the good guy we've always known him to be. Wonderful news. Sooo, I'll ask again. Who's looking over your shoulder?"

Claire glared. She didn't appreciate what was being implied. What was her point, anyway? That she was too fussy? Or, was her mother just making comments to stir the pot? Whatever the case, as far as Claire was concerned, she didn't have time for any of it. She had a family to raise.

"Found some!" Noah burst into the kitchen through the back door. His fists were clenched around a bundle of newly picked dandelions and specks of dirt and grass were dropping delicately onto Claire's recently washed tile floor.

Evan followed closely behind, a huge grin on his face as he held his equally messy handful aloft.

"Brilliant, boys!" Josephine clapped her hands in delight while Bear danced around her feet. "Time for some water and a vase."

Claire looked at her sons' filthy hands, then shifted her gaze to their green stained knees below their once pristine tan shorts, and sighed. She wouldn't think about the already teetering pile of clothing awaiting her attention in her *have to do* pile in her laundry room.

"Maybe some tall cups would work best," she said, reaching into her cupboard one more time.

* * * *

CHAPTER 5

"I just don't understand why you think this is a good place to drop your toys," Claire said, while snaking her hand and arm into the vent in their family room. "One of these days I'm not going to be able to reach it and then it will be lost forever."

Noah shuffled his feet on the hardwood, thinking. Finally he spoke up. "That's why I don't put small stuff in there, Mommy. That way you can reach."

Claire bit her lip to keep from grinning. Out of the mouths of babes. "How about you just stop altogether," she said, reaching a teeny bit further and finally making contact with the toy dump truck. "Find another place to drop your stuff, like in your toy box. Okay?"

"Okay. Sorry, Mommy."

Claire grasped the edge of the dump truck and pulled, yanking it from the hidden depths of the vent. "There," she said, grimacing. Man, it was dusty in there. She'd have to look up vent cleaners. "Now go and wash it in the bathroom sink before you play with it."

Noah's face broke into a huge grin. He nodded, grabbed the truck from Claire's hand and bolted up the stairs.

"I'm coming right up," she called behind him as she replaced the grate cover and stood up from the floor. "No splashing water all over the bathroom!"

Suddenly, a sharp knock came from the back door and a woman's voice rang out. "Yoohoo!"

"Oh, nuts," Claire muttered, under her breath, recognizing the owner of the voice. She brushed vent lint from her hands and halfheartedly straightened her ponytail.

"Anybody home?"

"In here," she called back, making her way toward the kitchen with a reluctant heart.

"THERE you are!" The woman, Jake's mother and subsequently Claire's mother-in-law, clapped her hands excitedly when Claire entered the kitchen.

"Hi, Peggy," Claire just barely managed to utter, before Peggy grabbed her and wrapped her in a tight, almost breathtaking, hug.

"You made it! You're here!" Peggy enthused. She pushed Claire back and beamed at her, her round face full of delight.

"We did," Claire said, taking a large breath when Peggy released her and suppressing the urge to rub her ribs.

"Oh, I could just kick myself for planning our vacation at the same time as your move!" Peggy looked around the room, her brown eyes almost ravaging in their curiosity. "But, nothing could be done. Nothing! The tickets were booked and we had no choice. We had to go."

"It's fine, really," Claire assured her, privately wishing she and her husband, Jake's father Earl, were still on vacation. "Nothing exciting was going on, anyway. We've just been settling in—"

"The boys!" Peggy blurted, cutting her off. "Where are my grandsons?"

She set off through the kitchen toward the family room, scanning as she moved. The way she seemed to know her way around was slightly alarming. As though she'd scoped the place - say, during an open house - before Claire and her family had made their move.

"Upstairs," Claire said, attempting to get ahead of her to lead the way. Why she even bothered, she didn't know. Her mother-in-law, while short in stature and plump all around, was a force of nature all her own.

"Noah! Evan!" Peggy called in a sing-song voice, before she arrived at the staircase to the second floor. "Grandma Peggy is finally here!"

Shrieks of excitement drifted toward them from the upper floor and a moment later both boys came thundering down the stairs.

"There you are!" Peggy gushed, standing at the bottom with open arms.

Claire winced. "Slow down," she cautioned, ready to catch them as they nearly tripped over their own feet in their rush. "Grandma Peggy's not going anywhere."

"Oh, don't listen to *Mommy*," Peggy said, dismissively, making Claire grit her teeth. "You can be as excited as you like."

"Oh, yeah, won't that be great when they have to go see their father after they've knocked out their front teeth in their *excitement*," Claire muttered under her breath. Thankfully, Noah and Evan's chatter drowned her out.

Claire peered at Noah. He was soaked down the front of his shirt. And his hair looked damp, too. Of course. If he looked like that, who knew in what state he'd left the bathroom. She debated sending him back upstairs for dry clothes, but changed her mind. Peggy was sure to balk at that, too, and she didn't have the energy to do battle. Instead, she took a backseat as her sons greeted their Grandmother; water soaked and all.

"Just think," Peggy told them, clutching them cozily to her sides and shuffling them toward the sofa in the family room. "You'll be able to visit Grandpa Earl and I all the time, now. And we'll be able to come over lots and lots to see you, too! No more planning for visits."

Claire's eyes widened. No more planning? What did that mean? And, was that a not-so-subtle jab in her direction? As though she'd been out of line to want to schedule visits when they'd lived in the city? She clamped her lips shut. She couldn't be sure and she wasn't about to offer any sort of query, especially in front of Noah and Evan.

"You'll have to see our bedrooms, Grandma," Evan said, squirming under her grasp.

"Uh-huh," Noah agreed, also twisting to try and free himself from her squeezing hold.

Claire took pity on them.

"Boys," she said, lightly. "Why don't you each grab a juice box from the fridge and then you can show Grandma Peggy some of the new *Hot Wheels* you bought before we moved."

That was all the prompting they needed. Noah and Evan launched themselves from Peggy's embrace and she nearly fell over on the sofa from their rapid-fire departure. "Goodness," she said, pulling herself upright and straightening her tan blouse as they beetled out of the room. "They must be thirsty."

Claire smiled politely. She had a feeling they'd be debating for a while over their choice of juice. "Can I get you something, Peggy? A coffee? Tea? Juice?"

"No, no." She shook her head of greying pin curls. "Don't trouble yourself. You've still got so much to do around here, you don't need one more person to take care of."

Claire blinked, taken aback. Peggy seemed almost ... thoughtful. "Oh, it's nothing really," she began, perching on the arm of the chair beside the sofa.

"Did you paint in here?"

"Yes." Claire braced herself.

"I thought so." She nodded and smiled as she glanced at the room. "I love the color you chose. So simple and classic."

Claire blanched. Was that a compliment? Or a backhanded insult? She *had* said simple, which could mean so many things. Claire cleared her throat and took the high road. "Thank you, it's called Wheat. I wasn't sure when I picked it—"

"Oh, your instincts were bang on," Peggy assured her. "Very fresh and doesn't clutter up the space. Especially with the boys and all of their toys and such. Too much color can cause chaos."

Okaaaay, Claire thought. She glanced around the room, almost expecting a camera crew to jump out and yell, 'Gotch-ya!'

Peggy sat forward and interlaced her fingers. "And don't you worry, either. Whatever else you and Jakey need to do, like attend to that yellow kitchen for instance, Earl and I will happily take the boys off your hands. I remember how difficult it was to get things done with little ones running in and out."

Claire refrained from saying the kitchen was already painted, thank you very much. She wondered, should she have chosen a different color? Her mother had liked it. But, then, what did *that* say exactly?

"Even the simple things," she remarked with a small laugh, jarring Claire from her thoughts. "Like making sure they're in dry clothes, can be a challenge."

Ah-ha, Claire thought. With one hand she pats and the other she slaps.

"Why, I remember a time when the kids were little," Peggy went on, referring to Jake and his brother and sister. "I had nothing for them to wear for an entire afternoon but their pajamas! Can you imagine?"

"Ummm." Claire blinked, unsure what to say.

"Now, I grant you," she continued. "It may not sound like such a big deal, but trust me in my day it certainly was."

Claire felt her jaw go slightly slack and quickly snapped it shut. What the hell was going on? Was Peggy sharing a mom story? *Peggy*?

"Anyway," she finished, patting gently at the waves of hair that brushed her jawline. "As I said, feel free to call on us."

Claire felt slightly lightheaded from the exposure to the unexpected, decent side of her mother-in-law. "That's very kind. I'll tell Jake you said so and if we need to, we'll take you up on the offer."

Noah and Evan returned, juice boxes in hand, each dragging a blue carrying case full of *Hot Wheels* cars.

"Well, what do we have here?" Peggy asked, her eyes wide as the twins plunked their cases on the area rug and tossed open the lids to reveal shiny cars in a rainbow of colors.

Claire stood up, straightened the hem on her t-shirt and shuffled toward the kitchen. "I'm going to grab a coffee, Peggy," she said, over her shoulder. "Sure I can't interest you?"

Peggy looked up from the row of cars the boys were starting to line up on the coffee table. "I suppose, as long as you already have it made."

"I do," Claire replied. "Fresh pot."

"Okay, then," she relented. "We usually don't have coffee past eleven, but I suppose one cup mid-day wouldn't hurt."

"Coming right up," Claire called out, changing her gait from a shuffle to a speed walk. It was all a bit too surreal. The faster she made it to the kitchen for a breather, the better.

* * * *

"I think something's going on with your mother," Claire commented, while standing in front of the ensuite bathroom mirror and vigorously brushing her hair.

Jake, sprawled across the bed in the adjacent room, pulled himself up onto his elbow. "How so?"

"She was acting strangely when she came over today, not her usual self." Claire put her brush down on the granite countertop, clicked off the light and strode into the bedroom. "Or, maybe she was sort of herself, but not." She frowned, then shook her head. "Anyway, something was off."

Jake leaned back into his pillow and clasped his hands behind his head. "Off how?"

"Like, out of the blue, she started to sort of share a mom story—"

"Mom story?" he cut in, his brow furrowed in confusion.

She nodded. "Uh-huh. The 'I remember when my kids were young' sort of story."

"Oh."

"So, anyway, she started doing that, then suddenly shifted into her usual mode and asked Noah if our dryer was broken because his shirt was so wet."

Jake grimaced at the backhanded slight. His mother's specialty.

"Exactly," Claire said, responding to his wince. "Her normal sort of crap, right? But then, when she came upstairs, she turned it around—"

"She came up here? Why did she come up here?"

"The boys wanted to show her their new rooms."

Jake nodded. Made sense.

"So, she came up here, saw the mess Noah had made washing his toy in the bathroom sink and do you know what she said?"

Jake shook his head. He wasn't sure he wanted to know, but knew he wasn't really being asked.

Claire folded her arms across her chest. "Nothing."

"Nothing?" He found that very hard to believe.

"Well, okay, maybe not *nothing*, but as good as. Instead of seizing the obvious opportunity to make another backhanded crack about the mess of water and towels everywhere, she made a big show of saying how *adorable* she thought it was Noah had been cleaning his toy all on his own."

Jake raised his eyebrows, unsure of how to react. "Okaaay, I'm not following. That's bad, how?"

"That's the point!" Claire threw her hands in the air in exasperation. "One minute she was making cracks about his wet shirt and our supposedly broken dryer, indirectly jabbing at me for being a crap mother—"

"No." Jake sat upright and tried to protest. "She doesn't think that."

Claire rolled her eyes, then sat on the bed beside him. "*Riiight*. Anyway, she started with that lovely thread, then turned around and said, 'Aren't you such a big boy, Noah, washing your own toys', then did another switcheroo and capped things off by telling me she thought it was great how I'm letting them take more responsibility."

"Maybe she really did think that?" Jake offered, then immediately regretted it when her face darkened and she wagged a finger at him.

"No way. She's never told me she thinks I'm doing a good job. Not once. And now, suddenly, she's complimenting my parenting skills?" She dropped the finger and glared at him. "What the hell is her game?"

Jake kept his mouth shut, pretty certain she wasn't waiting for a reply.

"I'll tell you what I think her game is," she went on, making him glad he'd chosen silence. "Instead of saying directly that she thinks I'm a crap mother, she's tossing around pretty words to throw me off the scent—"

"Oh, come on," he interrupted, trying one more time to insert reason into the conversation. "She doesn't think you're crap. She's just opinionated."

"And passive aggressive," Claire added, before vigorously pummeling her pillow. Jake watched her, his face alarmed, and she paused. "What? I'm fluffing it."

Jake reserved comment. Instead, he said, "Yup, no question, she's passive aggressive. And, we've known this forever and know it's not going to change."

Claire sighed, flopped over onto her pillow and reached out to drag the duvet over her body.

"The real issue is," he pressed, while adjusting his side of the covers, "why is it bugging you so much now?"

Claire tucked her hair behind her ears and turned on her side to face him. "Because I know it's only the beginning."

"Meaning?"

"Meaning, when we lived in the city it was manageable. We arranged our visits - another thing she saw fit to make a dig about - and I could let her little comments and general controlling crap slide because I knew the time was finite. Now, well...." Claire squeezed her eyes shut, unable to finish her thought.

Jake reached over to stroke her hair. "It's going to be fine."

She kept her eyes closed. "And you know this *how*, exactly?"

"It's brand new right now," he told her, still stroking. "She's just excited because we're all so close together now."

Claire opened her eyes and sat upright. "Yeah, about that," she said, exasperated. "Did you know their new house is only four blocks away? Four! They were living on the other side of town when we first told them we were moving and now they live four bloody blocks from here!"

Jake swallowed uncomfortably. He'd been taken off guard by that fact, too. When his Mom had told him she and his Dad were thinking of downsizing and moving a bit closer to his and Claire's new house, he hadn't given it much thought. Finding out they were more or less a stone's throw away was a whole other ballgame.

"We shouldn't have done this, Jake," Claire moaned, before flopping back into the bed linens. "We should have done like you brother and sister and stayed in the city."

"And dealt with having to move to a bigger place in the suburbs because we wanted the boys to have some safety and security," he cut in. "Not to mention dealing with the grueling commute every day to work, and me missing out on all of the stuff at the boys' school because it would take me so long to get home from work."

Claire folded the free half of her pillow over her face, hoping it could hide her from the truth. It was no use. He was right. She knew he was right. They'd made the best choice for the boys by moving back to Boxwood Hills, no question about it. They'd have safety, security, a great neighborhood, grandparents nearby; it was the best thing.

"I know," she said, her voice muffled beneath her pink pillowcase.

Jake gently lifted it from her face, a smile twisting his mouth. "Pardon?"

Claire cleared her throat. "I said, I know all that. I guess I'm just trying to get my sea legs, you know?"

He nodded, then reached to turn off the lamp on his bedside table. He snuggled under the covers, wrapped his arm securely around her waist and spoke softly into the darkness. "We all are, Hon. It'll take a bit, but I know we can do it."

Claire snaked her hand out and laced her fingers through his. "Either that, or we'll have to become fugitives on the lam because I've finally offed your mother."

Jake snickered.

* * * *

CHAPTER 6

"Oooh, now things are going to get interesting." Jessica tossed a small handful of popcorn into her mouth, brushed salt from her fingertips, then pointed toward the large window in her living room.

She and Claire were having a coffee and chat while Noah and Evan played outside on the lawn with a new friend, Sophia. The little girl lived a couple of doors down from Jessica and Kevin and was thrilled to meet two new kids in the neighborhood. Claire had been leery about leaving them outside with strangers, without her, but they were being supervised by Sophia's Grandmother, Rosa; a lovely Italian woman who kept a watchful eye, while seemingly not.

"Oh, no." Claire's face drained of color to match Jessica's pale beige sofa. She turned toward the window. "What's wrong? Are the boys acting up?"

"No, no." Jessica shook her head and laughed, making her silver chandelier earrings shimmer in the light. "Of course not. They're playing fine. Look at them laughing with Sophia."

Claire nodded and relaxed her tense shoulders. She took a sip of coffee from the red mug clutched in her hands. "They seem to be getting along really well."

"I know. It's the best luck they're all the same age. Serendipity." Jessica reached out and scooped another handful of popcorn from a yellow bowl on the glass and metal coffee table. "And, seriously, if you were wondering at all, you couldn't ask for a better family for your boys to get friendly with. They're all wonderful people."

Claire placed her mug on the coffee table and stood up to get closer to the window. "Is that your neighbor, Thomas, over there?" she asked, while peering between the slats of the wooden blinds.

"That's what I was talking about." Jessica's grin grew wider. "Things will get interesting because he's been spotted."

"Spotted?" Claire's brow furrowed in confusion as she adjusted the threaded tie she'd used to pull her hair back into a nondescript ponytail.

"Thomas tends to keep a low profile around here."

Claire raised an eyebrow. From her limited experience, it appeared the man was around every time they were. Hardly hiding in the shadows. "So, you're saying we've just been lucky to see him when we're around?"

Jessica laughed and picked up her coffee cup. "That's one way of looking at it," she agreed, grabbing another handful of popcorn. "But seriously, visible or not, he keeps his own counsel, doesn't get into anyone's business and seems to like it best when we stay on the fringes of his."

"Sounds like an easy neighbor," Claire commented, while silently thinking it would be nice if his cat was the same way.

"He is." Jessica finished the popcorn in her hand and took a swallow of coffee. "And, get this, I've noticed a certain other person has taken a shine to him."

Claire twisted away from the window, her face a picture of surprise. "Really? Who?"

Jessica looked momentarily sheepish. "I hate to gossip."

"Oh, please." Claire waved her hand through the air, before snapping her arm swiftly down to her side. Good lord, the motion had her mother written all over it.

Jessica watched her with curiosity. "Everything okay?"

"Uh-huh." She nodded and urged the conversation forward. "Besides, who am I going to tell?"

"True." Jessica shrugged. "And, it's not like I'm telling you anything that's not obvious to anyone looking."

"Okay, then," Claire urged. "Spill."

"Rosa."

"The grandmother?" Claire found that amazing on many levels. She glanced around the room; took in the pale grey walls, the vibrantly colored abstract art, light wood floors and chocolate brown area rug, while she processed the information. Finally, she frowned and said, "*Him*? Rosa seriously has a thing for *him*?"

Jessica giggled and tucked a jade colored pillow under her hip. "Oh, yeah. No question about it. The woman is smitten. It's been going on since Sophia's mom, Cristina, went back to work part-time a few months ago. Rosa stepped in as chief babysitter for Sophia and Portia and, needless to say, Thomas' days have changed considerably."

"Wow." Claire returned to peeking out the window at Thomas, trying to wrap her brain around it. He was sporting black house slippers, baggy, navy blue pants that looked more like pajamas than street wear and a faded t-shirt of indeterminate color. His salt and pepper colored hair was all over the place as it always seemed to be when she saw him and, to finish off his *look*, a cigarette dangled from between his lips. Quite the sight.

"I know what you're thinking," Jessica offered, while playing with the fringe on her ruby red top. "But despite his off-beat appearance, he does have a certain live-life-by-his-own-rules charm."

"I'll take your word for it," Claire said, while watching the scene coming to life outside the window. Thomas had been hailed from between his overgrown trees, which was clear from Rosa's sweeping arm gestures, and the kids were swarming around him like a long lost family member. "Do you think we should go out there?" she asked, starting to feel nervous.

Jessica pushed her curls back from her face. "Only if you want to."

"I'm just thinking, if Rosa is so smitten, maybe I should go out and keep an eye on the boys."

Jessica smiled affectionately. Claire's mother hen nature was on full display. "No worries about that," she assured, with complete confidence. "She may appear distracted, but if any one of those kids moves an inch beyond what she thinks is her safety perimeter, she'll be on them so fast you'll be shocked at the blur she can become when she moves."

"Really?" Claire raised a skeptical eyebrow as she observed the curvaceous woman through the window. Outfitted in a cap sleeved, navy blue and white polka-dotted house dress, her short brown curls gleaming in the sunlight, Rosa looked positively tranquil. It was a challenge to think she was acutely aware of anything; except Thomas, of course. "She seems pretty laid back."

"Trust me," Jessica insisted. "She seems laid back, and to a great degree she is. But she can turn on a dime. I've witnessed her move when Sophia was about to go tailing after a butterfly. Greased lightning."

Claire laughed at the image. "Okay. Fine. Yet again, I'll take your word for it."

"Oh, look! We have contact!" Jessica pointed and giggled when Rosa reached out and touched Thomas' tanned arm. "Look at him squirm."

Claire, feeling more confident Rosa could keep up with the kids, giggled as well. "Wow. He has the same expression Noah and Evan get when I tell them they have to eat their broccoli before they can have dessert."

Jessica snickered harder. "Its been going on all summer and every time I get a glimpse, it cracks me up all over again. Its become Kevin's and my living soap opera."

"Has she made any progress?" Claire asked, while leaning forward to watch Thomas suddenly bend down to talk to Noah. "Because he's clearly using the 'talk to the child' defense; bending down well away from her advances."

"Actually, I think she has." Jessica picked up her cup and swallowed the last of her coffee. "At the start of the summer, she could barely get a word in to the man before he'd come up with some sort of work project that needed his immediate attention and bolt. The fact he's sticking around is, I think, a huge step forward."

"Oh, look now. Rosa's giving him the baby to hold."

Claire was referring to Sophia's baby sister, Portia. The child was just shy of a year old and friendly as all get out. They watched as Thomas dropped his cigarette to the pavement, snubbed it firmly out with his foot, retrieved the butt and tucked it into his pocket; all before receiving the smiling baby into his arms.

"That child took a shine to him from the get-go," Jessica stated, then smirked. "Takes after her grandmother."

"We should go out there." Claire smoothed her bangs away from her eyes, all business. "I need to get a closer look and feel for this romantic comedy."

Jessica laughed and stood up. "After you," she said, extending her hand.

* * * *

"Mommy! Mommy! Mommy! Mommy!" Noah and Evan cheered simultaneously as Claire and Jessica descended the porch steps of Jessica's house.

Jessica grinned when the boys came barreling toward them across the lawn, barely able to keep up with their own feet. Such joy. It was wonderful to witness.

"Slow down," Claire cautioned them, holding her hands out. They managed to stop themselves just shy of careening full tilt into her and Jessica's legs. "Where's the fire?" she asked as she reached out to steady them.

"No fires, Mommy," Evan said, matter of fact.

"Birthday parties, though!" Noah enthused. "And go-karts!"

Oh, nuts, Claire thought, clenching her teeth. She'd really hoped they'd let that idea go.

Evan turned a stern face to his brother and folded his arms across his chest in a perfect imitation of an adult. He reminded Claire of Peggy. "Noah!" he huffed. "You said we'd tell it *together.*"

"It's fine." Claire immediately jumped in, patting down any possible friction. "Noah said one part and you can tell me the other. Who's birthday party?"

Evan relaxed his arms and gestured across the lawn toward Sophia, Thomas, Rosa and Portia. "Sophia's baby sister is turning one and we've been invited to her party!"

"Oooh, that sounds like fun," Jessica said, catching a thread of his excitement. "Should we go and find out the details from Sophia's grandma?"

"Her name is Nonna," Evan informed her, while Noah nodded his agreement.

"Right." Jessica caught Claire's eye and grinned. "Should we go ask Sophia's Nonna?"

Evan grabbed Jessica's hand while Noah tucked his into Claire's. They allowed themselves to be lead across the grass to the edge of the yard.

"Luik who's 'ere, now," Thomas piped up, sounding far more enthused than Jessica had heard him in a long while. Granted, it could have been because Rosa was nearly plastered against his side, cooing at Portia in his arms.

"Hi." Claire smiled politely at Thomas and Rosa. She looked down at Sophia and the little girl twinkled up at her. "And hello to you as well, Sophia."

Sophia grinned, her chocolate colored eyes warm and friendly. Claire had a momentary physical tug - the one she usually had when her boys were being all *boyish* - of what it must be like to have a sweet, clean little girl around the house. Not that she didn't love her sons beyond words, that wasn't worth discussing. It was just that ... *sometimes* ... well.... She sighed and reined in her traitorous thoughts.

"Here." Jessica released Evan's hand and extended her arms toward Thomas. "Why don't you take a rest and let me hold Portia."

The look of relief on his face was almost comical. He handed over the cherubic baby, her dark curls begging to be touched and her eyes a startling, unexpected blue. "Of course, of course," he said, his grin shifting from strained to genuine. "Donna wanna be hoggin' the wee one."

Jessica raised an eyebrow and gathered Portia into her arms. Right. More like 'donna wanna' be giving Rosa any more reason to snuggle in close.

"Right," he said, clearing his throat as he pulled a package of cigarettes from his pant pocket and took a couple of slow steps backward from their group. "I shood be gettin' on."

"Oh, no." Rosa adjusted her dress over her ample bosom.

"Aye, 'fraid so."

"Well, it was just lovely seeing you, Thomas." She blinked her eyes flirtatiously at him. "*Meraviglioso.*"

"Do you have to go?" Noah's shoulders slumped in disappointment. He'd taken an obvious shine to the unconventional Scotsman.

"Aww, *bello ragazzo.*" Rosa immediately latched onto the opportunity to keep her crush in their group. "Do you want Mister Thomas to stay, Noah?"

"I canna do it," Thomas said, sounding slightly desperate as he fished in his other pant pocket for his lighter.

"You heard him, Noah." Claire stepped in, saving Thomas.

He shot her a grateful look.

"Mister Thomas is very busy with ... umm." Claire raised an eyebrow in his direction.

"Wuirk!" he blurted, pulling a cigarette from the package in his hand and taking another step backward. "In me shop oot back. Lots to do, lad. Lots to do."

"Right." Claire nodded firmly, agreeing with his story. "We understand. Work comes first."

Noah shuffled the toe of his red and black sneaker back and forth across the lawn. "Okay," he said, reluctantly understanding.

"I'm sure you'll get a chance to see Mister Thomas again very soon, Noah." Jessica attempted to help things along. "Maybe to talk some more about your box cart."

"Go-kart!" Evan cheered excitedly.

"Evan," Claire began to warn, but was cut off by Rosa's laughter.

"It's so darling." She clapped her hands together. "Some fun for the boys."

"What about me, Nonna?"

"Oh!" Rosa pulled Sophia into the ample curve of her hip. "Of course, of course. Boys and girls."

Jessica saw the frown on Claire's face and inwardly cringed. Oops. Wrong tactic, clearly. "Hey, I know," she piped up, pushing things along. "Why don't you all tell us about Portia's birthday party."

Evan and Noah both grinned and Sophia jumped in. "Portia is turning one!" she said, dancing a small jig on the spot.

Thomas took advantage of the distraction, lifted his hand briefly and spun on his heel to speed walk in the direction of his house.

Noah nodded enthusiastically, while Rosa watched Thomas disappear from sight. "Uh-huh, and Nonna said we can go to her party!"

Rosa, hearing her name, snapped back to attention. "Of course!" she said, before reaching out to take Portia from Jessica. "It's not a party unless everybody celebrates!"

"Nonna says the whole block is going to be there!" Evan said, his eyes wide as he swung his arm in a circle to indicate the entire crescent.

"Wow." Claire looked around the street and took in the number of houses as she absorbed the information. "Sounds like quite the party."

"I have another idea," Jessica said, bending slightly at the waist to address the kids. "Why don't you three go into the middle of the lawn and practice rolling toward the edge of the grass while we grownups discuss all the nit-picky details."

The children jumped at the suggestion. They charged toward the middle of the front yard and flopped down on the lawn to start their game.

Claire nodded at Jessica, impressed. "Not bad. Are you sure you don't have kids stashed away somewhere?"

Jessica laughed. "No. I just remember how much fun it was to roll in the grass."

Rosa smiled affectionately as she bounced Portia on her hip and watched the children rolling and cheering each other on, over Claire's shoulder. "They're such darlings, your boys," she said, reaching out to pat Claire on the wrist. "They're welcome any time to come and play with Sophia."

Claire swallowed, slightly overwhelmed by the unasked for praise. She was always so worried the boys would create some sort of bother, she was taken off guard when the feedback was positive. "Thank you," she said, suddenly shy in the face of the compliment.

"So, we've established that Portia's having a party?" Jessica commented, changing the subject when she noticed Claire clamoring to regroup.

"Yes!" Rosa's eyes twinkled in excitement, much as the children's had a moment before. "And it's going to be something." She threw a jovial glance at Jessica. "Of course, you know all about the children's parties."

"I'll say." Jessica turned to Claire. "They are such a treat. You and Jake and the boys should really try and make it."

"Yes!" Rosa said, again. "Your husband. You must bring the boys' father as well. The whole family!"

Claire looked over her shoulder at Noah and Evan, playing and laughing with Sophia. Did she have any other choice? No, of course not.

"We'd love to come," she said, smiling at Rosa. "Thank you so much for the invitation."

"Wonderful, *grandioso*. Sophia's going to help me make the invitations, it's at the end of this month." She tickled Portia, making her giggle, then nodded happily at Claire.

Jessica looked as pleased as Rosa when she said, "Kevin will be so glad to finally meet you. I've told him about you and the boys and Jake."

"Si, si, even more good news," Rosa said, matter of fact. "Families making friends. *Meraviglioso*. Nothing better in the whole world."

Claire watched her plant a loving kiss on the baby's cheek. She had a feeling her comment wasn't offered so much as an opinion, as a fact.

Oh, to have even a fraction of her confidence, she thought. What would that be like?

* * * *

CHAPTER 7

"Thank you, again, for rescuing me in my time of need. You are a prince among men."

Jake laughed and cut a large bite of his strawberry pie with his fork. He was enjoying his dessert, along with a great cup of coffee, in Josephine's eclectic kitchen. Looking around, it was hard to believe she was Claire's mother. The walls were sponged in gentle shades of gold and the cabinets alternated in hues of soft orchid, grass green and Egyptian blue. Her stainless steel countertops and appliances were littered with clay pots filled with flowers and herbs and, in the center of it all, was her monster of a kitchen table. Plank-style and made of well-worn maple, it rested heavily on the pale hardwood floor and looked like something she might have purchased at a farmhouse estate sale.

"Well, ya know," he said, gesturing to his plate before scooping up the piece of pie. "When the gratuity is in the form of homemade pastry, I'm pretty much guaranteed to be available. You grow the best strawberries."

Josephine, leaning up against the countertop, lifted the coffee cup in her hand in a silent toast. "Good to know because, judging from the bounty you picked from that tree, I think I'm also going to be making quite a few plum pies that will need consuming."

"You can count on me, and the boys as well I'd guess," he said, around a mouthful of filling and crust.

"Speaking of which, how's Claire doing?" She placed her mug on the table and settled herself into the chair opposite him. Bear got up from where he'd been wrapped around Jake's feet and walked under the table to snuggle up next to her fluffy yellow slippers.

Jake placed his fork across his empty plate and picked up his coffee. "I think she's doing okay," he said, thoughtfully, while rubbing his free hand across the stubble on his chin. "She's made a friend."

"Jessica?"

"She mentioned her?"

Josephine shook her head and cleared her throat. "No, the boys did. And her cookies."

Jake laughed out loud, then swallowed some coffee.

"Sounds like she's very nice," Josephine offered, cocking her head.

He put down his mug. "I think so. I haven't actually met her yet, but Claire seems really happy about her friendship."

"Hmm," she exhaled.

Jake leaned back in his chair and rested one ankle across his opposite knee. "What?"

"I'm a bit worried about her, to be frank."

His eyebrows lifted. "How come?"

"Call it mother's intuition," she offered, then rested her chin in her hands. "But I get a feeling she's covering."

"For what?"

"A number of things, I'm sure." She sat back and her hands flitted about as she spoke, punctuating her words. "Suppressing her creative side, being a mother of high-spirited twins while she craves control, her struggle with craving control, getting used to being back here in Boxwood Hills, the list goes on and on."

Jake nodded as he listened and thought she was pretty much bang on in her assessment. He ran his fingers through his dark hair, his brow furrowed in concern. "So, what do we do?"

"Honestly?" Josephine let her hands drop gently into her lap and shrugged. "I don't know if there's anything we can do. Until Claire has the desire to address things, it doesn't matter what we think."

He nodded, again. She was right, of course. He'd seen it time and again in his office; patients who didn't want to face their teeth issues and wouldn't commit to their oral health until things got really out of hand. He grimaced. Hopefully Claire wouldn't have to go to that sort of extreme.

"Oh, dear, such a face." Josephine chuckled and pointed at the frown he was wearing. "I'm sorry I brought it up."

Jake laughed and his expression immediately cleared. "No, no, don't be. I think you're right about all of it. I'm just hoping she'll be willing to talk about things before...." He didn't want to finish that sentence in a concrete manner.

Josephine looked at him with affection. He was a good man and she cared about him like a son. "I'm sure it will all work out fine, dear. The less we fret, the better things will get. Energy creates more energy, after all. We just need to put ours into believing Claire will get things sorted out and then get out of the way."

Jake considered her logic. He'd heard worse. He took a breath and reached for his cup. "So, tell me more about this new furry creature that's become a hugely welcomed part of our family."

Josephine smiled and let him change the subject.

* * * *

Thomas examined a chunky, black and white wheel from a child's wagon that matched three others laying on a bench in his workshop. He'd found the wheels at the hardware store in town and thought they'd be perfect for the go-kart Noah and Evan were so excited about building.

Not that they'd actually set anything in stone in that regard.

However, as the boys seemed unwilling to let the idea go, he had a strong hunch it was only a matter of time before they started bringing the cart to life.

Thomas grinned and ran a hand through his beard. While he wouldn't necessarily go around broadcasting it, he had to admit it at least to himself, the idea of working with the lads pleased him. He'd never had grandchildren and while he wasn't keen to be friends with every person he met, he did enjoy the occasional association with young people. They were open and enthused; straight forward and without pretense. Often much better company, he thought, than most adults.

He pulled a cigarette from a package laying on the bench adjacent to the wheels, pulled his silver zippo lighter from his pant pocket and struck a flame. "Claire will want it ta be very safe," he said, talking out loud to himself.

He lit his cigarette and exhaled a blue-grey plume of smoke. "Won't be a problem," he said, nodding to himself in answer and tucking the lighter back in his pocket. "Nay a problem at all. Should be a grand bit o'fun."

* * * *

Jake swung open the back door and stepped into the house. "Pizza delivery! Fresh and hot pepperoni pizza, come and get it!"

"Pizza!" Evan parroted enthusiastically while jumping to his feet from his spot on the family room floor, next to Noah. They'd been playing with their toy cars and watching *Bob the Builder* on TV, while Claire worked on cleaning the grout around the tiles in the guest bathroom.

"Claire?" Jake said, from the kitchen.

Claire, still in the bathroom, pulled off her yellow rubber gloves and nodded in satisfaction. The stains had been bothering her since they'd moved in, but no longer. She'd done a fine job and the grout looked brand new. Amazing what a little elbow grease could do.

"In here," she replied, while holding the gloves under the tap and giving them a quick rinse.

Jake poked his head around the corner of the doorway and smiled at his wife. "Better hurry. The boys charged in here like they were shot out of a cannon. We may have to resort to eating their abandoned crusts."

Claire chuckled and arranged the gloves beside the sink to dry. It was surprising how much food two little boys could put away. It made her wonder what they'd have to do when they were teenagers? Purchase a second fridge?

"Hey." Jake pointed to the grout and nodded in appreciation. "Nice job."

"And you said it was fine the way it was," Claire teased as she squirted vanilla scented lotion into her palm from a bottle on the countertop.

He grinned and tipped an imaginary hat. "I stand corrected."

"So, how was your day?" she asked, while rubbing the lotion into her hands.

"Busy." He backed out of the doorway and Claire followed him into the kitchen.

"That's good, right?"

"Very good," he agreed, while she efficiently pulled one green and one blue cup from the cupboard, filled them with water and placed them in front of Noah and Evan seated at the table. "I stopped in at your Mom's at lunch and she sent a bag of plums for us."

"Oh? Everything ok?" she asked, before grimacing at Noah and Evan's sauce and cheese smeared faces.

He loosened the top buttons on his grey dress shirt. "Fine."

Claire pulled napkins from a wicker basket on the table and handed them to both boys. "Faces wiped. And mouths closed when chewing, please."

Jake grinned when Noah made a concerted effort to chew with his lips pressed firmly together. "She just needed some help picking the fruit and I had the time, so I went by."

"That was nice of you." She walked over to the fridge and pulled a mixed salad from its depths.

"I didn't mind," he said, while taking a plate from the countertop and piling pizza onto it from the cardboard box in the middle of the table. "Brought me back to my youth, days spent picking crabapples for my grandfather."

"What's a crappy apple?" Noah asked, around a mouthful of cheese and dough.

Jake laughed and set his plate down on his yellow placemat. "Crabapple. It's a small red apple and it's delicious."

"We should have some," Evan said, matter of fact.

"We should. Maybe we'll go to the farmer's market one weekend and buy some."

"I think Sophia has apples," Noah commented, before taking a drink from his cup.

Claire closed the fridge with a bump of her hip and brought the salad bowl to the table. "Really? I don't remember a tree at their house."

"Who's Sophia?" Jake pulled out his chair and sat down.

"A new friend we met today." Noah smiled as he remembered the fun they'd had that afternoon. "And Portia is having a party and we're invited."

Jake raised an eyebrow at Claire.

"Jessica's neighbor, a couple doors down, has a little girl—"

"Sophia," Evan interjected.

"Yes, Sophia," Claire agreed, as she walked back over to the fridge and pulled out a bottle of Italian salad dressing. "And, her baby sister is turning one and the boys—"

"*All* of us, Mommy," Noah corrected. "You, me, Evan and Daddy."

"Right," Claire nodded. "All of us have all been invited."

Noah raised his eyebrows at Evan as Claire placed the dressing on the table, next to the salad. "That's what I said."

"Sounds like fun," Jake said, before taking a large bite of his pizza.

"Gramma isn't so worried about how clean our hands are," Evan told Jake, with a shrug of his slim shoulders.

Claire almost choked at the unexpectedness of the statement. Where the hell had that come from?

"Oh, yeah?" Jake offered, neutrally, clearly having the same thought. "What made you think of that, buddy?"

"The plums from Gramma."

"Ahh," he said, unsure of what to say next.

Claire sat down heavily in her chair. *She* wasn't unsure of what to ask next. "Did Gramma tell you that, Sweetie?"

Evan shrugged again. "No."

Claire waited.

"But," he elaborated, "when we play at her house she doesn't make us wash our hands, or change our clothes and stuff."

"She says," Noah tossed in, a happy grin on his face as he recalled his Grandmother's pearls of wisdom. "'Sometimes life can get messy and that's when the fun starts'."

Claire picked up the salad tongs and nodded slowly while serving a helping of greens onto all of their plates. Now she was stumped. What did she say to that?

"Well, ya know," Jake spoke up, grabbing the proverbial ball and attempting to run interference. "Grammas are allowed to be like that. In fact, it's one of the perks of being a Gramma."

"What's perks?" Evan's eyes were bright and interested as he awaited Jake's reply.

"Oh, umm." He paused to think of a simpler word. "It means something extra. Sort of a bonus." He looked at Noah's pajamas, the blue printed flannel showing off an array of colorful cars and traffic signs, and was hit with inspiration. "Like when you get a new toy car and there's a perk of getting a set of plastic traffic signs with it."

Evan's eyes widened in appreciation. "I like that."

"Me, too," Noah agreed, speedily, tracing one of the yellow yield signs on the leg of his green pajama bottoms with his finger. "Those signs are fun to use when we play traffic jam."

"So, you see," Jake said, realizing he was drifting dangerously close to Josephine territory with his *insight*. "Gramma gets to have perks and not have to worry about things like clean hands."

"But, Mommy does?"

"Uh-huh." He nodded at Evan and figured, what the heck, he had a toe in the pool. May as well dive in all the way. "It's in the Mommy handbook."

Noah and Evan looked thoughtful as they considered their father's information.

Claire said nothing and stuffed a forkful of salad into her mouth. She was at a loss as to what, if anything, to add to the conversation. The thought, *think about it*, nagged at the edges of her mind, but she dismissed it. It was a reasonable request, except for one small detail: she had no time to do so.

* * * *

CHAPTER 8

C laire tugged self-consciously on the hem of her beige, knee length skirt. She had considered wearing dress pants, but it was such a warm evening the skirt felt more appropriate.

"You look sensational, Hon," Jake said, reaching for her fidgeting hand and smiling understandingly into her eyes. "Nothing to worry about."

Claire clutched his fingers and looked around as they entered the elementary school gymnasium, Evan and Noah in tow. Wow, it was large for a grade school. She let out a small exhale of relief when she saw more than a few skirts amidst the chinos, jeans and shorts in the crowd. She didn't stand out like a sore thumb.

"Wow," Jake echoed her thoughts. "It's a lot larger than I thought it would be."

Claire nodded. "I'll say."

"Look, Daddy." Noah tugged on Jake's hand as he pointed to the other end of the gym.

Jake smiled at the basketball hoops secured to the backboards on the gym walls. "Yup, looks like they have some fun in here, doesn't it?"

"They're really far away," Evan commented, tucking his hand snuggly into Claire's as he looked up at the red hoops.

"Yeah." Jake nodded and inhaled the smell of freshly waxed floors with pleasure. "But you'll get bigger and then they won't seem so high."

Claire took in the large number of people milling about. "Quite the turn out. Jessica wasn't kidding about the parents in the community being hugely supportive."

"And then some," Jake agreed.

Evan squeezed Claire's hand. "Look, Mommy, snacks!" He pointed toward a long table teeming with pastries, bags of chips and popcorn, bottled water and juice boxes.

"Okay." She shared a grin with Jake as they let themselves be dragged across the wooden floor. "Let's go have a look."

* * * *

Claire watched Evan and Noah circling the snack table, making their choices. "Just a few," she instructed. "We can always come back a second time after we've looked around the school a bit."

"They have the same cookies Jessica gave us," Evan said, excitedly, pulling on the sleeve of Noah's navy blue polo shirt.

"Did you say Jessica is a tall redhead?"

Claire darted her eyes toward Jake, then swiftly back to the boys. "Why? Do you see her?"

"Is that her?" With a rise of his chin, he indicated toward a striking woman walking in their direction from the other side of the gym.

Claire looked up and a wave of relief washed over her. "Yes." She smiled as Jessica lifted a hand in greeting, and the stress disappeared from her face.

Jessica, resplendent in a sleeveless, cream colored dress splashed with yellow and green flowers, stopped in front of them. "Claire," she said, happily. "You came."

Evan's face lit up in delight upon seeing his favorite redhead. "We're choosing snacks!"

"I see that." Jessica repressed the urge to scoop him up in a hug. Even though she'd only known both boys for a few weeks, she was already completely taken with them. "Everything looks yummy."

"You smell nice," Noah said, referring to the soft floral scent Jessica was wearing.

Jessica giggled. "Thank you, Noah." She turned to Jake and smiled warmly. "And you must be Jake. I recognize you from your photos."

Jake extended his hand. "Got me in one."

Claire blushed and pushed her bangs from her forehead. "Sorry, I was distracted by the small land sharks," she said, shrugging her shoulders. "Jake meet Jessica. Jessica this is my husband, Jake."

Jessica shook his hand, then patted Claire affectionately on the arm. "It's nice to finally meet the man who was instrumental in bringing my lovely new friend home to Boxwood Hills."

Claire's eyebrows shot up in surprise. It was such a kind thing to say, she didn't know how to respond. Thankfully, she had the boys to watch and save her from more awkward blundering.

"Okay, I think that's good," she told Noah, before he started on his second go-around. "One Rice Crispy square and two oatmeal cookies is fine for now. Grab a juice box and you're set."

"Claire and I were saying you've got quite the turn out," Jake commented, folding his tan arms across the front of his teal dress shirt.

Jessica nodded. "Every year. It's nice to see so many of the parents show their support for their kids and the school. And, just so you know, there are a lot just like yourselves whose kids still have a year to go before they enter Kindergarten. That's why I suggested you come."

"I'm really glad you did," Claire said, then pointed a firm finger at Evan. "You're set, too. Choose a juice box like Noah did."

Jessica glanced around, trying to spot her husband. "Kevin's here somewhere. We can go and find him and he can take us for a tour of the school and his classroom if you like."

"Sounds great." Jake held out his hands to take the juice boxes Noah and Evan carried, freeing them up to focus on their plates.

"Look, Mommy!" Noah sprayed a fine mist of cookie crumbs from his lips in his excitement.

Claire swallowed the reflex to tell him not to speak with his mouth full and, instead, looked to her left where he was pointing. "Oh, nuts," she exhaled, blinking and staring in disbelieve.

"It's Gramma," Evan announced as they caught sight of a brightly dressed, animated woman chatting with a man twenty years her junior.

Jessica's eyebrows lifted in question when she saw the surprise on Claire's face. Clearly Gramma had not been expected. At least not by Claire.

"Hey, Hon," Jake said, a bright smile plastered on his face as the boys ran ahead, their shoes squeaking on the shiny floor, leaving the three of them to bring up the rear. "Look who's here."

"I see." Claire clenched her teeth and forced a tight grin as she made eye contact with Jake. "What an unexpected surprise."

Jessica watched Claire, then Jake. The tension in their voices made the hairs on her arms stand on end. "You won't believe this," she said, keeping her own voice light and cheery. "Gramma is actually talking to my Kevin, of all people."

Claire let out a slow exhale as she watched her mother clap her hands in delight at the arrival of her grandsons. "Of course she is."

* * * *

Just when you think you're in the clear, Claire thought, stretching her tense neck from side to side.

Not that she didn't love her mother, of course she did. It was just that, in nearly all of her memories of Josephine, the woman did not do well in social situations. Actually, that wasn't the truth. It was more the opposite. She did *too* well in social situations. Never one to sit on the sidelines, Josephine tried to drag whoever was in her sphere along for the ride. And, while Claire knew her mother's intentions were pure, she didn't share the same inclination to such a gregarious nature. It often made for a bumpy commute.

"Claire Rose!"

Claire jerked herself away from her thoughts and braced herself for her mother's extravagant greeting. She wasn't disappointed.

"My gorgeous daughter has finally come back home and brought her beautiful boys with her!" She wrapped her arms tightly around Claire's torso.

Claire suppressed the urge to roll her eyes. You'd think she hadn't seen them in years, as opposed to days.

"You must meet this lovely teacher," Josephine told them, while releasing her hold on Claire. "His name is Kevin and he teaches fourth grade at this school."

Hoping she sounded pleasant, instead of embarrassed, Claire replied, "Yes, mother. We know."

"Great to finally meet you." Kevin offered his hand, grinning easily all the while. "Jess has nothing but glowing praise to say about you."

Claire smiled at him while Jake shook his hand. He seemed as open and welcoming as her friend.

Josephine's eyebrows shot up in surprise and she pressed a hand to her chest, the gold and silver charm bracelets on her wrists jangling merrily. "You know of each other already?"

Claire cleared her throat and gestured to Jessica. "Yes. Kevin is married to my friend, Jessica."

Jessica watched with amusement, intrigued by the effervescence of Claire's mother. Never would she have expected such a vivacious woman.

"Well, of course! This is the much adored Jessica!"

Claire reflexively braced herself when her mother reached out and grabbed Jessica in a warm squeeze. Adverse to physical contact, she wasn't.

"So good to meet you!" she enthused, still hugging. "My, you're so pretty! I'm Josephine!"

Jessica laughed into Josephine's tangle of curls. She smelled lovely, like vanilla and cinnamon. When Josephine released her, she found herself caught up in her enthusiasm. "It's great to meet you, too. Claire didn't mention you were coming tonight."

Josephine shrugged her shoulders. "That's because she didn't know." She giggled and played with the charms on one of her bracelets. "I'm often a spur of the moment gal. Isn't that right, Claire?"

Claire nodded jerkily and took a deep breath to try and calm her sudden, increased heart rate. "Spot on, Mother."

Jake's eyes bounced back and forth between the two women. Claire didn't look good. "You okay?" he asked, quietly.

"Uh-huh," she said, swallowing. "Just a bit hot, all of a sudden."

Josephine patted Jessica's forearm affectionately. "My best girlfriend, Ginnie, is here with her grandkids and I figured what the heck, a night out is a night out! It's just a happy coincidence my grandsons are here, too!"

Jake shot another look at Claire, she seemed to be holding up, and dipped his toe into the conversation. "The more the merrier, right?"

"Exactly." She shot him an affectionate look before turning her attention to Noah and Evan. "So! Tell me boys, what do you think of the big kid's school so far?"

"Good snacks," Noah told her, smacking his lips in approval.

Josephine released a peel of girlish laughter, while Claire shot poignant looks at Jake and he shrugged his shoulders helplessly.

Jessica observed from the sidelines and inwardly cringed at the disconnect between mother and daughter. Although, watching Josephine's easygoing manner, she thought she might have to just feel pity for Claire. She was the only one who looked uncomfortable, as though she wanted to apologize for her mother, and Jessica wished she could assure her it wasn't necessary.

"Well, listen." Josephine adjusted her shimmery blouse and fluffed her hair. "I've taken enough of your time."

Kevin, standing beside Jessica, grinned. The woman was a real firecracker. "Listen, before you go, I meant what I said. I appreciate your interest in our art program. I'll be in touch if I find out we need extra thoughts or helping hands."

Josephine shot him a flirtatious look, then winked at Jessica. "Oh, you gorgeous thing. You flatter me. I'm sure the rest of the parents are dying to get an audience and put in their two cents worth with mister charming teacher."

Claire nearly doubled over in her mortification. "Mom!" she spat.

Jessica, on the other hand, burst out laughing.

"Sorry, sorry." Josephine shrugged her shoulders. "Sometimes my mouth forgets to censor my thoughts."

"Censor," Evan repeated. "What does censor mean?"

Jake turned to his son. "I'll tell you later."

Suddenly, the distinct sound of trumpets began to play, followed by Louie Armstrong singing, *When the Saints Go Marching In*. Claire looked at Jake with raised eyebrows and he shook his head.

"Oh! That's me!" Josephine began to fish around in the pocket of her purple, orange and red patterned gypsy skirt and pulled out her cellphone. She pointed to the screen. "It's Ginnie!" She slid her finger across the screen and laughed into the phone. "Ginnie! Where are you?"

Kevin jumped in, while Josephine began scanning the gymnasium for her friend. "Why don't we go and see my classroom," he said, taking a small step forward, breaking the sightline between Claire and her mother.

Claire, now looking at his shoulder, let her gaze drop to the floor as she regained her composure. Her heartbeat had calmed back down and she breathed steadily, relaxing into the steady flow of air, in and out.

Jessica reached out a hand and placed it gently on Claire's forearm, much as she had done the first day they'd met. "I'm going to do a couple more turns around the room, so if I don't see you in a bit," she said, looking directly into her eyes. "I'll call you tomorrow and we can arrange a get together, okay?"

Claire nodded, grateful for her kindness.

"Okay, then," Kevin said, all business. "Let's go see my classroom."

Noah and Evan offered their empty paper plates to Claire, then happily reached up to clasp their father's hands; ready for the next adventure.

* * * *

"Well, that was interesting," Jessica said as she and Kevin walked past the principal's office, toward the elementary school exit.

They were amongst the final few to leave, helping to clean up after the parents and children departed for the evening.

Kevin held the door open for her. "Which part?"

"Claire and her mother."

"Ahh." He followed her out of the building.

"Claire looked positively gobsmacked."

"I'd say that's an accurate description," he agreed, a small laugh in his voice as he reached for her hand, interlacing his fingers with hers.

"And a little sick," she added, as they made their way out of the parking lot and began walking down the quiet street.

"Really?"

"Uh-huh." Jessica recalled how Claire's skin had suddenly gone pale. "It didn't last long, but I saw it."

"And she seemed oblivious to any of it," he commented, strolling at an easy pace and enjoying the warm evening air.

"Who, Josephine?"

"Yeah."

"Truth be told, I was a little surprised at how, umm." Jessica paused, searching for the accurate word to describe Claire's mother.

"*Colorful* she was?"

She laughed. "Yeah, I guess that's as good a word as any." She shook her head, remembering the strong hug Josephine had pulled her into so unexpectedly. "I honestly don't think I would ever have pegged her as Claire's mom."

Kevin watched a calico cat slink across the street; the yellow street lamps illuminating it in the dusk. "Yeah, I wonder if people who know Josephine first think the same thing, in reverse."

"What do you mean?"

"Think about it. If you knew Josephine first, wouldn't you be surprised when you met Claire?"

Jessica nodded. She inhaled deeply, sure she could smell the sweetness of evening primrose on the breeze.

"They were really nice, though," Kevin offered.

"Claire and Jake?"

"Yeah. I liked them," he said, gently squeezing her hand.

Jessica grinned into the fading light, while the bark of a dog echoed in the distance. "Good. And their sons—"

"Are fantastic," he finished as they rounded the corner of their crescent and began walking up the street.

When they made it to the front of their house, Jessica stopped on the sidewalk.

Kevin stopped, too, and looked at her inquiringly. "What is it?"

"I'm ready."

His brow furrowed and he shook his head. "Ready?"

"To start trying," she said, a small excited smile playing at her lips.

"*Oh.*" He began to smile, too.

Jessica nodded. "Uh-huh. Something clicked tonight and seeing those boys again… well…." She lifted her arms to drape them around his shoulders.

Kevin slipped his hands around her waist and pulled her up against the length of him. It was dark and, besides, if the neighbors could see them in the yellow glow of the street lamps, let them look. He bent his head to hers and kissed her deeply, sending a shudder through both their bodies.

When they came up for air, Jessica said, "So, that's a yes?"

He chuckled and began pulling her up the path to their house. "Oh, yeah. A definite yes."

* * * *

CHAPTER 9

"How are things going in here?" Jake asked as he walked into the warm kitchen. "Need any help?"

Claire wiped her hands on the apron tied around her waist and pushed her bangs from her forehead with her wrist. "Umm, no. I think I've got it all covered," she said, a small wrinkle creasing the space between her eyebrows as she concentrated on the meal she was creating.

Jake inhaled the rich scents of roast chicken, garlic and onions with pleasure. "It smells fantastic."

"I think the potatoes need a few more minutes." Claire began to wring her hands inside her apron and Jake reached out to stop her.

"Hon," he said, massaging her tense fingers. "It will be delicious, just like it always is. And everyone will be happy and fed and no one is going to care if everything isn't perfectly timed."

Claire swallowed and nodded. "I know. I just get so flustered when I make a family meal, wanting everything to be perfect—"

"Smells like Heaven in here!" Josephine cut Claire off mid-sentence as she wandered in from the family room. "I don't know where you got your cooking skills from, Claire Rose, because it sure wasn't me!" She winked at Jake and added, "But, I'm sure as hell grateful!"

Peggy followed in Josephine's wake. "Claire, do you need any help with anything?"

Oh the irony, Claire thought. On the one hand her mother chattering about what was coming, and on the other Peggy offering to help get things done. She wasn't sure which was better, or worse for that matter.

Jake ran interference. "Almost there, Mom," he said, picking up a bottle of wine. "Can I pour you another glass?"

Peggy pulled a prune face. "No. I've reached my limit. At least until we've had some food."

Claire checked the potatoes and was relieved to discover they were finally ready. "Thanks anyway, Peggy," she said, politely. "Just going to mash these and we're good to go."

"I'll take another splash, please." Josephine extended the wine glass she'd carried with her into the kitchen and Jake poured her a heavy measure - more like that of a cannonball than a splash.

He put the wine bottle back on the kitchen table.

"I still can't get over the fact you made these, Claire." Josephine lifted her clear stemmed glass to the light. "The blue is stunning," she said, referring to the swirling threads of cobalt glass running in circles around the goblet.

Jake saw his wife's shoulders tense at her mother's words. Uh-oh. "I can mash the potatoes if you want,

Hon," he said, hoping to detour the conversational thread.

"Did you know that, Peggy?" Josephine asked. "That Claire made these with her own hands?"

Peggy nodded. "Yes, I recall. Before she put her attention on the boys."

"Or at least with a blow pipe, anyway," Jake said, evenly.

Josephine, starting to narrow her eyes at Peggy's dismissive tone, stopped short and looked at Jake. "What?"

"She used a blow pipe," he repeated. "Because the glass was liquefied?"

"Oh!" Josephine burst out laughing. "Right! Of course. I was thinking of something else, entirely."

Oh, jeez, Jake thought, picking up the masher and silently praying she wouldn't elaborate.

Claire smiled gratefully when he began working on the potatoes.

"You should think about getting those trimmed." Josephine cocked her head at Claire.

"Pardon?"

"Your bangs. You should think about getting them trimmed."

Claire stepped away from the stove and gritted her teeth. "I know."

"Rumor has it your friend, Jessica, is a great stylist. You should pop over to her and let her get her hands on you. Freshen you right up!"

Claire's mouth gaped slightly while she watched her mother take a large swallow from her glass. Had she hear correctly? What rumor? From whom? And, wait a minute, had she also called her stale? In front of everyone?

"I think Claire's hair is lovely." Peggy threw in her two cents worth. "She always has such a classic, sensible style. Perfect for her lifestyle with two young boys."

Claire smiled politely at Peggy. "Thanks," she said, trying to walk the middle line. "Although, Mom does have a point about needing these silly bangs trimmed."

Josephine rolled her eyes and took another sip from her glass. She knew Claire too well and knew exactly what she was doing. Careful Claire. Considerate Claire. Cautious Claire. When was it going to be Creative Claire? Colorful Claire? Curious Claire?

"Mommy!" Evan came speeding into the kitchen, Noah on his tail. "Grandpa Earl wants to know when we're going to eat."

"Yeah," Noah added, eyes wide. "He says his stomach's going to eat itself! Can it really do that?"

Josephine laughed and reached out to grab one of the many bowls of food awaiting transport to the dining room. "We don't want to find out!" She set her wine glass on the countertop and pointed at the serving trays with her free hand. "Each of you grab one and we'll get things onto the table, quick!"

Claire jumped into action, making sure each of her sons took a bowl that wouldn't tip, be too heavy, or too clumsy in their grasps as they followed behind Josephine. Just like her mother to assign a task with no intention of supervising its outcome. She sighed. Only another couple of hours to go.

* * * *

Jake refilled Claire's wineglass, hoping it would help. It was the best he could do under the circumstances.

"So, you're telling us you pulled on a hula skirt without any hesitation whatsoever and started shaking your hips for England?"

Josephine snorted at Peggy's description. "I'd say that pretty much describes it. What else was I to do? Look like some sort of stick in the mud?"

Earl, seated across the table from Josephine and on his third whiskey, let out a bark of laughter. It earned him a stern glare from Peggy, not that he noticed.

Claire reached for her wine. Normally a two glass sort of gal, she decided sipping at one more - just this once - couldn't make things worse.

"Oh, come on Peggy," Josephine teased, over the rim of her goblet. "Don't tell me you would have refused? Not when it was your best friend's daughter's wedding?" She took a swallow of wine and added, "Even you wouldn't be that uptight."

Peggy's nostrils flared and she sat up in her seat. "Now listen—"

"Okay, then!" Claire clapped her hands and everyone startled. "I think it's time we let the boys leave the table and start thinking about dessert." She pressed her lips together a couple of times, noticed they felt slightly numb, and muttered, "Otherwise, this evening will never end."

Peggy cast a sharp eye in her direction. "Pardon?"

Claire blinked and swallowed. Uh-oh.

"Boys," Jake interrupted, hoping to throw his mother off the scent. "If you want to go and play, that's fine."

Both boys slide off their seats. "How come Bear isn't here?" Noah asked, before leaving the room.

Jake winced. "He already had his dinner," he said, fudging the truth.

"*And,*" Claire piped up. "Not everybody got a vote about him coming. Otherwise, it might have swayed in his favor."

Jake raised an eyebrow. Claire was referring to his mother. Peggy had stressed she would not feel comfortable with *that animal* present at their gathering. Perhaps the extra wine he'd poured for his wife hadn't been such a great idea.

"We could send him some dessert though, right?" Evan queried, reasonably.

"You betchya!" Claire grinned and waved as they left the dining room. "Good idea!"

Josephine snorted into her glass. Watching her daughter loosen up a little was a treat. If it took a few extra measures of wine, so be it.

With narrowed eyes, Peggy pulled her napkin from her lap and rested it on her plate. "Can I help clear?" she asked, tightly.

Claire shrugged her shoulders. "Suit yourself."

Josephine snickered, while Jake ran yet more interference.

"Why don't you go in and join the boys, Mom." He nodded at Earl. "You too, Dad. Take a load off."

Earl tipped the last of his drink into his mouth and pulled himself unsteadily to his feet. "Sounds like a good idea. I think that couch needs some attention."

Peggy's mouth twisted, yet she said nothing. Instead, she stiffly pushed her chair away from the table and followed her husband into the living room.

Claire gave another small wave, then rubbed her nose. "My heart feels good," she said, with a slight slur.

Good God, Jake thought.

Josephine leaned back in her chair and smiled indulgently at her daughter. "Isn't that nice."

"We can just leave everything, you know." She shrugged her shoulders. "It's not like it's going anywhere."

Jake just stared. He wouldn't have believed it if he hadn't been right there to hear it. Who knew something as simple as some extra wine with dinner would transform his wife into someone else. He glanced at Josephine at the other end of the table and felt his gut clench. Not just any old someone else either. More like a shockingly spot-on imitation of her mother.

* * * *

"Thanks for coming," Jake said as he waved off his parents and Josephine. "We'll have to do this again."

Claire, having been hit by a sudden need to lie down, was absent.

He closed the door solidly and leaned up against its frame. "Jesus," he exhaled, finally relaxing his shoulders.

It had been a challenge, but he was pretty sure he'd met it head on. After delivering his looped wife upstairs, he'd put the boys to bed, then bravely stepped into the breach to serve coffee and dessert to the relatives, play referee to their conversation and, finally, send them all on their way.

Jake turned off the lights in the family room and padded into the kitchen to do the same. Pausing for a glass of water to bring upstairs to his wife, he silently congratulated himself on letting his mother do her bidding and clean up - giving him a break and allowing for a gap in the conversation between her and Josephine.

Talk about oil and water. He shook his head and couldn't help but chuckle. Josephine tossed Peggy so far out of her comfort zone it was comical. He quite liked the idea that, with enough association, some of Josephine's *joie de vivre* might rub off on his mother. Although, judging from the visible tension in her neck, it didn't appear that was going to happen anytime soon.

He turned off the under-cabinet lights, grinned into the darkness and made his way upstairs.

* * * *

CHAPTER 10

Noah and Evan sang along merrily to the radio from the backseat of Claire's minivan. She'd long ago given in and kept the dial tuned to the top-forty station they insisted they loved. While she sometimes cringed at the lyrics, she placated herself with the reminder the radio versions were always clean and, fingers crossed, they didn't understand the intent anyway.

In the passenger seat, Josephine hummed and sang under her breath as she watched the world sail past the windows. "Have you had a chance to think about when we'll all get together again?" she asked, interrupting herself. "I loved what you did with the mashed potatoes. Perhaps next time we can make it a potluck and you can give me your recipe."

Claire gripped the steering wheel. An image of her mother-in-law sending daggers across the dining room table at Josephine flashed through her head. Oy. The last thing she wanted was to host another get together. She still needed time to recover both emotionally and physically from the last one and a week wasn't nearly long enough.

Josephine bobbed her head in time with the music and looked at Claire with inquiring eyes. "Claire? What do you think?"

"I think—" Claire began.

"Or, even better," Josephine cut in. "I could host!"

Oh, yeah, Claire thought, wryly, as she stretched her neck from side to side. Even better.

"Are we getting cold drinks, Mommy?" Noah asked as he reached out to pat Bear affectionately. The small dog was nestled comfortably in his basket between the boys' booster seats.

Claire turned down the radio and flicked on her right turn signal. "Yes," she said, while steering the minivan into the parking lot of a small strip mall in Boxwood Hill's downtown.

"What a perfect afternoon this was," Josephine sighed.

"Sure was," Claire replied, half-heartedly. The truth was, she was exhausted after an entire afternoon spent minding the boys on a nearby beach. Having the dog with them had only added to the disarray; keeping up with snacks and drinks and making sure they all stayed free from harm while playing in the sand and splashing in the water.

"Cold drinks!" Evan enthused, when Claire drove toward the drive thru lane of a coffee shop on the northern corner of the parking lot.

Josephine shifted so she could lean around her seat and better see the twins. "And what sort of cold drinks tickle your fancy, young man?"

Evan giggled. "I want iced lemonade, Gramma."

"Me, too," Noah said, nodding.

"Regular, or…." Josephine began, before Claire knocked her with her elbow across the front seat as she rummaged in the center console for money. "Goodness, Claire! You nearly took my eye out! Be careful."

"Sorry," Claire muttered, ignoring her mother's blatant exaggeration as she tried to focus on both driving and searching at the same time. "Yes," she said, when her hand brushed the top of the small jar of change she kept in the vehicle's console for just these types of stops and pulled it triumphantly from its depths.

"Gramma," Evan said, pointing. "You have to order for Mommy."

"I do?" Josephine's voice was full of surprise as she turned back around in her seat.

Claire's eyes widened in horror. "Oh-my-God."

"Oh, my." Josephine lifted her large, rose-tinted sunglasses from her nose. She laughed loudly and began to roll down her window. "It's certainly an unconventional approach, Claire. But I'm all for it."

Claire's cheeks burned with embarrassment as she took in the full brunt of what she'd done. "I can't believe I did this," she sputtered, as they sat at the takeout window, completely backwards and facing the front bumper of a car waiting in line from the correct direction.

"We seem to have gotten a bit turned around." Josephine used the sunglasses she held in her right hand to gesture at their vehicle as she addressed the girl behind the window. "Can you still take our order, dear?"

The girl smiled professionally and nodded. "Of course. What can I get you?"

While Josephine gave the boys' requests to the girl, Claire took a few deep breaths and tried to get her bearings. Her heart was beating very fast, so fast she was finding it uncomfortable. How could she have driven through the drive thru lane in the wrong direction? Had she really been that tired and distracted?

"Claire," Josephine said, merrily, cutting into her thoughts. "You wanted an iced coffee, right?"

Claire wasn't sure a coffee was the best thing, her hands were trembling, but she wanted to get the hell out of there. She nodded and tried to avoid making eye contact with the girl behind the window. She had a sinking feeling her blunder was going to become a well-worn story in the shop by the end of the day. Oh God.

* * * *

Claire pulled her van up to the curb in front of her mother's two bedroom bungalow and threw the gear stick into park. She was still reeling from the coffee shop incident, reliving the slow backward crawl of the van as she'd maneuvered it out of the drive thru in reverse; all the while being cheered on by Noah and Evan.

"I thank you again for a lovely afternoon, dear." Josephine smoothed her calf length cotton skirt and twinkled at Claire. With her red curls held off her face by a soft ponytail, a few tendrils drifting delicately around her shoulders, she looked as though she'd just arrived fresh from a shower as opposed to spending the day on a hot, sandy beach.

Claire sighed, glanced at her own clothes - a faded green t-shirt and baggy, beige shorts - and rolled her tense shoulders. "Glad you had a good time, Mom."

"Is there something wrong, dear?" Josephine cocked her head and sucked on the straw of the iced coffee she held in her hand.

Claire frowned and shifted in her seat to face her mother. "Umm, well, let's see. Not only was it a long day at the beach spent chasing after the boys and the dog, but then I had the overwhelmingly embarrassing experience of going through a drive-thru backwards!"

Josephine's eyes widened as Claire's voice rose and she huffed and puffed, trying to catch her breath. "Are you okay?"

Claire swallowed and tried to shake off her agitation. She took a breath, then frowned when a flash of yellow and silver caught her eye. "What on Earth is on your house?"

Josephine looked out the window to where she was pointing. "Mylar."

"Mylar?" Claire watched as strips of thin metallic film flapped merrily against the side of Josephine's house, as though dancing on the breeze. "You mean like gift wrap?"

"Uh-huh."

"Are you having a party, or something?"

Josephine chuckled and shook her head. "It keeps the woodpeckers away."

Claire took a second look. "Really?"

"Yup."

"Huh."

Josephine placed her drink in a cup holder between the seats. "So, are we good now?"

"What do you mean?" Claire pulled her sunglasses from her face.

Josephine shrugged her shoulders. "You got pretty bent out of shape there, so—"

"Can you blame me?"

"I don't know. *I* think we had a perfectly lovely day. We had a chance to play in the sun and relax in the shade." Josephine smiled, then bit her lip. "And, *yes*, we had the amusing mishap at the coffee shop—"

"For *you*, maybe," Claire cut in, frowning.

"Oh, *Claire*." Josephine rolled her eyes. "Lighten up. It was funny. *And* it could have been funny for you, too, if you hadn't been so caught up in worrying what everyone else thought."

Claire's frown deepened.

"Life is going to throw you all sorts of stuff, my dear," she said, while slipping the gold flip-flops she'd shucked off onto the floor back onto her feet. "Why not try to catch the ball, instead of always worrying about ducking it?"

"That's your philosophy for life, isn't it, Mother?" Claire's comment was thick with reproach, her mouth set in a rigid line on her face. "Do whatever you want, catch the ball or throw the ball, and who cares what anyone else thinks about it."

Josephine ached for her daughter. She was so hard on herself, so needlessly. She tried another approach. "And that's a bad thing *why*, exactly?"

Claire paused, taken aback. She'd been prepared for her mother to go off on some sort of spiel about life and fun and her usual blather. This was an entirely different angle.

Josephine picked up her coffee and waited. She'd discovered that, often, the best way to get results was to let the other person find them.

Claire glanced at her sons in the backseat, their eyes closed as they began to nod off. Their hair was still damp and their clothes dusted with sand; she needed to get them home and into a bath. "You know what, Mother? I don't have time for that question, or this discussion." She shoved her sunglasses back onto her face and squared her shoulders against her seat.

Josephine offered no argument. Instead, she put down her cup, unclipped her seatbelt and reached into the backseat for Bear. "Thanks again, dear," she said, as she unclipped the warm animal's harness and lifted him into her arms. "I'll get the basket later, I have a spare in the house. Please tell the boys I said bye."

Claire scrambled for a suitable reply, but Josephine had slipped out the door before she could utter another word. All she left behind was her coffee cup and her question, hanging in the air, waiting for an answer.

* * * *

"And then we had lemonades and Gramma got to order because she was at the window instead of Mommy!" Noah doubled over in mirth at the memory, slapping his pajama clad knee like an elderly man as he told Jake about their day.

Jake sent Claire a puzzled expression across their kitchen table while he tried to follow Noah's story. "At the window?" he asked, picking up his water glass. "Do you mean the counter inside the coffee shop?"

"No, *Daddy*." Evan's voice was filled with exaggerated patience.

After her mother's commentary that afternoon, Claire wondered if he'd learned the tone from her.

"We stayed in the van and it was pointed backwards in the forward lane," Evan explained, before forking up a mouthful of corn from his dinner plate.

Claire reflexively pressed her hand to her chest as a phantom feeling of her heart racing that afternoon swept through her. She'd hoped they'd let it drop, but no such luck.

"Backwards in the forward lane," Jake repeated, still looking very puzzled.

"I made a mistake today," Claire said, swallowing against the reoccurring embarrassment.

Jake sipped his water and gave her his undivided attention.

"After we went to the beach we decided to stop for drinks."

"Lemonade," Noah repeated himself.

"Right." Claire nodded. "And I guess I was so tired and distracted trying to find my money jar that...." She paused, took a breath and then spoke at a rapid fire pace. "I accidentally drove into the drive-thru lane from the exit, instead of the entrance."

Jake's eyebrows shot up and, as comprehension dawned, a grin spread across his face.

Here we go, Claire thought, bracing herself. She wasn't disappointed. Jake began to chuckle, then Evan and Noah joined in and she wanted to melt into a puddle and disappear.

"Sounds like an interesting adventure," he said, finally, putting his glass back on the table.

"Finish your broccoli, too." Claire pointed at the boys' plates, trying to avoid her husband's eye.

"A fun ride," he elaborated.

"Ha, ha." She finally gave up and looked across the table to glare at him.

"Oh, come on. It *is* funny, Hon. You have to lighten up a little—"

"Do *not* say that to me!" Claire shot upward from her chair, shoving it back with a sharp scrap across the tile floor. Her heart kicked into high gear and she pressed her palm against her chest.

Jake frowned. "You okay?"

Claire looked at the wide eyes on her sons' faces and breathed steadily in and out, forcing herself to get a grip. "Boys, you look like you're done. Good job. You can go and play now and Daddy and I will clean up and I'll call you in a little bit for some dessert."

Noah and Evan looked at each other in surprise. They each had a few stalks of broccoli left on their plates, but they weren't about to argue. They jumped from their chairs and beetled from the kitchen without a backward glance.

"What happened?" Jake said, as soon as they were out of earshot. "Are you okay? What'd I say?"

"I'm fine," Claire said, relieved her pulse had calmed down. She began clearing the dishes from the table as the sounds of *Bob the Builder* drifted in from the TV in the family room.

"Okay, so what happened there?"

"I'm sorry, but you sounded exactly like my Mother and it really pissed me off."

"Exactly like your Mom?" Jake repeated as he picked up cutlery and cups.

Claire placed the dishes on the countertop and spun around on her heel, her mouth a grim line on her face. "Yes, as a matter of fact. She started doing her usual thing today, going on about how I took the whole incident too seriously. As though I should be like her, merrily skipping along and not caring that people think I'm a flake."

"No one thinks your Mom's a flake." Jake opened the dishwasher.

"Oh, please," Claire retorted, pushing her hands through her hair. "They've thought it since I was a kid and still do."

Jake turned around and leaned up against the cabinets. "Claire, honestly, I've always thought your Mom was a bit of a wild card, but—"

"A wild card?" Claire scraped the leftover food from the plates into the garbage can beneath the sink. "Seriously? That's the term you'd use?"

"Yes. She's unpredictable, but she's no flake and definitely not stupid."

Claire stacked the plates in the dishwasher, all the while digesting Jake's comments. "So," she said, finally. "Are you saying you agree with her, then? The *wild card* is right and I should lighten up?"

Jake ran a hand through his hair. He was in dangerous territory. "I don't think this is about agreeing, or disagreeing, Hon. Do I sometimes think you make life hard on yourself? Occasionally." He sped up when he saw her face twist with annoyance. "*But*, I know your reasons are sound, so I'm not judging what you do. I just wish, sometimes, you'd be a bit easier on yourself."

Claire chewed her lower lip. She felt both intensely annoyed and slightly touched. He'd managed to find the middle ground and she wasn't sure what to give back. He didn't understand her life, *obviously*; he was at work all day. But, on the other hand, he did care she was happy.

Evan's face peeked around the side of the kitchen doorway, his eyes bright and hopeful. Claire wondered how much of their discussion he had heard.

"Looking for something sweet?" Jake asked, while closing the door on the dishwasher.

"Yes!" Evan stepped fully into the doorway.

"What about ice cream?"

"Ice cream, Noah!" Evan bellowed above the sounds of *Bob the Builder* and his gang of machines.

Claire grabbed a sponge and picked up a dirty pot from the sink. Turned out she didn't have just food for dinner, but for thought as well.

* * * *

CHAPTER 11

The door to *A Cut Above* swung wide and a gust of warm, late summer air swept into the salon. Jessica, behind the front desk, turned in time to watch Claire lean her shoulder on the glass door, pushing it closed behind her.

"Whew!" she exhaled, smoothing her hair away from her face. "That's some wind!"

"I know!" Jessica skirted the stone desk. "I feel like I've been watching people blow past all morning."

Claire clutched her purse under her arm. "I'm on time, right?"

Jessica glanced at the large clock on the wall and nodded. "One o'clock, right on the nose."

"It's a miracle for me, truth be told. But the boys were so eager to get over to play with Sophia, it was shockingly easy to get them out of the house."

"Aww," Jessica said. "That's so nice they all get along so well."

"You're telling me. Having Sophia, never mind Rosa, so close by is a Godsend. It's the first time I've ever had this sort of thing."

Jessica cocked her head. "What sort of thing?"

"A person I feel I can trust with the boys. I mean, other than my Mom."

"What about Jake's Mom?"

"Oh. Right. Sure." Claire cleared her throat and diverted. "Anyway, turns out I really like it."

"And, Noah and Evan are so good." Jessica smiled at the thought of their happy faces. "It seems like they never fight."

Claire laughed and shook her head. "Oh, believe me, they fight. Jake and I still talk about the piñata incident on their fourth birthday."

"Piñata incident?" Jessica motioned for her to follow her into the salon.

Claire trailed behind. "I don't know what happened, but somewhere between three and four, sharing certain things became taboo. It would have been nice to know that ahead of time, but we didn't."

Jessica led them to the brown leather chair at her station. "Uh-oh," she said, crinkling her nose.

Claire chuckled. "Yeah, pretty much. We got them a piñata and they got all bent out of shape, having to share it, and the next thing we knew there was shrieking and crying, and pushing and shoving, and ripping and tearing...." Claire shook her head, again. "It was a miracle they didn't seriously hurt themselves in the process."

Jessica bit her lip, trying not to laugh.

Claire saw her face and snickered. "Go ahead, it is funny, *now*."

"So, I guess if a piñata ever shows up again at your house, there will be two?" she asked, between giggles.

"You've got that right," Claire agreed, while stepping back to get a good look at *A Cut Above*. It was gorgeous.

The floors were a dark distressed hardwood and covered the entire length of the space. The walls, painted a cool, creamy butter, were accented by wide panels of the same rock that made up the front desk. And, finally, there were eight workstations that ran the length of the outer walls; each with their own padded, chocolate brown leather chair and perfectly lit oversized mirror.

"Wow," she said, gushing in appreciation. "I have to say, your salon is fantastic."

Jessica grinned and placed her hands on the back of her chair. It was the exact reaction she liked to hear. "Thanks. I had things renovated a couple of months ago and I love it."

"You should. It's perfect." She sighed. A sense of calm enveloped her and her shoulders relaxed. "Fresh, yet soothing."

Jessica's pleasure at the compliments brightened her whole face. "That's pretty much exactly what I was going for."

"Well, you've succeeded. I feel ready for my hair appointment and then a nap."

Jessica laughed out loud. "The hair I can do," she said, gesturing to the chair in front of her. "The nap is in your court. Have a seat and we'll discuss what you want to do before it gets crazy in here."

"Yeah," Claire said. It hadn't escaped her notice they were completely alone in the shop. "I was going to ask about that. Where is everybody?"

"Oh, believe me, this is the calm before the storm. I wanted a chance for us to chat before this place gets deep in blow dryers and chatter, so I booked you in a half hour before the other girls start."

Claire was touched. How kind. "That's so nice," she said, sitting down in the chair.

"Can I get you anything?" Jessica asked, while reaching out to run her fingers through Claire's sandy blonde hair; appraising. "A coffee? Juice? Water?"

"No, no, I'm good, thanks." Her cheeks grew warm as Jessica lifted strand after strand of her hair. She'd left it so long without any attention. She hoped she wouldn't be appalled. "But, you'll have to do me a favor and forgive the state of my hair. It's just that, with the boys and the move and such, I haven't had a chance to do much with it."

Jessica smiled kindly. She'd heard it all before. She patted Claire's shoulder comfortingly. "It's fine, really. And it's often better it's had a chance to grow, especially if you have something in mind you'd like to do with it. Are you thinking of a change, or staying in the same style?"

"Maybe." She shrugged her shoulders. "Or not. I don't know." She wrung her hands. "I mean, I've had it this way for a while now and I know what to do with it. I don't have a lot of time to fuss, you know?"

Jessica folded her arms across her chest and cocked her head. "Okay, let's break it down. First, do you want to stay with blonde?"

"I've always been blonde," Claire said, while a slightly nervy feeling overtook her body.

Jessica waited.

"I think I should probably stay blonde, at least for a little while longer...." She tapered off and raised her eyebrows.

Jessica grinned. "Sounds good. We'll refresh it."

"Okay."

Jessica explained further. "And by refresh I mean that your highlights have grown out a lot, so I could work with your base and build in some other colors to give it texture. Maybe add some darker strands for contrast and keep some of the lighter strands for accent. Whatever strikes your fancy."

"Oh, boy." Claire's eyebrows knotted together. "I'm not very good at these sort of decisions. I think I should just stay in the same hair color area, but make it look fresher. Natural."

Jessica nodded. "Okay, got it."

Claire grinned, relieved. When she'd first decided to get her hair done, she'd thought she'd go for something radically different. Prove to her mother she could lighten up. But, if she was to be honest with herself, the idea made her stomach do flip flops.

"Alright, you hang tight and give me a minute to get some color made up, then we'll get things going." She grabbed a black cape and deftly wrapped it around Claire's shoulders. "Sure I can't get you something? A coffee? A magazine?"

Claire shook her head. "No, thanks. I'll just enjoy the quiet while I can."

* * * *

Claire reveled in the hum of the dryer over her head as she flipped through her magazine. It had been so long since she'd been pampered in any way, it was a treat to sit and do nothing. She pulled her gaze away from the glossy pages and watched the activity around the salon. Gone was the quiet she'd first stepped into; five stylists had since arrived and had been working non-stop for the past hour, filling the salon with busy animation.

"How are you doing?"

"Great," Claire said, while Jessica pulled the dryer away from her head and began checking the color of her hair. "It's so nice to sit and be responsible for nothing more than flipping these pages."

Jessica laughed. "I think you deserve it. You're done, so come on over to the sink and we'll rinse it out."

Claire rose from her seat, just as the shop door opened. Two women and two men crossed the threshold, their boisterous voices surging forth, sending a fresh burst of energy into the salon.

Jessica turned toward the sound and grinned. "Oh, boy," she warned. "Get ready for a party."

* * * *

Jessica had not been exaggerating. In fact, Claire was pretty sure she'd never seen anything quite like the foursome who'd entered the salon. Discreetly informed their names were Heidi, Denise, Travis and Gerry, they lit the place up like a fireworks display. They were exuberance personified.

Claire sat in Jessica's styling chair and used the mirror's reflection to watch them on the opposite side of the room, much like a wide-eyed child would the circus for the first time.

"And did you notice how low her blouse was cut?" Travis whooped, his green eyes dancing as he giggled and fidgeted like an excited puppy in his chair.

Claire peeked at him covertly, hoping it would appear she was watching Jessica cut her hair. Married or not, she couldn't help but notice he was magazine model gorgeous. Lean and muscular beneath slim cut white jeans and a sleek black t-shirt, his short blonde hair fashionably mussed, Travis was a head turner.

"I know!" Gerry effused. "I think she was banking on the judge being a man!" Seated to the left of Travis, he winked at his stylist in the mirror as she snipped his thick, chocolate brown hair with precise movements.

Jessica had whispered to Claire that Gerry was Travis' partner. She was trying her best not to stare back and forth between them. It was very likely she was failing.

It was just that the two men couldn't have been more opposite! Gerry, handsome in his own right, was thick and muscular where Travis was lean. He possessed dark hair and eyes while Travis was fair and golden. Even his laugh, a low and rumbling wave, was the antithesis of Travis' peals of mirth. Claire felt she was witnessing the adage of opposites attracting coming to life right before her eyes.

"Oh, *puh-lease*." Heidi, seated next to Gerry, twisted toward him and leaned forward to catch Denise's eye in the mirror. "It was a *dog* show, for God's sake! She was supposed to be showcasing her dachshund, not her Poms!"

Denise, at the opposite end of the row on Travis' right, cackled. "We should have starting singing how much are *those* doggies in the window!"

Heidi burst out laughing and leaned further forward, making her stylist follow her with the strawberry blonde hair color she was applying to her roots. Claire noticed that, just like the men, the two women were also the complete opposite of each other.

Heidi clearly had some sort of Nordic heritage, whereas Denise was dark; her bobbed hair black as coal. Claire saw her wink at Heidi in their mirrored reflections and thought the woman's bright, almond shaped eyes were an exotic accent to her porcelain, Chinese features. That is until they locked with her's across the floor and Denise slowly spun around in her chair.

"Oh, nuts." Claire averted her eyes from the mirror as Jessica finished the last few snips on her cut.

Jessica raised an eyebrow. "Pardon? Is everything okay? I didn't change much, just added a few layers and cleaned up the rest like we agreed."

"No, no." Claire flushed slightly at being overheard. "It's perfect. Honest." She stopped talking when Denise sidled up beside her, her dark eyes glittering with obvious interest.

"Hey, Denise," Jessica said, before picking up the blow dryer. "Meet Claire."

Denise extended her hand from beneath the black salon cape she wore wrapped around her shoulders. "Nice to meet you."

Claire smiled shyly and shook the perfectly manicured hand being offered. God, her own nails were a mess.

Denise cocked her head. "You look familiar, but from where?"

Claire was one hundred percent certain she'd never before crossed this woman's path. If she had, she'd remember. "Maybe I just look like someone you know," she said, shrugging and tucking her hands back under her cape. "I haven't been here that long, or been very many places, so...."

"Claire and her family just relocated back from the city a couple of months ago," Jessica offered. "Maybe you've seen her at the grocery, or something."

"The new dentist!" Denise snapped her fingers and pointed her index finger at Claire.

"Pardon?"

"Is your husband the new dentist that joined the Oakwood practice on 2nd street?"

"Umm, yes," Claire said, taken aback by the question.

"Ah-ha!" Denise spun around and marched over to Heidi's chair. "That woman, Claire, is the new dentist's wife."

Heidi visibly perked up and smiled in, what could only be called, a knowing manner. So knowing, in fact, that a shiver involuntarily ran up Claire's spine. Why the sudden Cheshire grin, she wanted to ask. But then, just as quickly, wasn't sure she really wanted the answer.

"Oooh, I've heard about *him*, Honey." Heidi, still having her hair color applied, spoke to Claire via her reflection. "Apparently you've got yourself quite the dish there, with a fabulous chair side manner."

"Oh, boy." Jessica cringed on Claire's behalf. She'd been on the receiving end of Denise and Heidi's lascivious remarks when she'd first started dating Kevin.

Gerry snickered at Heidi's remarks and Travis reached out to slap playfully at her arm. "Be nice," he said, wagging a warning finger.

"What?" Heidi's eyes widened and she blinked a few times.

Travis rolled his eyes and shook his head as Denise returned her to chair beside him. "You're terrible, the both of you."

"What?" Denise echoed, a smirk playing at her lips. "We're just being friendly."

Acute discomfort clutched at Claire's stomach. Fabulous chair side manner? What on Earth did they mean by that?

"Okay, then," Jessica said, trying to help by swiftly switching on the blow dryer. She pointed it at Claire's wet hair and effectively shut down further conversation. It was the most efficient way she could think of to stop her replying and inadvertently adding fuel to Denise and Heidi's already well-tended fire.

* * * *

Claire's thoughts were muddled as she closed the door to her minivan and started the engine. She flicked on the air conditioning while she took a deep, bracing breath and collected herself. She felt a little like she'd exited some sort of strange battlefield; where she'd been thrown directly into a verbal sparring pit and had only her wits to dodge her way out.

Heidi and Denise had been relentless. Jessica and her hairdryer had only postponed their inquisition about Jake. Or, as Denise kept calling him, 'Boxwood Hills' answer to Mr. Big'.

God. Claire shuddered, despite the warm temperature in the vehicle. They'd fallen all over themselves when they'd found out she and Jake had twin boys, or 'Mini Bigs' as Heidi had coined them; loving the idea of Jake being a father. They'd painted a picture of he and the boys that could only exist on the pages of a cheesy romance novel. Oy.

Focus, Claire told herself when her pulse began to increase. Get a grip. There was absolutely no reason to be rattled by a couple of nosey, over-sexed women. However, that being said, she also had to acknowledge she had legitimate reason to be unsettled by the discovery that Travis and Gerry were her neighbors a few doors down. Not that they didn't seem perfectly friendly. No. It was the close friendship they shared with the Tactless Twins that gave her a case of heartburn.

The Tactless Twins. Claire grinned. The nickname wasn't her creation, but she'd take it. Jessica had divulged she and Kevin had coined it when they'd been on the receiving end of Heidi and Denise's overly curious attention. While it didn't necessarily make the onslaught any easier to bear in the moment, it did take the sting out of things once it was behind her.

Claire ran her fingers through her freshly styled hair, slid her sunglasses over the bridge of her nose and turned her key in the ignition. Enough obsessing. She had to pick up the boys.

* * * *

Claire pulled her minivan up to the curb in front of Sophia's house. Rosa's house she mentally amended, while cutting the engine. Or, rather, Matt and Cristina's house she further corrected. She sighed. It really was no use. The facts were, while it was Matt and Cristina's house, it had become their daughter's house in Claire's mind because of her friendship with Evan and Noah. It was just the way things happened when kids were involved.

Claire eased out of the vehicle and closed the door behind her, listening for the sound of children's voices. Nothing. Only birdsong, a distant thumping of either music or someone working and the occasional dog barking disturbed the quiet, sun splashed crescent. The wind that had practically blown her into Jessica's salon earlier that afternoon had disappeared, leaving a still, oppressive heat to shimmer off the pavement. Moving indoors to play was a wise decision.

Claire blotted a thin film of moisture that had collected above her lip with the back of her hand, smoothed the creases from her tan, cotton skirt, then followed the crushed rock path that led her through Sophia's front yard. As she approached the house, she regarded with appreciation the wide, shaded wooden porch spanning the entire length of the home. Decorated with terracotta pots overflowing with rich purple lavender and melon orange cape daisies, inviting sun bleached wooden rocking chairs and a well-worn welcome mat at the front door, Claire was charmed. All that was missing was a calico cat, or lazy farm dog.

She pressed the bell and waited. Silence. She lifted her hand to press it a second time when the inside door creaked and opened and Rosa's smiling face greeted her from the other side of the screen.

"Claire! *Bella*!" Rosa enthused, while holding Portia on one hip. "*Vieni dentro.*" She stepped back, bumped the screen door open with her knee and waved Claire inside with her free hand.

Claire stepped through the opening, the screen door tapping at her heels as she crossed the threshold. "It smells absolutely heavenly in here, Rosa," she complimented, inhaling the mouth-watering, heady smells of fresh garden tomatoes, cilantro and baked bread.

"*Grazie.*" Rosa pushed the inside door closed with her barefoot.

Claire reveled in the foyer's coolness and pulled her sunglasses from her face. She couldn't help but notice that everything from Rosa's cotton, green and white flowered house dress, to the tantalizing cooking smells, to the untidy pile of summer shoes on the floor, seemed to say family. Did her own house do the same? she wondered. She had the uncomfortable feeling it did not.

"The children," Rosa said, while gently bouncing a delighted looking Portia up and down. "They hadda bruschetta for *pranzo*."

"Pranzo?"

"Yes, yes," Rosa confirmed. "Their lunch, yes?"

"Oh! Right." Claire nodded. "Of course, their lunch." She paused, a small frown creasing her brow when she realized what the woman had said. "Did you say bruschetta? *My* boys ate bruschetta?"

"*Si*, bruschetta."

"Evan and Noah?"

Rosa nodded. "Si. Yes. Evan and Noah."

"Bruschetta? With tomatoes?" Claire was aware Rosa was beginning to look at her as though she was a little slow on the uptake.

"Yes, tomatoes." She laughed and bounced Portia some more. "They love the tomato dance."

"Tomato dance?" Claire parroted, confused again.

"Si." Rosa grinned and began shaking her hips back and forth. "We do a shimmy, shimmy dance before we cut the tomatoes. I taught it to Sophia and she gave it to Noah and Evan. Everyone dancing and laughing and eating, suddenly tomatoes are fun, yes?"

Claire digested the information. The 'shimmy, shimmy dance' certainly sounded like a whole lot more fun than the information she gave to the boys about how they'd end up with scurvy if they didn't eat their vegetables. Hands down, more fun.

"So, umm." Claire returned to the reason she'd arrived. "Are the boys around?"

"Oh, yes, of course. You're here to get them after hair salon visit."

"Yes."

"Lovely hair Jessica gave to you," Rosa complimented. "Very sharp, very sensible, yes?"

Claire inwardly cringed. While she knew Rosa was being kind, that word *sensible* had really started to grate on her nerves. What with Peggy saying it as her version of a compliment, then her mother using it as something to avoid; either way, it didn't feel like a word she wanted being used in conversations to describe her.

"Thank you," she said, instead of voicing her thoughts. Rosa was an innocent bystander, after all. "So, the boys. They would be *where*, exactly?"

"Right!" Rosa straightened her shoulders and pointed to the door. "The children are with Thomas, next door. *Mi segua.* You come with me and we'll go and tell them you're back."

Oh, great, Claire thought as she trailed behind. Just fabulous.

* * * *

"Yoo-hoo! *Bambini!*" Rosa called out as she swept through the tall grass in Thomas' backyard.

Claire, in her wake, was gob smacked. The height of it! Why, the lawn had to be standing at least a foot tall, maybe more. Did the man not own a lawn mower? Better yet, did living next door to such blatant horticultural disregard drive Jessica batty?

"In here!" Thomas called back over the music thumping from the depths of his workshop at the rear of the property.

"Ah, yes! Come, Claire. The bambini are in the shop."

Rosa patted Claire's forearm, then set off at a brisk pace toward the small outbuilding; her ample hips swaying from side to side and Portia bobbing along in rhythm. Claire nearly tripped over her sandals in her effort to keep up and marveled at the woman's energy; privately wishing it was something she could bottle for herself.

Rosa pushed against the partially opened shop door and grinned. "We're here!"

Claire arrived a pace behind and inhaled to catch her breath. Thank goodness they'd had the kindness to turn down the music, she thought, before her face warped into a frown. Good God, what on Earth had they been up to?

The children were each wearing a white t-shirt over their clothes, presumably to keep them clean. Judging by the state of them - paint splashed in a riot of colors - the shirts hadn't stood a chance.

"Mommy!" Noah jumped up and down in his enthusiasm. "We've been painting!"

"I can see that," Claire said, clutching her sunglasses to keep herself from wiping a smudge of black from his cheek. "Good afternoon, Mister... uhh, Thomas."

Thomas inclined his head. "Ta."

"We've been trying to find our favorite colors for the go-kart," Noah further explained, using his paint brush to gesture at freshly splattered planks of plywood laid out on the floor. "We've even had music to paint to."

"Ahh, right, the infamous go-kart." Claire nodded, as though she was on board with the whole idea. Which she really was not.

"Did you find a favorite?" Rosa asked as Portia began wiggling in her arms.

"Yes, Nonna," Sophia replied, stepping out from behind Evan. "I picked purple and yellow."

"I want orange and blue." Evan pointed out the two colors smattered on his board.

"And you, Noah?" Rosa shifted Portia to her other hip in an attempt to distract her from her squirming.

"Black and red." Noah's confident manner so resembled his father, Claire was slightly stunned.

Rosa grinned at Thomas while she gently bounced the baby in her arms. "That's a lotta color."

Thomas chuckled and puffed on a cigarette between his lips. "Aye. It'll werk oot fine. Enuf space on the cart for all of them."

Claire eyed the cigarette and pursed her lips. She was itching to tell the man to put the damned thing out. She didn't want him smoking around her boys, but it was his shop. The one saving grace was all of the windows were open and, if pressed, she'd have to reluctantly admit she'd never have known he was smoking if it wasn't for the blatant evidence.

"Well, boys," she stated, hoping to move things along. There was so much clutter; she was feeling a touch claustrophobic.

The workbench was full of every tool imaginable, pieces of metal and what-not hung from every available space of wall, rags and paint cans and overflowing makeshift ashtrays were tucked in-between the rest. Whew. Claire craved fresh air.

"Aww," Evan pouted. He knew from her simple statement the direction his mother's thoughts were headed.

"There's no need for that," Claire said, patting down the weak protest in hopes it wouldn't grow any further. "You can come back again."

"Of course you can!" Rosa reached out and pulled Evan to her in a warm hug. "You and Noah, you come any time. Isn't that right, Sophia? They're your *migliori amici*, yes?

Sophia grinned and nodded. "Yes, Nonna."

"Mee-lyoh-ray ah-mee-chee?" Noah's face was seriously puzzled. "What's mee-lyoh-ray ah-mee-chee?"

Rosa's face lit up with pleasure as she released Evan. "Best friends. You and Evan."

Noah's confusion cleared and he smiled at his brother. "We're mee-lyoh-ray ah-mee-chee."

"Okay, then!" Claire brushed her hands together, as though she too had been working and had finally finished cleaning up. She turned to Thomas. "Thank you so much for entertaining them."

Thomas pulled his cigarette from his lips and flicked the long ash in the direction of one of the makeshift ashtrays. It almost made it. "No need ta thank me, lass. I donna do what I donna wanta do, right?"

"Of course." Claire stiffened, suddenly feeling wrong-footed. She wasn't meaning to imply he was associating with them against his will, or anything.

"They're guid lads," Thomas added with a curt nod.

Claire shifted from one foot to the other, she really needed fresh air. "Well, thanks," she said, then quickly clarified. "For the compliment, I mean."

Thomas grinned and, just like that, it changed the entire state of his face. His blue eyes sparkled, his laugh lines were on display, he looked so friendly and welcoming, Claire was slightly staggered. Suddenly, she could see what the children saw.

Evan yawned and put down his paintbrush. "I'm thirsty."

"And hot," Noah sighed, the heat finally making an impression as he rubbed his eyes.

"Off we go, then." Claire urged them toward the door, tucking away the new information about Thomas. "Oh, wait," she said, pausing in the doorway. "The shirts."

"Keep 'em," Thomas swiftly interjected. "They can use 'em again, next time."

"Right." She forced herself to sound agreeable. "Next time." She turned to Rosa. "Thanks again for having them."

"*Prego*," Rosa replied, warmly. "Anytime."

Noah and Even filed out of the shop then turned to wave good-bye to Sophia. Claire brought up the rear and with great gusto inhaled the air beyond the shop door.

* * * *

(HAPTER 12

"Please, come in." Josephine opened her front door and smiled warmly at Peggy.

Peggy dimpled at the invitation and tentatively crossed the threshold, almost as though she was nervous about what she might find.

Bear, standing next to Josephine, wagged his tail in a friendly manner and wandered forward to sniff at Peggy's shoes.

"Oh," she said, blinking rapidly.

"Bear," Josephine called the dog away. "Come on now. Let's not crowd the woman."

"Oh, I'm fine," Peggy said, tightly.

Josephine, sympathetic to Jake's mother, suppressed an amused smile. She understood not everyone was an *animal person* and judging from Peggy's frozen stance, she'd hazard to guess the woman was about as distant as one could get from being just that.

Bear stepped away from Peggy, his toenails clicking lightly on the scuffed hardwood floor, and Josephine gently nudged him even further with her bare foot.

"Off you go," she said, giving his backside a little bump to get him moving. "To your bed."

Peggy visibly relaxed when the small dog trotted out of the foyer and disappeared from sight. "I hope I'm not intruding," she began, peering at Josephine's outfit. It looked like she was dressed for something menial, like painting, but Peggy couldn't be sure.

"Of course not. We just came back from a walk. Beautiful day." She put her hands on her hips. "But I hope you didn't come out of your way to get the fruit. Jake offered to pick it up and bring it back to their place, what with you living so close to them now."

Peggy stared. A walk? Really? Dressed like *that,* in a pair of baggy, beige chinos and some sort of pink, brown and grey cotton blouse; her hair piled messily on top of her head?

"Oh, no!" she finally said, shaking her head. "I didn't mind at all. I was running errands anyway and I knew Jake was busy with the boys, so...."

Josephine nodded. "Well, that's good to hear. Did you want to come inside for a cool drink? Or, do you have to get back right away?"

Peggy clutched her purse under her arm. The desire to leave was warring with her curiosity and she wasn't sure which one to follow. She glanced again at Josephine, thought of the small dog in the neighboring room and made her decision.

"That's really nice of you to offer, but I do have to get back. I'll take a rain check, if that's okay? Or, maybe you could stop over at our place the next time you visit the kids?"

Josephine bit her lip to keep from giggling. Peggy's discomfort was glaringly obvious and while she felt for her, she also found it humorous. "Of course," she said, and couldn't resist adding a second time, "since you live so close by now."

"Isn't that a blessing?" Peggy said.

Josephine cocked her head.

"I mean," she went on, looking pleased as punch. "We wanted to move closer, but never thought we'd get so lucky and find a house available only a short walk away." She giggled and added, "It was so much fun to surprise the kids after they were here."

Josephine was speechless. *Surprised* was the operative word, considering Claire had nearly lost her nut when she'd found out just how close to home Peggy and Earl had moved.

"I look forward to many more opportunities for us to all get together. Sunday gatherings, barbecues, birthdays, holidays...." Peggy's face turned dreamy, before she suddenly snapped to. "I mean all of us, of course."

"Of course," Josephine agreed, blandly. Poor Claire. Her daughter could be in for a battle to defend her corner. She spun on her heel. "Hang on and I'll get the fruit."

"Need a hand?"

"No, thanks," she said, over her shoulder. "It's just in the kitchen. Won't be more than a moment."

Peggy nodded as she disappeared from sight and glanced again at the foyer. The walls were a brilliant blue, the area rug cherry red and the hanging artwork depicted butterflies so vibrantly colored, she almost expected them to fly off the canvas. The only normal thing to be seen were the white baseboards. Peggy shrugged. Everything was in perfect tune with what she knew of Josephine. The mystery, in her opinion, was how Claire had managed to turn out like the baseboards and not the area rug.

* * * *

Thomas ran his fingers through his hair, leaving it in unkempt, salt and pepper colored spikes. Not that he was remotely aware. No, his attention was utterly focused on a large, plastic bin in his favorite hardware store labeled, *Odds and Ends*. Whenever he frequented the store, which was often, he kept his eyes peeled for bits and bobs that could end up being the perfect thing to assist him in the creation of his next invention. He was a hands-on guy and would always be a hands-on guy.

Not that he had anything against the new, computer generation; who often spent more time at their screens than getting their hands dirty in the actual creation. Absolutely not. He was well aware inspiration was to be found in many different ways. It just so happened that, for him, inspiration only struck when he had his hands in the muck. Sometimes, figuratively. Other times, literally.

"Ahh," he exhaled, when a flash of metal caught his attention. He'd been seeking out pieces for a braking system for the go-kart and that steel looked like it might bring him closer to his goal.

"What are these things, Daddy?"

Thomas, raising a hand to free the metal from the bin, paused mid-reach to cock an ear. If he was a betting man, he'd put cash on guessing it was Noah's voice he was hearing from the other side of the hardware stacks.

"Umm," a male voice replied, "looks like camping equipment. Not what we're looking for today."

"How about over here!" the child's voice declared.

Thomas listened to the sound of footsteps stamping rapidly around the corner of the aisle.

"Mister Thomas!" Noah cheered, coming to a halt in front of the wild haired Scotsman.

Thomas gave him an amused grin. Yup, he'd called it.

"Hey, Daddy!" Evan, also rounding the corner, called out excitedly to Jake before nearly wiping out on the concrete floor in his eagerness to join his brother.

"Whoa, thare," Thomas said, wincing. He exhaled in relief when Evan regained his footing.

Jake appeared at the end of the aisle, his expression curious. "Boys?" he said, before catching sight of his sons. He grinned.

Thomas was impressed. Judging from his easy smile, it appeared 'Daddy' was a whole lot more welcoming, right from the get-go, than 'Mommy' had been.

"This is Mister Thomas," Evan said, hopping up and down on the spot as Jake strode over. "The man we told you about who's gonna help us make the go-kart."

"Right." Jake extended his hand. "Nice to meet you, Sir. I'm Jake."

"No, Daddy," Noah said, his voice amused. "Mister Thomas, not sir."

Thomas chuckled. "I'd say Thomas will do juist fine." He reached out and shook the hand Jake offered. "Good ta meet ya, Jake."

"My sons have nothing but the highest praise to offer about you," Jake said as he tucked his hands comfortably into the pockets of his shorts.

"Ah, *well*." Thomas stroked his beard and cleared his throat. "They're guid lads, so."

"Are you shopping for go-kart stuff?" Evan asked, his eyes bright and curious.

"Aye. I am."

"Goody!" Noah enthused, a grin decorating his entire face.

"You know," Jake said. "You're welcome over to our house anytime you want to work with the boys. I understand you have a workshop at your place, but if you want to try anything out over at ours, please know you're welcome."

Thomas studied Jake. He appreciated his honest and earnest attitude. It was easy to see where his sons had acquired their agreeable, approachable natures.

"That's good of ya, Jake," he said, meaning it. "I'll take ya up on it. Be juist great ta have a clean space ta put things tagether and have another man there ta help oot."

"Goody," Noah repeated himself. "Daddy's gonna help."

Jake ruffled Noah's hair. "If I might ask, what part are you working on now?"

"Ahh, right," Thomas replied, nodding. "Trying ta find the pieces ta make the brakes for the soap box."

"Go-kart," Evan corrected.

"Evan." Jake shot his son a warning look. "Manners."

"Sorry," Evan said, immediately.

"Nah, nah." Thomas shook his head and pointed at Evan. "The lad's right on it, thare. A go-kart is the thing, not a soap box."

Jake let it slide, but raised an eyebrow at his son.

"What?" Evan asked.

Jake dropped the eyebrow and sighed. Subtlety was lost on four year olds. "Never mind," he said, before turning back to Thomas. "I have something that might work."

"Gae on," Thomas said, intrigued.

"We still have an old carriage that we used when the boys were babies and it has a brake on it—"

"Perfect!" Thomas blurted. "Spot on, lad. I used juist that sort ta thing before. I dinnae know why it didn't come ta mind."

Jake was pleased. And, a little surprised. Claire's description of the man didn't do him any sort of justice. Yes, he was a bit off the beaten track insofar as how he dressed, but that aside, he was actually a very approachable guy.

"Excellent." Jake squared his shoulders and stood a little taller. "I'll fish it out of the garage for you and we can go from there."

"Aye, that's sound, eh," Thomas agreed, pleased. He liked Jake. He liked Noah and Evan. He liked building and creating. This project was getting better and better.

* * * *

Peggy lifted the bag of fruit she'd received from Josephine from the trunk of her car with a grunt. She hadn't expected so much and was wondering how she would make use of it all before it turned. There was only so much jam and pie a woman could make before she could no longer stand the sight, or smell, of prune plums.

Resting the bag on the ground, she slammed the trunk closed, the sound reverberating off the side of the house. She blinked at the ringing in her ears, then grimaced when it was replaced by the cacophonous, high pitched sound of barking dogs.

"What's this now," she muttered under her breath as she turned around to face the street.

"Good afternoon!" A tall, dark-haired and very handsome well-dressed man beckoned from the curb.

Peggy's manners immediately kicked in. She smiled politely in return. "Hello."

"You're new to the neighborhood, yes?" he asked, taking her smile as an invitation while leading four, short, long bodied dogs forward across the driveway in her direction.

Peggy glanced at the bag of fruit, then at the dogs. They wouldn't try to eat it, would they?

"Only, I've seen you a few times and I noticed the sign on the lawn was gone, so I've been waiting for the opportunity to welcome you to the area." He stopped in front of Peggy and his dogs immediately sat their backsides on the pavement.

Peggy was relieved. They'd stopped barking and seemed well behaved. "Yes," she said, extending a hand. "I'm Peggy Jamieson."

"Gerry Carrion," he replied, shifting the dog's vibrantly colored leashes to his left hand and shaking the hand she offered with his right. "And these charmers are Cee-Cee, Buddy, Romeo and Tank."

He smiled at the nearly identical wire haired Dachshunds gazing up at him and Peggy wondered how he kept them straight. Each one was attached to a different colored leash, perhaps that helped? But, would that mean he'd have to keep them leashed all the time?

"Lovely to meet you." she snapped to. She refrained from greeting the dogs - *please* - and clasped her hands together demurely in front of her beige slacks. "Do you and your wife live close by?"

"Sort of," Gerry said. "My *partner*, Travis, and I live a couple of blocks over."

"Oh." Peggy blinked, digesting the word *partner*. What exactly was she was to assume by that? Workmate? Roommate? *Or ...?* Oh, boy.

"We're in the business." He gestured to the house. "We own *G&T Real Estate* in town, which is why I noticed your listing had been sold."

Peggy glanced at his electric blue boat shoes, lifted her gaze to take in his tan and white checked polo shorts and fitted, chocolate brown tee shirt, and reaffixed her polite smile on her face. "Isn't that nice. Does that mean you might have sold my son's house to him when he and his family moved in?"

"Where did they buy?"

"Close to here, actually—"

"Oh, wait," Gerry interrupted, snapping his fingers. The dogs immediately stood up. "Is your son the new dentist?"

Peggy smiled in delight. "Yes, he is! Jake Jamieson. That's him."

Gerry suppressed a grin. If this woman only knew. Whew. "Right," he said, keeping things on the level. "I met his wife at the hair salon not long ago."

"Claire," Peggy stated.

"Right. Lovely woman."

"So, does that mean you didn't sell them their house?"

Gerry shook his head. "Sorry, no. Although, interestingly, we actually only live a couple of doors down from them."

"Oh." Peggy wrinkled her nose. "*That* must have been awkward."

"No, not at all." He fiddled with the leashes, separating them where they'd become tangled. "The couple that lived there were great, but they have a relative in the business, so he got to do the deed with Jake instead of us."

Peggy nodded and Gerry caught his breath when his words rang back in his ears. Got to do the deed? Good lord. Thank goodness Travis wasn't with him. He would have cracked up at the double entendre.

"Well," Peggy said, her tone consoling. "I'm sure you and your ... *Travis* are just fine at your jobs, too."

Gerry glanced down at his dogs waiting patiently for his lead. He wasn't touching that comment with a ten foot pole. Time to go. "Well, it's been great meeting you, Peggy. I really should get the fur kids back home for some water. Perhaps we'll see you again, sometime."

"Bye." She waved him off as he walked purposefully down the street, small dogs at his heels. "Well, that was certainly interesting," she commented, to no one in particular, as she hoisted her bag of fruit upright and made her way to her front door.

* * * *

CHAPTER 13

"I'll be back out to check on you in a bit!"

Claire grimaced when she heard her mother's voice and footsteps on the back porch. She sounded so chipper, so cheerful, so *encouraging* - ugg. The last thing Claire wanted.

"Hi-ho!" Josephine trilled, as she pushed open the screen door that led into the kitchen.

"Hey, Mom," she said, rinsing dishes at the sink.

Josephine grinned and padded on bare feet, Bear at her heels, to the cabinets.

"Where are your shoes?"

Josephine looked down and shrugged. "In the yard? Or, maybe in the car? I'm not sure."

Claire stared at her. Not sure? How could she not be sure of where her shoes were? Was she a child disguised in an adult's body?

"Looks like things are really coming along out there with that go-kart, hey?" Josephine opened a cupboard door and peered inside.

"Umm-hmm," Claire muttered, her voice anything but enthused.

Josephine closed the cupboard door and opened another. "Something wrong?"

"Are you looking for something specific?" Claire placed the last dish in the draining board beside the sink and reached for a towel to dry her hands.

"Just a bowl for some water for Bear."

Claire dropped the towel on the countertop. "Next cupboard over. There are some blue plastic bowls."

"Ahh," Josephine said, following her directions. "There we go."

Claire moved aside to let her get to the tap at the sink. Bear sat on the tile floor, his head slightly cocked and one front foot raised as he waited. She couldn't help but grin at the furry little thing. Against her better judgement, he had grown on her.

"So, you were saying," Josephine prompted as she turned off the tap and carefully placed the bowl on the floor for Bear.

"What?" Claire reached out to the paper towel dispenser and pulled off a few sheets in readiness for when Bear was finished.

"I asked you about the go-kart and your face got all pruney, like you'd been sucking lemons."

"*Nice.*" Claire shot her a reproachful glance. "If you must know, I'm not all that thrilled with what's going on out there."

"Where?"

"In the yard."

"In the yard?" Josephine parroted. "What's going on in the yard?"

Claire rolled her eyes and said, with exaggerated patience, "The go-kart?"

"Oh." Josephine picked up the emptied bowl from the floor and placed it in the sink, then shrugged her shoulders. "I don't follow."

"It's dangerous," Claire stated, bluntly, bending to wipe the floor where the bowl had been.

"Oh, for goodness sake. It's a go-kart, not a formula one racer."

"And messy," she went on, tossing the paper towel into the garbage. "And what about other kids wanting to ride in it? Huh? What then? Suddenly, we have the issue of making sure they don't get hurt on our watch."

"Highly unlikely," Josephine commented. "How fast will they really be going, after all—?"

"*And* I know it's going to cause fights for whose turn it is and...." She paused to catch her breath, then started up again. "Where will we even store it!"

"Claire!" Josephine blurted.

Claire clamped her mouth shut and wrung her hands together.

"Honestly," Josephine exhaled. "You're getting way ahead of yourself." She gestured toward the back door. "The damned thing isn't even fully built yet and you have the boys, and their friends, careening out of control and in battle over whose turn is next."

Claire shrugged and walked over to the fridge. "Iced tea?" she offered, opening the door and reaching inside for a jug.

"Yes, please." Josephine ran her fingers through her wind-blown hair and pulled a chair out from the kitchen table. "And, even though you're trying to change the subject, I still suggest you stop overthinking everything, put aside your incessant worries and live in the moment. It's the only one you've got."

Claire bit her tongue. She wasn't going to argue. It was pointless.

"Anyway, what we really should be discussing is that dish of a man out there with them."

"Excuse me?"

Josephine raised an eyebrow and grinned lasciviously.

"Oh, God." Claire's face twisted, appalled. "*Thomas*?"

"I'm sure as heck not talking about your husband."

"Mother!" Claire poured them both a glass of tea and visibly shuddered.

"Oh, come on," Josephine cajoled as she picked up her glass. "He's not conventional, I'll give you that. But, what he lacks in blatant—"

"Grooming?" Claire said, wryly.

"*Polish*," Josephine corrected, with a smile. "He more than makes up for in rugged, Scottish charm. That accent of his is gorgeous, don't you think? Could make a girl willing to do all sorts of unspeakable things."

Claire stared at her mother. Gorgeous was the absolute last word she ever would have come up with to describe Thomas. As for *unspeakable*.... "I'm speechless," was what she finally managed to utter.

"That's a first," her mother shot back, giggling.

Claire couldn't help herself and smirked.

Josephine pointed at her and laughed out loud.

"Oh, shut up." Claire snickered and attempted to hide it behind her glass of iced tea. God. Just when she wanted to huff at the woman, she made things funny. She couldn't win for losing.

* * * *

"We should have a gathering."

"A gathering?" Gerry repeated, looking up from where he was brushing the dogs in the shade of his awning covered patio.

Travis, sprawled across one of their padded chaise lounge chairs, nodded; his green eyes hidden by dark sunglasses. "We haven't had one this summer."

"What about the birthday party for Gil?" Gerry patted Cee-Cee affectionately to let her know she was done. "Good girl, off you go."

Travis leaned over and plucked a half piece of bacon from a paper plate on the patio table and reached down to give it to Cee-Cee as her reward for being good during her grooming. "I don't count that," he said, with a shrug.

Gerry laughed. "He's your brother and you don't count it?"

"It was pretty much all family, not a gathering on purpose." Travis handed the other half piece of bacon to Buddy when Gerry sent him over. "Good boy," he said, stroking his soft, brown head.

Gerry stood up. "You have a point," he conceded. "Could you pass the sticky roller over?"

Travis picked up the lint brush and tossed it to him. "Come closer and I'll clean the back of your shorts for you."

Gerry caught it and swiftly ran it over the front of his black cargo shorts, gathering whatever stray bits of hair the dogs left behind. He rolled his eyes before stepping closer to the lounge chair. "Seriously?" he teased. "You couldn't just get up?"

Travis giggled and grabbed the brush from his hand. "This seemed easier. Turn around."

Gerry stood facing their lush backyard as Travis finished rolling the brush over the back of his shorts and short sleeved, blue plaid shirt. He sighed. He loved their outdoor space. They'd paid top dollar to have it remodeled. When they'd bought their home a couple of years ago, the backyard had been so unsightly its mere memory made him grimace. The previous owners had small children and no time and, as such, had left it to run wild. Now, with a pile of money thrown at it, it was a haven.

Where once there had been dirt, was now a flagstone patio; the tiles resplendent in colors of terra-cotta, marbled grey and black. Instead of weeds passing for grass, there was a rich, green synthetic lawn canvass. It was perfect for entertaining, perfect for the dogs to play and perfectly wonderful in that it required no maintenance or upkeep. Add in the Japanese maple trees throwing their dappled shadows across the blooming, yellow Potentilla shrubs in the boarder garden and the clay pots filled with herbs, and Gerry was confident the former owners wouldn't recognize the space.

"What's that sigh about?" Travis asked, finishing up and placing the brush on the patio table.

Gerry turned around, grinning. "Our yard makes me happy."

Travis settled back into the pillows on his lounger and crossed his legs at the ankle. "Yes?" he prompted.

Gerry laughed and sat on the end of the chaise. "And, you," he said, reaching out to affectionately squeeze Travis' bare calf. "You make me happy."

"So, does that mean you're on board for a gathering?"

Gerry gazed at his partner, drank in his blonde good looks and shrugged. "How could I resist?"

"Excellent!" Travis' face lit up. "We'll invite the whole gang and some new faces, too."

"New faces?"

Travis waggled his eyebrows before reaching out to pull Cee-Cee into his lap. "Well, it only seems right to include the newest neighbors. Make them feel welcome."

Gerry sighed. Only this time it wasn't with contentment. "You just can't let sleeping dogs lie."

"Oh, come on," Travis pet Cee-Cee and grinned. "It'll be fun. *And*," he added, before Gerry could speak up again. "I promise it will all be above board, no shenanigans."

Gerry shrugged, again. "Okay. I'll leave it to you."

Travis kissed the top of Cee-Cee's small head. "Deal."

* * * *

(HAPTER 14

"My goodness, Claire," Josephine called out, from the family room. "How long does it take to wrap a few bowls in saran wrap? It's only going to be torn off, anyway."

"I want them to stay fresh," Claire replied, her tongue sticking out slightly from between her lips as she concentrated upon getting a glass smooth seal across the bowl tops.

"I don't know why she's bringing food in the first place," Josephine muttered under her breath, before shrugging at Jake sitting beside her on the couch.

Jake refused comment. He wasn't about to get into that discussion. Again.

"*Because*," Claire said, her words carrying a sarcastic edge from the kitchen. "I was taught it's only polite to bring something to a party."

Josephine's eyes widened and Jake grinned. "She has the hearing of a bat," he said, in a hushed voice.

Josephine giggled and offered back to Claire, "That's true, but it's a birthday party. The gift is the thing you're supposed to bring. Not the banquet. Is your gift for Sophia's little sister, food?"

Jake shook his head at Josephine. She was so bad. Stirring the pot.

"I'm only asking," she added, "as I'd be inclined to think that a party throw by Italians will have more than its fair share of food."

"Mother!"

"What?"

"Seriously?" Claire walked into the family room and placed her hands on her hips. "You don't think that that comment sounds just a bit politically incorrect?"

"Oh, for goodness sake." Josephine rolled her eyes. "You know that's not what I meant at all. I love and embrace everyone; race, creed or color. And, saying that, I know for a fact Italians don't skimp on food."

Noah and Evan chose that moment to come thundering down the staircase, much to Jake's relief. Any interruption was welcome.

"Is it almost time to go to Portia's party?" Noah's cherubic face was alive with eagerness and excitement.

Claire cast a critical eye over her boys. They'd managed to keep their matching, blue polo shirts and tan shorts clean; much to her amazement.

Josephine's mouth twisted in a smirk. "As soon as Mommy is finished hermetically sealing her crockery."

"What's herman-cally sealing, Gramma?" Evan asked, his eyebrows knotted together in a frown.

"Never mind." Claire shot Josephine a scathing look. "Have you boys both used the bathroom?"

"Yup!" Noah nodded.

"Uh-huh," Evan agreed.

"Alrighty then," Jake said, standing up and stretching his arms over his head. "I'll pack the cooler for Mommy, you grab the gift and we'll go."

"Yay!" Noah and Evan simultaneously cheered.

"Need me to help with anything?" Josephine asked, just as the doorbell rang.

"You could answer the door," Claire said, over her shoulder, as she followed Jake into the kitchen. She wanted to make sure he packed the cooler correctly.

"Boys," Josephine spoke to her grandsons. "Wanna get that?"

Claire stopped short and Josephine laughed. "Kidding!" she said, walking toward the foyer, Noah and Evan trailing behind.

"Hilarious," Claire shot back as they disappeared around the corner.

Noah opened the front door. "Hello?" he said, to the blonde man standing on his porch.

"Hey, there!" the man replied. "Is your...." He stopped short, gasped and slapped a hand to his chest when Josephine pulled the door open wider and stepped into view. "Ms. Wright! What are you doing here?"

Josephine's face broke into a huge smile. "Travis!" She put a hand on both Noah's and Evan's shoulders. "Boys, I'd like you to meet my good friend Travis. And Travis, these are my grandsons, Noah and Evan."

Noah and Evan each said "Hello" in turn.

Travis put his hands on his slim hips, a delighted grin decorating his handsome face. "Well, hello yourselves, boys!" He wagged a finger at Josephine. "Ms. Wright, I'm having a hard time believing you're a Grandma, not to mention you never once mentioned these adorable boys lived in my neighborhood."

Josephine pushed her curls off her shoulders and laughed raucously at the scolding tone in Travis' voice. "In my defense—"

"Mom?" Claire cut the conversation off as she came up behind Josephine and the twins. "What's taking you so long? Is something wrong?"

"Well, hello again!" Travis sparkled at Claire.

Claire blanched and the air left her lungs in a whoosh. What on Earth was he doing at her doorstep?

"Again?" Josephine turned to face Claire. "You've met Travis before?"

"Uh-huh." Much to her chagrin, Claire's face flushed. "At Jessica's salon." Her eyebrows knitted together as she glanced at her mother, then Travis. "How do you two know one another?"

"Oh, dear," Josephine said, reaching out to grab his arm. "Where are our manners? Come inside, for goodness sake."

Claire stepped back into the foyer, Noah and Evan followed, and the next thing she knew Travis and her mother were herding them forward and they were all assembled in her family room. Claire blinked, trying to get up to speed.

"Jake!" Josephine called out. "Come in here for a moment."

Jake walked in from the kitchen, took in the tableau, and shot a questioning look at Claire as he asked, "What's up?"

"This is my friend, Travis," Josephine said, giving Travis' arm an affectionate squeeze. "We know each other from our pottery class."

Ahh, Claire thought. Of course. That made perfect sense. Her mother couldn't participate in anything without acquiring at least one or two new followers ... or rather, friends.

Jake, still looking confused, nodded. "Hi," he said, politely, while offering his hand to Travis. "Nice to meet you."

"The pleasure is all mine," Travis replied, his eyes dancing as he shook Jake's hand.

Claire held her breath. Was he going to call him *Mister Big*?

"However, what Ms. Wright is forgetting to mention," he clarified, winking at Josephine. "Is that I'm also your neighbor a few doors down."

"Oh. Are you joining us for the party?" Jake asked, trying to clear up his confusion.

"No, no." Josephine spoke for Travis. "No, Travis was popping in for...." She paused and cocked her head at him. "Did we say why you stopped in?"

Travis giggled and shook his head. "No, but it seems we're all on the same page for the party theme." He reached into the breast pocket of his short sleeved, violet colored dress shirt and pulled out a folded piece of paper. "I'm here to invite you and Claire to a gathering at our house, next weekend."

"Oh, how nice!" Josephine released her grip on his arm and clapped delightedly.

"I know it's a bit old fashioned," Travis said, self-deprecatingly, while handing the paper with *We're Having a Party!* emblazoned on the front in large purple print to Claire. "But, I still love the formality of hand written invitations."

"Oh, so do I," Josephine practically purred.

"What's a gathering?" Noah asked.

Travis beamed at him. "It's a get together, where grown-ups talk."

Evan nodded, his face thoughtful. "Kind of like a meeting?"

"Uh-huh," Travis agreed. "Something like that."

"Did you say next weekend?" Claire asked, holding the invitation tentatively between her fingertips and wracking her brain for a reason to decline. She had nothing.

"Yes," Travis said, before wrapping an arm around Josephine's shoulders. "And, even though I don't have an invitation for you Ms. Wright, consider yourself officially invited as well."

Josephine wrapped her arm around Travis' waist. "I'd be delighted," she trilled.

Claire exchanged a look with Jake. What the hell was happening? Her mother was turning into some sort of southern belle before their eyes.

Jake shrugged his shoulders.

"Anyway," Travis interrupted Claire and Jake's silent communication and untangled himself from Josephine. "I understand you're on your way out, so I won't keep you any longer."

Josephine trailed after him toward the foyer. "I'll see you out, dear."

"Remember," he called over his shoulder, just before he left the house. "Next Saturday. It's going to be *live*, as the kids say. Mark it on your calendar!"

"Live?" Claire repeated, raising her eyebrows at Jake.

Jake laughed. "No idea."

"Can we go now?" Noah shuffled back and forth on his feet.

"You betchya, buddy." Jake clapped his hands together. "Let's get to Portia's party."

Claire gave herself a shake. She felt as though she was coming out of a fog. She looked at the invitation, still in her hand, then set it carefully on the coffee table. One step at a time.

* * * *

"Bella! Bella!" Rosa enthused when she saw Claire and her family walking up the street toward the party girl's house.

Noah and Evan broke ranks and ran full barrel toward her welcoming hugs.

Claire admired her flowing summer dress, the color of new roses, and immediately felt underdressed. She'd chosen her tan shorts and blue cotton top because she wasn't sure how much time she'd be spending chasing after the boys. Maybe she should have put in a bit more effort.

"Wow," Jake said, referring to the display that encompassed the entire crescent ahead. "These people really know how to put on a party."

Claire looked past Rosa and the boys and her eyes widened as she took it all in. Jake was right.

Multi-sized hot pink, lemon yellow and candy purple helium balloons waved merrily from the front porches of every house; even Thomas'. White streamers trailed from tree branches and multi-colored, butterfly shaped birthday banners were strung from tall poles set up in each yard.

The center of the crescent was nearly obscured by a vast, canopy-styled white tent rimmed with plum purple, squash yellow and fuchsia pink colored paper lanterns. It was providing shade to numerous tables overflowing with an array of food and drink to rival a cruise ship.

And it didn't stop there.

The resident's properties all boasted some sort of fun to be had. There were garishly colored bouncy castles set up next door to face painting stations. Craft tables and water balloon games neighbored bean bag and ring toss venues. There was even an ice cream truck with a lineup forming at its open window.

"Oh, look," Josephine pointed at Matt and Cristina's front yard. "They have a pool and a *Slip 'N Slide*. The boys will love that."

Claire looked over at the birthday girl's front yard. Sure enough, a large, green rectangular pool and a long, blue water tarp were open for business.

"It feels like a carnival," Jake observed, moving slowly along the street. "Are those steel drums?"

Claire dragged her eyes away from the pool to see two men dressed in vibrantly patterned shirts, their skin the color of rich cocoa, and one woman in a matching sheath dress and sandals, her long hair the color of summer strawberries, setting up their drums next to the ice cream truck. Moments later, beneath a large honey yellow umbrella, a relaxed calypso beat began to wash over the party.

Jake, unconsciously strolling in time to the beat, asked, "Do all of the people manning the stations live here, or did they bring people in?"

"Umm, no. Pretty sure they live here," Claire said, her focus drawn back to the pool. She was slightly agog, marveling at how Matt and Cristina were smiling and laughing as they casually presided over the children splashing in the shallow water. She was sure she would have been a wreck, worrying about someone losing their footing and getting hurt.

"What a hoot!" Josephine proclaimed, as they caught up to the boys and Rosa. "Those drummers make me feel like having a rum punch!"

"Si, si," Rosa agreed, a bright smile on her face beneath her teal, wide-rimmed, straw shade hat. "It's a great party! Lotsa fun for everyone. We're so happy you come. And you bring your family."

Claire, caught up in the cheerful spirit, grinned and gestured to her Mom and Jake. "Rosa, I'd like you to meet my mother, Josephine, and my husband, Jake."

"It's wonderful to meet you," Josephine said, throwing her arms around Rosa in a warm embrace. "I've heard so many wonderful things about you from Noah and Evan," she added, into Rosa's silver streaked hair.

Claire flinched, slightly embarrassed by her mother's effusive greeting. Rosa, on the other hand, was clearly fine with it and hugged Josephine back with the same vigor.

"I hear so many wonderful things from Noah and Evan about their Gramma, too," she said, patting Josephine's back affectionately. "It's such a good thing to finally meet you."

Josephine broke the hug and stepped back, then looked expectantly at Jake. "Well," she said, inclining her head. "Don't just stand there holding that cooler. Get in there."

"*Mom*," Claire warned through a tight smile on her face.

Jake quickly intervened. He placed the blue and white cooler on the pavement and opened his arms. "If Rosa will have me."

Rosa laughed and hugged him, making Claire feel like the stick in the mud. She refused to make eye contact with Josephine, knowing her mug would be decorated with an 'I told you so' expression.

"Come," Rosa said, when she and Jake had untangled themselves. "You join the party, mingle, eat." It was then she took notice of Claire's cooler. "What's this? Did you bring food, sweet Claire?"

"Oh, well." Claire cleared her throat, uncomfortable in the knowledge it appeared she was so picky she'd brought her own lunch.

Rosa's face lit up in genuine delight. "What a nice girl. And generous, too."

Claire flushed and smoothed her t-shirt. "It was nothing," she began.

That was as far as she got.

Rosa patted Josephine's arm, as though it was her accomplishment her daughter was so nice, and Claire snapped her mouth shut. Then, when Josephine grinned, it took all of Claire's effort not to snort derisively.

"How about I take it for you to the table and get it all set up, yes?" Rosa pointed at the white tent, the sheer, lavender colored curtains hanging at each corner billowing softly in the gentle breeze.

"Alright," Claire said, still feeling slightly wrong-footed. "I mean, if that's really fine with you. I don't want to upset any sort of food plan you might have created for the party."

"Food plan?" Rosa parroted, her eyebrows furrowed as she tried to grasp what Claire meant.

"Oh, good god," Josephine muttered, before sprang into action. "Thank you, Rosa," she said, grabbing the handles of the cooler and lifting it off the ground. "I'll help you and we'll let the young people go mingle. I think the boys are nearly coming apart at the seams to get into this fabulous party."

"*Grazie*," Rosa said, as she led Josephine away.

"I adore your hat," was the last thing Claire hear her mother say, before being swallowed up into the festivities.

* * * *

Claire sipped at a glass of mango punch and wished she had something stronger available to spike it. Perhaps that rum her mother had been going on about. It had been a stressful couple of hours keeping up with her sons and if it wasn't for the fact they were having the time of their lives, she'd have happily bailed out.

"There you are." Jake sidled up beside her under the shade of the large, white tent.

"Where are the boys?" she said, automatically.

"At the craft table."

Claire began to scan the street. "Which one?"

"They're fine. I told them where I was going."

"Have you seen my mother?" Claire frowned and surveyed the block one more time.

"She's fine, too," he said, with a laugh. "The last I saw her, she was sporting an oversized, red sunhat and shaking her booty near Thomas' house."

Claire rolled her eyes, but held her tongue. Jake reached out and wrapped an affectionate arm around her shoulders, swaying them both back and forth to the gentle rhythm. "Man, that band is something, right?"

Claire nodded. Even she had to admit, they were really great. She pulled back and stared at his head. "Speaking of which, where did that come from?" she said, pointing at the wheat colored, straw fedora he was wearing.

He reached up and touched the hat's rim. "Matt gave it to me. The party girl's Dad?"

Claire knew who he was. She'd met both Sophia's parents.

"He's a good guy. When I was over at their yard, he said he was giving them to all of the Dad's, or Uncles, or whoever came with their kids to the party."

Claire regarded the crescent, suddenly aware of the sea of straw hats.

Jake stuck out his chin, striking a model pose. "Is it me?"

Claire couldn't help but giggle. With his strong jaw, sparkling green eyes and thick, brown hair, he really was handsome. "Totally you," she said, grinning. "It brings out the navy blue of your shirt."

He laughed.

"Seriously, though, that was really decent of him."

"Yeah," he agreed. "And it keeps the sun off my head, which is a bonus."

"Oh, that reminds me." Claire snapped her fingers. "The boys' hats—"

"Are on their heads," Jake answered smoothly, then looked at her butterfly decorated cup and raised his eyebrows. "Is that plain punch, or—"

Claire looked at the cup, then set it on the table. "Plain," she confirmed.

Jake frowned. "We need to remedy that, I think. Gotta raise the stakes at this party." He started looking around for Kevin, spotted him near Josephine and Thomas and grinned. "Wait here. I'll be back."

"Check on the boys," Claire called after him as he took off at a brisk pace toward Jessica's husband.

"Excuse me, but have we met?"

Claire twisted around at the sound of a friendly voice and was rewarded with a cheerful smile from a short, middle aged woman with curly blonde hair and intelligent eyes. She was being trailed by the same fluffy dog Evan and Noah had spotted on their first day in the crescent, when they'd been returning Corkscrew.

"You look familiar," the woman continued. "I'm Carol, by the way, and I'm sure I've seen your boys around. Twins, aren't they?"

Claire nodded. "Yes. I'm Claire, their Mom."

"It's lovely to meet you." Carol extended a hand for Claire to shake, then made a sweeping gesture with her arm to the party. "So, how do you know the birthday girl?"

"I'm a friend of Jessica's," Claire explained. "I think she's your neighbor?"

"Yes, she and Kevin."

"Right. We just live on the next block over—"

"Mountainview Terrace?"

"Yes," Claire confirmed. "And Jessica introduced me and my sons to Sophia and her family; thus, the invitation to Portia's party."

"Just you and your boys?" Carol asked, pointedly, her mouth set in a sympathetic line.

Claire paused, surprised by her blatant nosiness. Carol waited. Claire sighed and gave in.

"Well, my *husband*, too," she said, a bit irritated at herself for folding.

Carol's face brightened, much like a squirrel who'd found an unexpected nut. "Oh, good. You're married."

Claire's eyebrows knotted together. She wasn't sure what she was supposed to say to that.

"Quite something how the two of them got together isn't it?" Carol suddenly leaned in closer, as though they were sharing some sort of confidence.

Claire tilted backward. "The two of them?" she asked.

"Uh-huh."

She shrugged, still none the wiser.

"Jessica and Kevin, of course," Carol said, squinting at her as though she was a bit slow on the uptake.

Claire cocked her head in a perfect imitation of a dog trying to understand. There had been no transition from one topic to the next and she felt she'd skipped a vital step in the conversation. "Umm," she said, straightening her neck and trying to keep up. "I'm not sure I follow."

"Oh, I know it doesn't matter *now*," Carol said, swatting dismissively at the air. "But, still, it's quite the amazing thing when you think about it. I mean, can you imagine how odd it would be to know your husband used to be engaged to, never mind shacked up with, your sister? I mean, sure, we've all gotten used to it now. Old news here on Sunrise Place. But, at first…."

Claire blinked and swallowed. Say what?

Carol peered at Claire. "Are you okay, dear? You look a little startled? You *did* know that Jessica's sister was the person who unintentionally brought the two of them together, right?"

"No," Claire said, bluntly. "I'm afraid I didn't."

"Oh." Carol looked as though she'd swallowed something particularly unappetizing. She cleared her throat and patted at her blonde curls. "Well, I guess I just assumed, you two girls being friends and all, she would have shared that with you."

"Shared what?" Jessica asked, striding into the shade of the tent.

Oh, marvelous, Claire thought, scouring the crowd for Jake and his promised remedy for the punch.

Carol visibly jumped. "Oh! You startled me, dear!" She laughed and attempted to change the subject. "Such a party, isn't it? The band just makes everything so happy."

"What should I have shared with Claire, Carol?" Jessica pressed, not to be deterred.

"Oh, it's nothing," Carol said, shrugging and fiddling with the hem of her yellow, cotton shirt to avoid direct eye contact.

"Well, if so, why suddenly so secretive?"

"Listen, Jess," Claire said, attempting to move things along. "It really wasn't anything. Carol was just chatting about how great you and Kevin are together." She cleared her throat and added, in a mutter, "How you met...."

Jessica's face twisted and became a perfect picture of pissed off. Carol dared to peek in her direction, saw her expression and beat a hasty retreat. "Oh, dear, I think I see Deborah having some difficulties with the water balloon toss." She stepped clear of them and beckoned to her small dog. "Peaches! Come on!"

Before Jessica could utter a single word of reprimand, Carol was long gone.

"Wow," Claire said. "You wouldn't know it to look at her, but that woman really can move if she needs to."

Jessica, against her better judgement, chuckled. "Well, you know, if you're caught telling tales you'd better be ready to scatter as necessary."

"Look," Claire began, hoping to pat things down. "It doesn't matter what she said."

"Oh, I know," Jessica assured her. "I was just hoping to share the sordid tale of how Kevin and I got together in my own way. Not as casual, souvlaki dip conversation."

Claire smiled. "If it helps, it didn't sound *that* sordid."

Jessica laughed and ran her fingers through her curls, pushing them back from her neck. "It isn't, really. Just... awkward. Telling people that you met your husband because he was dating... okay, *engaged* to your sister sounds a little Ozarks, if you get my drift."

Claire bit her lip. What to say. "No, no," she tried.

"Oh, please." Jessica rolled her eyes. "It does, too. But, the important thing is everybody is fine about it. Absolutely fine. My sister is actually happy about how things turned out, believe it or not."

"Really?"

"Really. Once there was some time and distance and everything calmed down after their breakup, Kevin and I discovered our friendship was slowly turning into something more. By that point, April said she wished she'd realized it sooner and got us together."

"Wow," Claire said, impressed.

"I know," Jessica agreed. "I didn't believe her at first; I was sure she'd finally come clean at one point and tell me she hated that he and I had a connection, but she didn't. She's amazing like that. She knew she and Kev weren't a good match and because she loved us both, was thrilled we'd found happiness together."

Claire shook her head. "That is a seriously cool sister you have."

"Don't I know it," Jessica said, smiling. "Now, can we put aside the souvlaki dip conversation and find your boys?"

Claire nodded. "Absolutely."

* * * *

"Such a party," Peggy said, for what felt to Claire like the hundredth time. "Such extravagance, just for one little girl's first birthday."

Claire rolled her eyes. It was one thing to think it, but to say it out loud... well, that was Peggy. In an attempt to cut off the conversational path her mother-in-law had chosen to follow, she nodded noncommittally and murmured, "Umm-hmm."

"Not that a person shouldn't celebrate, of course," Peggy was quick to clarify.

Darn, Claire thought. Didn't work.

"I just think that asking all of your neighbors to get involved seems so...." She paused, searching to find her exact thought. "Well, *so...."*

Claire jumped in and tried again. "They were all more than happy to do it, Peggy. Jessica told me."

Peggy shrugged. "Oh, well, if they were okay with it, who am I to say anything." She sniffed and looked around for Jake's father. "Have you seen Earl anywhere?"

"No." Claire stifled a yawn. She was beat.

"I have to say, when the boys told us about the party and insisted we come along, Earl lit up like a small child." She nudged Claire with an elbow and shot her a conspiratorial look. "I suppose it's the boy in all men that gets awakened over such things."

Help, Claire thought, her head starting to hurt. And where had Jake managed to disappear to?

"Oh, did you happen to get a look at that mangy, grey cat hanging around that unkempt house? Or, for that matter, the rough looking man who lived there?"

Peggy grimaced. "I mean, really. I understand about wanting to include all of your neighbors, but there should be a line drawn—"

"There's Earl!" Claire blurted and jabbed her finger toward the face painting table.

Peggy followed her directions and gasped. "Oh! He's not getting his face painted, is he?"

"Maybe," Claire said, hoping to set her on her way. It worked.

"For goodness sake!" Peggy set off at a brisk pace, her tan slacks nothing but a blur.

Claire watched her go and sighed, relieved. Peggy was a woman to be taken in small doses and when she and Earl had rolled up unexpectedly to the party, Claire had groaned in disbelief. Just one more thing to get through.

"Mommy!" Noah called out, snapping her to attention.

He was at the wading pool and while she'd had a lovely chat there earlier with Sophia's parents, Claire wasn't all that confident Matt was watching as closely as he should have been.

"Careful," she called back, leaving the cover of the tent and striding across the pavement toward the lawn.

"I am!" Noah said, joyfully, before throwing himself face first down the water slide connected to the pool.

Claire stopped short and held her breath. It wasn't until he hit the bottom of the shallow pool, laughing merrily, that she exhaled shakily.

"Did you see?" he asked, grabbing for his orange towel.

"Yes, but seriously, Noah," she said, firmly, while marching up the lawn. "You have to be careful." Before he could argue, she added pointedly, "You're not the only one in the pool and you might hurt someone else."

There. That should do it. She sounded like she was looking out for the other children, not fussing over her own.

"Okay." He nodded and swiped at the water dripping from his green swim trunks.

Claire backed off slightly and attempted to affect a casual air while still keeping close watch.

"Is your Mommy angry?" Sophia, dressed in a rainbow colored swimsuit and sitting on a pink towel just outside the edge of the pool, asked Noah.

Claire's ears perked up.

"No." Noah shook his damp head, then turned to watch his brother approach.

"She sounded angry," Sophia offered, while fiddling with the edge of her lavender colored sunhat.

"She's like that sometimes," he said, sagely, his voice sounding so wise it startled Claire.

"Yeah." Evan tossed his opinion into the conversation, while sitting down and making himself comfortable on the grass beside Sophia. "She's just a scared Mommy a lot, that's all."

"A lot," Noah echoed as he wrapped his towel around his shoulders and sat next to Evan.

"But," Evan added. "She says it's only 'cause she loves us."

Claire's heart began to race and she felt slightly lightheaded. Had she just heard what she'd thought she'd heard? Her sons, her dear and treasured boys, thought of her as a 'scared Mommy'?

Sophia, meanwhile, shrugged. "Yeah, my Mommy sometimes tells Portia stuff, too."

Oh, God. Claire clutched her hands together. Her mothering skills were being compared to that of a mother of a *one year old*. It felt like a kick, adding insult to injury. She waited, her heart thumping in her chest, but the kids moved on and started discussing whether or not they wanted another ice cream. Eavesdropping was over. All that was left was to ask herself the question: what the hell was she supposed to do with that information?

* * * *

CHAPTER 15

Jessica drove carefully through the quiet, Sunday morning streets of her neighborhood toward her salon. It was closed for the day, but after the somewhat scattered and confusing phone call from Claire, asking if she'd meet her there, she'd agreed and set out.

She wasn't sure *what* was going on, but knew for sure *something* was going on. Claire had sounded so disjointed, it was completely unlike her; at least in the time she'd known her. Jessica sincerely hoped that, whatever the problem was, she could help.

* * * *

Claire looked up from the curb she was sitting on in front of the doors of *A Cut Above* when she heard the sound of a car pulling into the parking lot and heaved a sigh of relief when she recognized Jessica's Jeep. Finally.

Jessica parked the vehicle and stepped out, her face a picture of concern. "Hey," she said, feeling more alarmed when she saw Claire had a small cloth shopping bag beside her and the distinct shape of wine bottles were peeking out of the top.

Claire stood up, brushed off the seat of her shorts and picked up the bag. "Thank you for meeting me here," she said, meaning it wholeheartedly.

Jessica walked past her and reached out to unlock the salon door. "What's going on?"

"There's a loaded question," she replied, her voice heavy.

Jessica pushed open the door and motioned for her to go inside. "Well, start at the beginning then. I've got time."

* * * *

Once inside, Jessica locked the doors and kept the reception lights off. No need to make any passers-by think she was open for business. She and Claire moved into the heart of the salon and only then did she turn on a few lights to illuminate their path.

"Do you want to go back into the lunch room?" she asked, eyeing Claire's bag.

Claire rubbed her makeup free face and shrugged. "Whatever you like. Do you have glasses there?" She raised the bag and added, "I think this conversation needs a splash of wine."

Jessica couldn't help it and laughed. Despite her subdued demeanor, Claire still had her wits about her. "We do, and mugs," she said, a glint of amusement in her eye.

"Perfect." Claire flashed a small smile. Life wasn't all bad, after all.

* * * *

"And there I was," Claire said, before taking another gulp of wine from her cup. "Standing not a few feet away, listening to the horrible information that my lovely, lovely boys think of me as their scared Mommy." She put her mug down on the low coffee table in front of the cushy sofa in the lunch room and dropped her head into her hands. "I felt as though my heart had been punched."

Jessica wasn't sure what to say. In all of her thoughts, it hadn't occurred to her Claire's crisis might be because her sons had unintentionally revealed one of their truths. And while she wasn't a mother yet, she could only imagine it would cut to the core to have such an unflattering picture presented in such a startling way.

"And do you know what the worst part is?"

Jessica shook her head.

"They're right."

"Oh, Claire," she said, trying to find a way to cushion things.

"No, no." Claire pulled her head from her hands. "It's true. I am a nervous parent. Horribly so. I didn't realize it until they were about three, because up until then it was sort of normal to be running around behind them, you know?"

Jessica nodded, again.

"But, then, when they got older and made it to four, I had to face up to the fact I was still pretty nervous about letting them get too far away. Too out of hand. Too…." She sighed and ran her fingers through her lank hair. "And, still, I justified it by telling myself I was being a responsible parent."

"And you are," Jessica insisted. "You're a fabulous Mom."

Claire smiled, gratefully. "Thank you. But, the facts are in. I still treat them like they're toddlers and they're not."

Jessica couldn't stand it. She looked so down on herself. "Why do you think you this happened?" she asked, trying to help her get to the root of things and stop being so hard on herself. The first step, after all, was admitting it.

Claire reached out and grabbed a bottle of wine from the table, topped up her mug, then reached out and did the same for Jessica. "You know, I've been asking myself the same damned question."

"And?"

"And," she said, thoughtfully. "I think it stems right back to my childhood."

"You think your Mom is the reason?" Jessica picked up her mug and took a sip. Despite the early hour and that they'd soon have to make a run to the bakery next door if they didn't want to end up seriously tipsy, it was really nice to be relaxing and enjoying a great bottle of wine.

"Well, yes and no." Claire leaned back into the couch cushions. "For as long as I can remember, my Mom's been a free spirit. No surprise to you, I'm sure."

Jessica shook her head. It wasn't.

"And, apparently, I'm more responsible in nature - more *scared*."

When Jessica opened her mouth to protest, Claire held up her hand. "No, it's fine," she said. "Really. I'll never be the free spirit my mother is. I think she was born that way. It's okay. I accepted it a long time ago."

"I feel like there's a *but* coming."

Claire laughed. "*But*, because she was that way when I was growing up, I pushed against it and tried to make up for her carefree attitude by being almost obsessively responsible."

Jessica nodded. Made sense.

"It's actually kind of funny, in a sad sort of way." A small smile played at Claire's lips. "She was the adult and I was the child, but very often it felt as though the roles were reversed."

"Are you saying she didn't take care of you the way that you needed?" Jessica suddenly felt badly for the young Claire. Trying to cope with an irresponsible mother.

"No, not at all," she said, swiftly shattering that image. "She got everything done that needed to be done, she just did it her own way and with a well-developed sense of silly and humor to dress it up. I was the one who made issues with everything, I'm now realizing."

Jessica digested the information while Claire sipped her wine and, finally, spoke up. "Okay, so you were a cautious child, then what?"

"Cautious." Claire snickered. "That's a kind way of putting it. I made cautious look whimsical." She sighed and added, "I did finally loosen up, though. After I met Jake."

Ahhh, Jessica thought.

Claire grew wistful, her shoulders softening. "It was like he released me, you know? I'd left home, was living a fairly routine life, working and dating here and there and then, bam! Along came Jake. And suddenly this whole other side of me, I like to call it the Josephine genetic, was stirred up and I found myself ready to jump head first into any adventure he offered."

Jessica smiled at the youthful expression that had washed over Claire's face, making her look ten years younger than her current thirty eight. Clearly, Jake was a good thing in her life. "So, what happened between then and now?"

"The boys," she said, simply. "Once I got pregnant and found out we were having not just one, but two boys, the Josephine genetic was systematically trampled by a wave of responsibility and practicality."

"Just like that?"

"No," Claire admitted. "It took a while for that responsible part of me to shove the Josephine genetic to the curb. It was like every ultrasound test we saw, combined with every kick and nudge in my belly as they grew bigger, congealed together to weight me down and thrust me into a state of almost panic at the awesome responsibility I was going to be embracing."

Jessica suddenly realized she'd been holding her breath as Claire unburdened her truth and exhaled. "And Jake?"

"Oh, he was fantastic." Claire placed her mug back down on the table and slumped back into the sofa. "He still is. I know he's concerned about me, but he just goes along steadily by my side, doing what he can to pat me down. I know it's been terribly difficult on him to watch the once willing and happy woman he married turn into a nervous wreck over two, four year old boys." Her face crumpled and she pressed her hands over her eyes. "God, the poor guy. Stuck with a sap like me."

"Hey, hey," Jessica said, getting up swiftly from the chair adjacent to the couch and sitting beside her. "You're not a sap. Not even close. You've had a tough time, had to take on a lot of responsibility all at once and you caved a bit under the pressure."

Claire didn't say anything, just sighed and wiped her teary eyes.

Jessica reached out and gave her a hug. "What matters is you see it."

"Oh." Claire shrugged. "*Well….*"

"No, really," Jessica insisted. "You being able to see it means you can change it. Most people never face up to their stuff, Claire. And then they end up victims of their own making."

Claire sniffed and nodded. That was true. She hugged Jessica back and smiled.

"There you go," Jessica said, thrilled to see the smile light up her face. Hope. "And, if you're willing, I think we can get started on the first stage of the change right here."

Claire looked at her, interested. "I'm listening."

"First, we have to get some solid food into us to soak up all of this wine."

Claire giggled and nodded.

"Then, once I'm back in control of my faculties, we can put this quiet salon to good use and—"

"Change my hair!" Claire sat up straight and grinned widely. It was a perfect idea. Start with the outside, change what she saw every time she looked in the mirror and work her way inward; transforming her thoughts to match her new look.

"You're in?" Jessica asked, eagerly.

"One hundred percent."

* * * *

Claire giggled to herself as she shunned her garage in favor of her driveway and pulled the minivan to a stop on the concrete pad in front of the large door. She didn't want to alert her family she'd arrived; instead desiring to make an entrance.

Jake was going to be so startled. When she'd fled the house without a backward glance that morning, wine bottles clinking together in her cloth grocery bag, he'd watched her go with wide, startled eyes.

Claire didn't blame him. She'd looked exactly as she'd been feeling; upset, inconsolable and scattered. Not a combination anyone would want to see in their beloved, especially when operating heavy machinery.

But that was water under the bridge. She'd taken the first step toward change and was eager to keep on stepping. She'd left her careful, sensible style on the floor of Jessica's salon, then joined her in a spur of the moment shopping trip to add some much needed pizzazz to her wardrobe and now felt excited to wow the socks off all three of her boys.

Taking a deep breath, Claire grabbed the colorful shopping bags on the adjacent passenger seat and exited her van. Show time. She walked up the path to the doorway in her new, bright yellow ballet flats, twisted her key in the lock and threw open the front door with a flourish.

"Tadaaaaa!"

Nothing.

Claire stood in her foyer, arms thrown outward and shopping bags dangling from her hands, and was met with dead silence. Where the hell was everyone?

She dropped her arms back down, shucked the bags to the floor and closed the front door. "Well, this is a fine how-do-you-do," she said, to nobody but herself.

Then she heard it. The sound of voices and laughter coming from the backyard. Well, it was *nice* to know they weren't sitting around wringing their hands with worry over her. Okay, *fine*, she *had* phoned and left a message for Jake, informing him of her plans with Jessica, but *still*.

Claire walked through the family room and into the kitchen to peek out the window. There they were, Jake and the boys, her mother and... oh good god in heaven... Thomas.

Jake and Thomas were drinking beers and seemed to be tinkering with the go-kart. Noah and Evan were in green swim shorts, matching blue capes tied around their shoulders; jumping through a spinning sprinkler and cheering each other on. And, not to be missed, her mother was lounging gracefully on a beige deck chair, a glass of wine held aloft as her mouth moved a mile a minute, entertaining the troops with some sort of tale. *Que sera sera.*

Claire frowned. God, she couldn't leave the house for half a day without all semblance of order being thrown out the window. She moved closer to the glass when she saw a shadow lurking beneath her mother's chair and felt more annoyance drape over her like a heavy blanket. Corkscrew. That mangy cat of Thomas' was a part of the backyard show and Claire was sure Jake hadn't thought to make sure the boys wash their hands after touching it. Or rather, *him*.

No, instead, they were all goofing around, carefree as all get out. And who would have to think about things like clean hands and dinner? Her. Claire gritted her teeth and prepared to march out into the yard and get things into order. After all, if she didn't….

WAIT.

She's a scared Mommy rang in her ears and Claire practically lurched forward on her feet as she responded to the brakes she slammed on her mental chatter. She spun away from the window and caught a glimpse of her newly refreshed self in the reflection of the mirror she'd hung on the wall over the table and took a steadying breath.

No, she silently corrected herself. She was *not* going to straighten anything, or anyone, out. Clearly they'd been getting along just fine without her and there was nothing she needed to do. Except for get a grip.

She straightened her spine, winked at herself in the mirror - then felt silly for doing so - and decided that, instead of a *tadaaa* moment, she'd stroll out to the yard, casual as all get-out and let the reactions fall where they may.

But first, pizza.

* * * *

"Hey, boys!"

Claire opened the back door in time to hear her mother calling out to Evan and Noah, making them turn swiftly around from their sprinkler jumping game. She hesitated and listened.

"Guess what happened to me?" Josephine went on.

Noah cocked his head. "What?"

"I had a dream last night that I was eating a giant marshmallow."

Evan looked at her, curious. "And then what happened? Was it good?"

"It was," Josephine said, grinning. "But the strange thing was, when I woke up my fluffy white pillow was missing!"

Noah's eyes widened in surprise and Josephine cracked up. Claire smirked and shook her head. Her mother had told her the very same joke when she was little and she'd ran into the house to see if it was true.

"Gramma!" Evan piped up, his voice accusing as he watched the adults laughing. "You made that up!"

Noah started to giggle when realization dawned Josephine was having a bit of fun. His giggles turned into all out belly laughing when the image of his Gramma eating her pillow took over his thoughts.

Claire smiled as she watched, relieved her sons hadn't been infected with her cautiousness. It was one thing to recognize your Achilles heel, it was another to find out you'd passed it along. Thank goodness she hadn't.

She pushed the door wide and stepped outside. "Hello!" she called out, closing the door behind her.

Josephine spun around in her chair, looked at her daughter and let out a gasp. "Claire!" she shouted, making Corkscrew shoot out from beneath her chair and dart for the tree house. Josephine ignored the cat, pulled herself swiftly upright and threw her hands in the air. "Oh my goodness! Claire Rose you are an absolute vision! Look at you!"

Claire couldn't suppress the grin capturing her mouth, nor the delight swirling through her stomach, when she saw the surprise and pleasure that swept across Jake's face.

"Hey, you," he said, putting down his beer bottle and getting up from where he sat on the grass, next to Thomas. "Busy afternoon?"

Claire didn't get a chance to answer. Noah and Even launched themselves at her, talking a mile a minute.

"Mommy!" Noah practically shouted, while pointing at her flouncy, flowered skirt. "You look different!"

Evan wrapped his arms around her upper thighs. "Your shoes are different."

"And your hair is different," Noah observed, looking at the short, flirty, layered bob Jessica had created.

"And your face!" Evan tilted his head back and pointed at her.

"My face?" Claire asked, slightly bewildered.

Evan nodded. "Uh-huh. Did you have a nap?"

Josephine laughed and smoothed her hand affectionately down Claire's arm. "I think Evan might mean you look very relaxed, dear. Rested. I'd hazard to guess it's a compliment."

Jake took his opportunity and leaned in for a quick kiss. "It definitely is," he said, his eyes twinkling. "You look fantastic."

"And you look like you're feeling a whole lot better than when you left, this morning," Josephine threw in.

Claire's eyebrows shot up in surprise and she cast an accusing glance at Jake.

"Oh, don't get your knickers in a knot," Josephine said, when she saw her face. "It was like pulling teeth to get him to say anything at all. I put two and two together all on my own."

Claire took a breath, reminded herself of *scared Mommy* and nodded. She would let it go. Instead of making a fuss, she looked past Josephine at Thomas. "Hello," she said, giving a small wave. "Nice to see you, again."

Thomas tipped an imaginary hat and grinned, startling her yet again with the friendliness he exuded when she least expected it.

"Thom and I've been working on the go-cart," Jake began to explain. "We were just taking a break, that's why we have the beers."

Claire could hear the nervousness in her husband's voice and realized she'd put it there. Apparently, she wasn't just scared Mommy, she'd become shrew wife as well.

"Great!" she said, making sure she sounded enthused. "I'm sure the boys will love it when it's done."

Jake raised an eyebrow and Josephine cocked her head, her face curious.

"And," she went on, reaching out to pull Noah and Evan into a hug. "Guess what I did?"

"Eat your pillow?" Evan asked.

"What?" She paused, taken aback, until she remembered her mother's joke.

Josephine, meanwhile, broke into fits of giggles and returned to her lawn chair to sit down.

"That's what Gramma said, after guess what," Noah informed her.

"Oh, well, no. I didn't eat my pillow. But, I did order pizza for you to eat!"

"Pepperoni?" Evan asked, while Noah threw in, "Ham and pineapple?"

"Yes," Claire agreed. "Both of those. And two other types as well." She turned to Thomas. "I hope you'll stay, I've ordered more than enough."

Thomas raised his beer bottle in a small salute. "Aye, thank you kindly, lass."

Claire grinned. Okay, maybe not a man of many words, but the ones he did use were genuine. Maybe he'd grow on her. She saw Josephine give her an approving look and tucked it away for later. She hadn't had many of them from her mother, usually the glances were of a more pitying variety; it was a balm to her heart.

"Why don't we get you boys cleaned up before the pizza arrives," Jake said.

Claire felt another wave of delight course through her. She'd wanted so badly to say it, but she'd squelched it, and now it was Jake taking the reins. She could do this. She had to do this. Scared Mommy had to be eliminated.

Baby steps, she thought, watching Jake lead the boys into the house.

* * * *

CHAPTER 16

C laire drove her minivan into an empty parking space in front of *Fitness Zone*, turned it off and pulled up the parking break. She swallowed against her nerves. It was silly, she was well aware, to be nervous about taking a yoga class. However, as it was Jessica who was teaching, not to mention an advanced class, she was feeling a bit squiggly inside. She'd been so surprised when Jessica had revealed she taught yoga part-time. A woman of many talents.

Get a grip, she silently counseled as she grabbed her bag and stepped out of the vehicle. At its barest of bones, it's just Jessica and some stretching with some other women; it would be fine.

* * * *

Jessica checked the number of students she was supposed to be receiving in her class that morning and was pleased to see all fifteen spots taken. She loved when her class was full, it really amped up the positive energy and got the ladies in a 'can do' mood.

She adjusted the levels for her music, straightened her lilac colored tank top and checked her hair in the mirror on the wall to make sure her newly purchased, purple and fuchsia flower patterned hair band was securely in place. It was. Check.

Now, it was just a matter of.... Oh, there went the door to the studio. She turned away from the mirrors, a large grin on her face when she saw Claire walk in.

"Hey!" She raised her hand in a small wave and crossed the hardwood floor. "I saw your name on the list, I'm so glad you came for a class."

Claire smiled and shrugged. "I figured I may as well get it over with, or you'd never let me hear the end of it."

Jessica snickered. "I'll help you get so loose and flexible, Jake will be startled."

Claire couldn't help herself and laughed out loud. "Either that, or he'll just shake his head at me when I turn up stiff as a board from doing a class way more advanced than I can handle."

"Uh-uh." Jessica shook her head. "I told you, I have modified moves for everything I do. They call it an advanced class so people who are looking for that will know they'll get the instruction they're looking for. I'm actually pushing for them to change the name to something like *multi-levels yoga*. That way people will be prompted to ask what it means and we can explain that everyone is welcome, regardless of the level they're at."

"Okay, okay, fine." Claire held her hands up in mock surrender. "You've convinced me. Just be kind, okay?"

Jessica grinned. "You got it."

* * * *

The class was beginning to fill up, so while Jessica greeted her other students, Claire went to find a place (not up front) to unfurl her yoga mat. She took a deep breath and felt better. It was going to be a fun class, she was sure. Jessica was so kind and encouraging with her kids, there was no doubt she was a fantastic teacher and—

"Stop the presses!"

Claire jumped, her train of thought derailed.

"Or, should I say, *stop the plank poses*! We're here and ready to get bendy!"

Claire froze. Oh, no. She turned her head forty five degrees and quietly groaned. Yup. It was exactly who she thought it was. Denise Chang and Heidi Miller, the Tactless Twins.

"Ahahaha!" Heidi exploded, clutching Denise's shoulder. "You're ridiculous, but I love it!"

Claire turned her focus back to her mat, maybe they'd be too busy being... *themselves*, to notice her.

"Mrs. Big? Is that you?"

"Denise!" Heidi gently slapped her best friend's bicep.

"What?" Denise held her hands outward, palms up. "It's a compliment! She knows it's a compliment, right Claire?"

Claire exhaled and plastered a pleasant smile on her face. "Of course," she said, trying to keep her teeth from gritting. "How could it be anything but?"

"See!" Denise playfully slapped Heidi's shoulder in return. "I *told* you. How could it be anything but flattering, you ninny."

Heidi looked slightly skeptical, but chose to leave it. Instead, she queried Claire. "So, what brings you here, other than the obvious? Preventative medicine?"

Claire wasn't sure exactly to what Heidi was referring, the possibilities were too many to ponder, so she kept things simple. "The obvious," she said, then gestured toward Jessica at the front of the room. "And Jessica insisted she thought I'd enjoy the class."

"There's something different about you." Heidi cocked her head and narrowed her eyes.

"Ooh! She's been made over since we last saw her!" Denise nodded, her face approving.

Heidi snapped her fingers. "Yes!" She grinned, looking like the Cheshire Cat and raised an eyebrow. "Very nice. Very, *very* nice."

Catching the thread of the conversation, and Heidi's intonation, Jessica cringed on Claire's behalf. She walked over and broke things up. "Ready for class, girls?"

"You bet!" Denise turned her focus from Claire and smoothed her hands down her yoga pant clad backside.

Claire shot Jessica a grateful look.

"You're going to love the class, Mrs. Big," Heidi said, before adjusting her blonde ponytail. "She's great. Top notch."

Claire gave them her first genuine smile. It was just the sort of thing she wanted to hear about her friend.

* * * *

An hour had passed, or to be precise an hour and ten minutes, since Claire had sat down cross legged on her yoga mat and prepared to follow Jessica through her class. Now, she was lying prone on her back and she thought she might never get up again.

"So," Jessica began as she came over and eased herself effortlessly to the hardwood floor. "What'd ya think?"

Claire blinked. What did she think? "I think you're a sick and twisted soul."

Jessica laughed. "Oh, come on—"

"You assured me you'd have alternate postures—"

"Which I did!"

Claire cut her eyes at her and continued. "Which you did; *however*, I foolishly got warmed up and figured I could try some of the more advanced stuff—"

"I *told* you," Jessica gently reminded, "and the rest of the class, to go at your own pace."

"Yes," Claire countered. "But you did not take into account how fabulous you are at your job."

"Oh, come on." Jessica shrugged, but Claire cut her off from saying anything further.

"And because you're so damned good at it, you make us want to strive further and; therefore, you've left me feeling like an overstretched rubber band!"

Jessica bit her lip to keep from laughing, again. "Are you going to be okay? Do I have to call in the medics?"

Claire stuck out her tongue and slowly pulled herself upright. So far, so good. "Ha, ha," she said, easing herself into a sitting position. "But, I meant it. You're amazing."

Jessica blushed and waved her words away.

"No, seriously," she pressed. "You know how I said it was upsetting that the boys were calling me *scared Mommy*?"

"Uh-huh."

"Well, every time that thought comes into my head, I'm pulling out yoga Jessica."

"Yoga Jessica?"

"Absolutely," Claire told her. "Yoga Jessica is strong, self-assured, patient, calm, and just generally kicks ass! She'll get rid of scared Mommy in a heartbeat!"

Jessica felt tears prickling behind her eyes. She'd never looked at herself in that light. It was one of the kindest things she'd heard in a long time. She extended her hand and said, "Thank you."

Claire took the hand offered and groaned while she stood upright. She looked her friend in the eye and smiled. "You're welcome."

* * * *

CHAPTER 17

Jake let out a low, wolf whistle when Claire descended the stairs in her burgundy skirt. She blushed.

"You look fabulous," he complimented.

She grinned and smoothed her black halter top. "It's not too much?"

Jake chuckled and shook his head. "No."

"Are you sure?" She swallowed against the nerves threatening to surface. "Because I don't want to be *too*... you know, over the top and feel out of place."

"According to your Mom," he assured her. "Travis and Gerry are the kind of guys who live for over the top."

Claire frowned. "So, you're saying you think I'm over the top?"

"No." He laughed. "I'm just saying, Travis brought us a formal invitation. I think sexy skirt and top will fit right in."

Peggy sniffed loudly from the family room. "Language."

Jake raised an eyebrow at Claire.

She shrugged.

"Pardon?" he asked, walking in to face his mother.

She inclined her head in the direction of the twins. "Saying s-e-x-y might not be the best language to use around the b-o-y-s."

Jake looked at his father. Earl held his hands up in mock surrender and returned his attention to the TV.

"I think it's fine, Mom," Jake told her. "Anyway, we're ready to go, you know where we are."

Peggy shot a quick look at Claire, gave her the up-down and nodded curtly. "I'm sure everything will be fine while you take time off."

"Is something wrong, Peggy?" Claire asked, catching the look.

Peggy held a hand lightly to her chest and blinked. "No. Not at all. Why do you ask, dear?"

"No reason, I must have misunderstood," Claire replied. She wasn't about to start anything when they were getting ready to leave. Clearly, Peggy had issue with them daring to take *time off* for something other than, say, grocery shopping.

"See you guys in a bit." Jake leaned over and hugged Noah and Evan.

"You're going to your gathering now?" Noah asked.

Claire grinned. He remembered the conversation with Travis.

"You bet," Jake said, while Peggy sniffed a second time.

Claire waved and walked out the door.

* * * *

"Here, try this one." Josephine extended a fruity concoction in a long-necked cocktail glass decorated with hand painted flowers.

Claire took the glass and nodded at it approvingly. "Wow. Almost looks too good to drink." She winked at her mother. "Almost."

Josephine giggled girlishly as Claire took a long swallow then smacked her lips together in appreciation. She was rather enjoying this reinvention of her daughter and had her fingers crossed it was a permanent change. It was about time Claire had some fun.

"*Another* one?"

Claire turned toward Jake and grinned. "I was thirsty and Mom offered, so what was I to do?"

"Of course," he said, before shaking his head at Josephine. "Careful there, Josie. She's a bit of a light weight."

Josephine snickered and nodded. "Yes, sir." She reached around to the bar and grabbed another glass of the same creation. "Want one?"

Jake narrowed his eyes, before taking the drink. "You're good," he told her.

Josephine laughed loud and long.

* * * *

"Dance with me," Claire said, grabbing Jake by the hand and pulling him close.

A couple of hours had passed and the light was getting low, Travis had turned on twinkle lights and paper lanterns and turned up the music. The party was getting into its stride.

Jake wrapped his arms around her waist and drew her in, enjoying the way she relaxed against him. He began to sway them back and forth, letting the warm evening breeze wash over them and the music hum through their bodies.

"May I cut in?"

Jake stopped moving and pulled back from Claire. Gerry stood waiting, a friendly grin on his face. "You bet," he said, nodding at his host.

Before Claire could say a word, Gerry pulled her into his arms and began to dance her around the yard. He was a brilliant partner and she threw her head back in laughter at how she felt lighter than air.

"Why, Mister Carrion, you are a surprise," she told him.

Gerry laughed. "My mother insisted I learn to dance when I was in grade school. At the time, I wasn't thrilled, but now...." He twirled her away from him, then speedily back into his arms. "I'm glad she did."

Claire grinned up at him, enchanted. "Me, too."

From across the yard, Josephine watched her daughter and her friend, delighted. Gerry and Travis' party was just what Claire needed.

"She's having fun." Jake pulled up a chair and sat down next to Josephine.

"I have to tell you," she confided. "I don't remember the last time I saw her so... free."

Jake followed her gaze and sighed. "It's been a long time."

"Uh-huh. I think she needs more of this, don't you?"

He was about to reply, when he was interrupted by his mother's voice in his ear. "Well, this is *quite* the party."

He spun around, startled. "Mom? What are you doing here? Is something wrong with the boys?"

Josephine leaned forward, her face a picture of concern.

"No." Peggy practically sneered when she said it. "They're fine. They're with your father. I just thought

I'd get a bit of air and I heard the... *music* and decided to see what all the fuss was about."

Josephine's eyes widened at Peggy's tone. What on Earth?

Peggy looked across the yard to where Claire was still dancing with Gerry and pulled a sour lemon face. "Do you think that's wise, Jake? Letting her drape herself on other men?"

Jake stood up. "Hey, hey," he said. It was as far as he got.

"Watch it, *Peggy Sue*." Josephine stood up, too, and pointed a finger at Jake's mother. "You're on thin ice with that attitude."

Peggy stiffened. "Excuse me?"

"Hey," Claire said, charging forward, having seen them all from across the yard. "What's going on? Is something wrong at home?"

Peggy sniffed. "No."

Gerry came up behind Claire, saw the obvious tension and went into hyper-drive hosting. "Is that Mrs. Jamieson?"

Peggy, Claire, Jake and Josephine swiveled their heads in his direction.

"It is!" He plastered a smile on his face and reached out for her hand. "How nice of you to stop in. You must come with me and meet Travis. I've told him all about you."

"I'm not staying," Peggy managed to utter, as he tugged her away through his sea of friends.

Claire turned back around to Jake and Josephine. "What was that about?"

"She said she was taking a walk," Jake offered.

Josephine narrowed her eyes, exchanged a look with her son-in-law, and nodded.

"A walk?" Claire frowned.

"Uh-huh." Jake reached out and took her by the elbow, leading her towards the bar. "Want another drink?"

* * * *

"It's fine, Mom," Jake said, quietly, as he led Peggy to the back door.

It was late, the boys were in bed and Earl was waiting out in the dark backyard, reclining on a lounger while he waited for his wife.

Peggy shook her head. "I don't usually interfere, but this time I feel I must."

Jake groaned and held his tongue. Instead of calling her out on her meddling, he said, "Everything is fine. We had a few drinks, danced a bit and now we're back home."

High pitched laughter rang out from inside the house and Peggy's face pinched even further into itself. "Really? Because that doesn't sound like fine to me. It sounds like a slippery slope, with children ending up neglected."

"Oh, for god's sake." Jake ran his fingers through his hair.

"What's going on?" Claire padded into the kitchen, Josephine right behind.

"Nothing," Jake said. "Mom's just leaving."

Peggy sniffed and clutched her purse under her arm.

"What's that about?"

Peggy's eyes widened at Claire's tone. "I'm sorry?" she asked.

Claire folded her arms across her chest and cocked her hip. She was still feeling the effects of her many cocktails and, suddenly, she wanted answers. "That little sniff. You seem to be sharing it a lot lately, especially at me, and I'd like to know *what's that about*?"

Oh, boy, Josephine thought, stepping back.

"Hon," Jake said. "The boys are sleeping."

"So?"

"So, your voice is kind-of loud."

Claire took a breath and pulled her voice down a notch. "Fine. But, I'm staying here until I get an answer to my question."

"I don't know what you want me to say." Peggy tightened her grip on her bag.

"I want you to be honest." Claire threw her arms up in the air in exasperation. "Can you do that for once, Peggy? Huh? Be honest?"

Peggy's eyes bugged and she opened and closed her mouth like a fish.

"Oh, forget it." Claire waved her hand at her in disgust and turned to her mother. "I'm going back inside. Are you coming?"

"Of course," Josephine said, smoothly, following on her daughter's heels.

Jake, his back to his mother, watched them leave. His gut clenched and he wondered how the heck he was going to diffuse things.

"Listen," he started to say, turning around. He shut his mouth. He was talking to nothing but an empty doorway.

* * * *

(HAPTER 18

"So, tell me all about your first day of school."
Peggy clasped her hands earnestly in front of
her as she spoke to Noah and Evan. They
were sitting in the family room while Claire attended to
dinner in the kitchen.

Claire smiled to herself, they'd managed a polite
truce in the past couple of weeks since *the party incident*,
and she listened happily to the boys launch into tales
about their first day of play school; the teacher, the
other children, how they each had their own hook for
their jackets and a cubby for their snacks.

"It sounds just perfect," Peggy said, enthusiastically,
before spontaneously reaching out to pull them to her
ample bosom in a tight hug. "Did Mommy stay, or did
she leave you all on your own?"

Claire jerked to a halt at the stove. What was that?
Had she heard correctly?

Evan squirmed in Peggy's embrace until she let go.
"Mommy stayed, Grandma Peggy," he told her, as he
reached out to tug Noah from her other side.

"*Mom*," Jake said, lifting his hands, palms upward, as he questioned her. "Why would you ask that?"

Peggy released Noah and carefully straightened her flower patterned blouse, not meeting Jake's eye. "It's a valid question, Jacob. *Considering....*"

Considering? Claire thought, her stirring spoon poised above her pot of stew. Considering what?

"Considering what?" Jake probed, vocalizing her thoughts as he leaned back into the armchair and rested his left ankle atop his right knee.

Claire began to stir her stew again in small circles, all the while cocking an ear to listen to the conversation.

Peggy inclined her head toward Noah and Evan, now playing with their cars on the mat on the floor, then looked pointedly at Jake while raising her eyebrows.

"Oh, for hell's sake," Earl practically growled from his seat on the sofa beside Peggy. "She thinks Claire's gone all fussy and is neglecting the boys."

"What?" Jake frowned and stared at his Dad, but Earl just kept on watching the muted TV on the wall across from the couch.

"Earl!" Peggy swatted his arm. "I didn't say neglected."

Claire, feeling equally aghast, stirred faster.

"Oh, for the…." Jake gritted his teeth, took a breath and modified what he really wanted to say. "Seriously, Mom. How could you even think such a thing? You know damned well—"

"Language," Peggy said.

He cleared his throat. "*Darn* well what a great mother Claire is."

Tears began to well in Claire's eyes. She knew he always had her corner, it was just touching to hear it when he didn't know she was listening. She swiftly grabbed for a tissue from a box on the counter and blotted her eyes.

"Yes, yes," Peggy said, shifting uncomfortably at being put on the spot. "But, ever since this...."

"What?" Jake cocked his head, waiting.

Peggy sniffed. "This *makeover business*, you have to admit Claire's been...."

Claire waited with baited breath. What else did she believe she'd *been*?

"Been?" Jake questioned, when she left the comment hanging. "Been? What do you think she's been?"

"Well, all I know is, when I was raising you kids, the last thing I was worrying about was makeovers and the like. A mother has to put her kids first, end of story."

"Oh, for...." Jake huffed, inwardly editing once more. "So she decided to give herself a change, so what?" He tried to engage Earl, again. "Dad, are you hearing this?"

Earl cleared his throat, but kept his eyes firmly focused on the TV. "Leave me out of it."

"Yeah, but surely you know the last thing Claire is as a mother is negligent, or self-absorbed."

"I never said that," Peggy insisted, folding her hands primly in her lap.

"Oh, please." Jake snorted. "As good as."

Peggy went silent and turned her eyes to the TV.

Claire swallowed and turned off the burner beneath the pot of stew. The conversation had ground to a halt and while she hadn't been a participant, she felt as though she still needed to defend her corner. The problem was, she was seriously rattled. Was Peggy right? Was it possible she was giving not just her opinion, but insight into what others might be thinking, too? Maybe they all secretly thought she was being a bad mother, going all *city* and forgetting her kids as she swanned around in her new haircut and clothes. Oh, God.

"Hey, Hon," Jake said, coming up behind her and jerking her from her spiraling thoughts. "Is there anything I can do to help things along?"

She took a breath and plastered a smile on her face as she turned around. "Nope. Everything is set and everyone can come on in and dish up."

He leaned down and gave her a quick kiss on the lips. "Gorgeous, talented, smart and a great cook. How'd I get so lucky?"

Claire thought of her in-laws seated on the family room sofa. The real question was, with those two for role models, how had he turned out to be so decent?

* * * *

CHAPTER 19

Claire wrung her hands together as she looked outside her dining room window. Rain. Not good. On any other day she'd barely notice, but today....

Jake came up behind her, carrying a cup of coffee. "Man, those two are keyed up. I was just upstairs and they're talking a mile a minute."

"It's raining," she said, by way of reply.

He leaned around her to look out the window. "Barely. Won't make any difference."

"I don't know." Claire wrung her hands some more. "If it's too wet, won't it be dangerous?"

He took a sip from his mug before turning away from the rain smattered glass. "Hardly. It's not like they're going to be competing in a race. It's really only a test drive for the kart, so Thomas can see where it may need some tweaking."

"Can't he do that without the boys being involved?"

Jake walked into the family room, Claire tailing him. "No. Pushing it isn't the same as one of them being inside and steering it."

Claire sighed. If only she could come up with something more exciting for the boys to do, instead of test driving the go-kart. Was it too short notice to get them booked on a flight for Disneyland?

"Go-kart day!" Evan charged down the staircase and into the family room.

"Yes, well," she began, hoping to temper his excitement in case of a rain delay.

"Roller blades!" Noah thundering down the same stairs a moment later.

Claire looked at him, alarmed. "What?"

Noah climbed up onto the sofa. "We can wear them over to Mister Thomas' house."

"I don't think so."

"Why not?" Evan sat down on the floor and pulled a dump truck from a bin of toys sitting on a shelf built into the wall.

"Because it's too dangerous."

Jake, having sat himself in their oversized armchair, listened to the conversation. He had a feeling, any minute now, he was going to be dragged into it against his will.

"And, I'm sure Daddy would agree with me because it's starting to rain outside."

Bingo, he thought, drinking the last of his coffee.

"Awww," Noah whined and hauled himself from the couch to run to the large window behind the chair.

Evan abandoned his dump truck to join his brother.

"I'm just warning you." Claire felt better, now she'd started the ball rolling. "In case we have to postpone the test drive."

Noah jerked away from the window and ran around the chair to face Jake. "We won't, will we Daddy?"

Oh, brother, he thought, before putting his mug on the coffee table and laying a comforting hand on his son's shoulder.

"It's almost stopped," Evan said, his eyes glued to the front yard through the glass.

Jake looked into Noah's crumpled face and took pity. "We'll watch and see, and I'm sure it will be fine and we'll go over to Mister Thomas' as planned."

Noah's face immediately changed, a huge grin replacing his anguish.

"Yay!" Evan ran around the other side of the chair to add his smile into the mix.

Claire slumped into the sofa and raised an eyebrow at Jake, silently thanking him for his help. *Not.*

He winked at her and shrugged. What else could a guy do?

* * * *

Claire walked a few paces behind her group made up of Jake, Evan, Noah and her mother. The boys were wearing matching orange slickers and, against her protests, sporting their black roller blades. She'd been outnumbered not just by them, but by Jake and Josephine as well. Thankfully, the rain was remaining more of a drizzle, so they seemed to be doing just fine on the damp pavement. However, if either of them had a tumble, she was *soooo* going to make Jake deal with the cleanup.

She watched her mother, chatting away to Jake in her yellow slicker and matching hat - they made her look a lot like Curious George - and wondered how she'd managed to get involved in the first place. She needed answers.

"Hey, Mom?"

Josephine stopped mid-sentence and turned her yellow hatted head. "Yes, dear?"

"Tell me, how did you know we were doing this today?"

Evan glided to a stop slightly ahead and called back to Claire, speaking for Josephine. "We invited Gramma, Mommy. When you were getting your haircut."

"That's right." Josephine smiled at her grandson, then slipped a companionable arm through Jake's as they rounded the corner and began striding along the sidewalk of Sunrise Place. "And I confirmed the date with Thomas when I saw him last week."

Claire's eyebrows shot up beneath her bangs. Excuse me? What the hell did *that* mean?

"You mean on a date, Gramma?" Noah queried, rolling alongside Evan.

Josephine laughed loudly. "No, not quite, my dear."

Claire waited for more, but her mother gave nothing else. Instead, she returned to chatting to Jake, finishing her story as they arrived at Thomas' house. Nuts, she thought. She'd have to interrogate her later.

Jake adjusted the baseball cap on his head and spoke to his sons. "Okay, now that we're here, why don't you go on up and let Mister Thomas know."

Claire watched as they efficiently rolled up the pathway, despite the cracks and dips that might have tripped them up, and disappeared around the side of the house. Like it or not, this plan was in motion.

* * * *

"Right. Think that's got it." Thomas' cigarette bobbed up and down in the corner of his mouth as he finished checking the torque on the wheels.

Claire was sitting on the curb in front of Jessica's house, trying to appear relaxed instead of tense. It had been about a half hour since the boys had returned with Thomas and the go-kart in tow, and she'd watched them with steadily growing trepidation. Granted, her mother hadn't been helping in any way.

Seated on Claire's right, her legs stretched out and crossed coquettish at the heels, Josephine was causing some serious ripples in the fabric of Sunrise Place. More directly to the point, the woman was seriously getting under Rosa's skin.

Rosa had initially been pleased to see Josephine when she'd come outside with Sophia, remembering her from Portia's birthday party bash. All good. Or, so one would think.

Her expression had turned grim; however, as she observed Claire's raven haired mother flirt unabashedly with Thomas. Claire was beginning to have serious concerns that, if they didn't get things going right away, there might be *words* spoken. She sighed from beneath the hood of her hunter green rain jacket. Wouldn't it be fitting if her mother caused the normally unflappable Rosa to lose her cool and start yelling in Italian?

"It's ready?" Evan clapped his hands in his excitement.

Claire sat up straight and her pulse kicked up a notch. Like it or not, *scared Mommy* was starting to kick up a fuss.

"Aye, lad, 'tis." Thomas slicked his damp hair back from his forehead. "Who's taking the first ride, then?"

Noah stood up tall. "Me. We tossed a coin and my side won."

Evan nodded easily. They'd been solving their 'who goes first' dilemmas in that manner for as long as they'd been alive.

"Right," Thomas said, as though Noah's comment made perfect sense. "Then in you get, lad."

Jake stepped forward to assist Noah in sliding into the go-kart's black, padded seat. His young face was a picture of eager delight. Claire watched, her insides churning from a mixture of happiness on his behalf and dread about what was to come. She sighed a second time.

"What's with you?" Josephine leaned over and nudged Claire's shoulder with her own. "You sound like you've got too much hot air, or something."

"Just thinking." Claire shrugged. "It's nothing."

Josephine reached into the pocket of her rain jacket and pulled out a package of gum. "Want one?" She held the package up for Claire to see.

She shook her head. "No, thanks."

"Thinking about what?" Josephine unwrapped a stick of bright pink gum, then popped it into her mouth.

"I've come to a conclusion," she replied, unusually candid for once. "Having kids has been one of the best and worst experiences of my life."

Josephine laughed and snapped her gum. "You don't say?"

Claire suddenly realized what she'd said, out loud, and quickly tried to backpedal. "I mean, *obviously*, I'd never trade having the boys. I just meant that—"

"Oh, no explanation needed," Josephine cut her off, an amused grin decorating her face. "Trust me, sweetheart, you're not alone."

Claire wrinkled her forehead and glanced at her mother.

"Every mother has felt that way, and more often than once I can absolutely assure you." Josephine nodded in a knowing manner and blew a small bubble.

Against her better judgement, Claire felt better. She wasn't a terrible person for thinking it. Granted her mother wasn't going to win any awards for her past parenting, but in that instance she had a feeling she was sharing an honest truth.

Josephine patted her arm affectionately. "Just roll with it," she said. "Some days are glorious. Others, you wish you could run far and never look back." She shrugged, then pointed. "I think they're going to start."

Claire looked over and took a deep breath. "I think this day is a bit of both."

* * * *

Thomas crouched down beside Noah, seated in the go-kart. They'd rolled it manually down the block and the plan was for him to drive it back up the street, following the road into the closed top of the crescent.

"Right," he said, before taking a last drag on his cigarette then dropping it to the pavement and grinding it out with the toe of his boot. "You know what to do?"

Noah looked down the street. "The brown ones?"

"Aye." Thomas picked up the cigarette butt and tucked it into his pant pocket. "Juist like we talked aboot."

Noah looked back down the street, then again to Thomas. "Okay."

"Got it?"

Noah nodded. "Got it."

Thomas snuck a glance at the obviously twitching blinds on the front window of Deborah's house and grinned. He'd said no mishaps, but that didn't mean he couldn't have a bit of fun. "Guid lad. Should be a laugh all around. Give it a go."

"I'm ready," Evan said, standing behind the kart, prepared to start pushing it along.

Noah looked at his brother and grinned. "Okay, but…." He gestured for Evan to come closer, so no one else would hear.

Claire straightened her spine and exchanged a look with Jake. What was that all about? What were they saying that they wanted to keep private?

Josephine snickered and reached out to tap Claire. "Seems they have something secret going on."

"They shouldn't," she said, irritated by her mother's blatant amusement. "They know we don't keep secrets."

"Oh, pish." Josephine waved her hand dismissively, before catching Thomas' eye and sending him a saucy grin. "They're not even five years old, how sinister could their secret be?"

Claire shrugged. She hated when her mother was right.

"They're going to go!" Sophia jumped up and down in her excitement.

Claire startled, having forgotten the little girl was there. She turned to her left and was pleased to see Rosa grinning at her granddaughter's excitement, as opposed to glaring at Josephine. Thank goodness. She returned her focus to Noah, Evan and the go-kart. They were, as Sophia had stated, 'going to go'.

Claire held her breath when Evan gave the kart a push. She was impressed by how easily it began to roll.

She'd held a secret worry it would turn out there was no way either of her boys would be able to move it with the other seated inside and she'd end up being the one stuck shoving them along, after all was said and done.

Noah steered the kart straight down the middle of the road as coached, Evan rolling steadily along on his blades behind him. They seemed to be doing fine, much to Claire's relief; however, her ease began to waver when it became glaringly apparent Noah was drifting and headed directly for Jessica's neighbor's garbage cans.

"Be careful!" she called out, shifting from one foot to the next as she physically restrained herself from running down the street.

If either of the boys had heard her, it wasn't apparent. They kept right on going toward the cans, not seeming to have any clue Noah could turn his wheels.

"Jake!" Claire strode briskly over to her husband. "Do something! He's off course. He could get hurt."

Jake shook his head, watching intently. "No, I don't think so. I'm sure he'll swerve if he needs to. He's been practicing. It'll be fine."

Claire wanted to stamp her feet in frustration. She looked over at Thomas for back up and not only did he not appear the least bit concerned, he actually looked amused.

"Mister... umm." She took a breath and corrected herself. "*Thomas.*"

"Aye?" He kept his eyes focused on the boys.

"I think Noah's going to get hurt if you don't hurry––"

"Thare he goes," he interrupted, with a sharp nod of his head.

"What?" Claire looked down the street just in time to see Noah effortlessly swerve and clear the trash cans. Evan stepped swiftly to the side, keeping pace beside him, and both boys laughed delightedly.

"There you go!" Jake pumped his fist in the air.

Ahh, Claire thought, an image flashing in her head of Evan doing the exact same thing. That's where he'd learned it. One mystery solved.

"Magnifico!" Rosa enthused as Sophia hugged her, sharing the happiness of Noah's success.

"He's a terrific driver." Josephine tipped her head toward Jake. "His father's son."

Claire cut her eyes at her mother. What was that supposed to mean? She was about to take umbrage with the comment, but then saw the expression of pure pride on Jake's face and decided to keep quiet.

"Great job, guys!" Jake jogged up the block to meet the boys.

Claire took, what felt like, her first full breath since they'd arrived and glanced once more at Thomas. He was grinning like it was Christmas.

"He's so charming," Josephine whispered in her ear, making her jump.

"Stop it," Claire admonished, swatting her on the arm before she strode off to join the boys. Maybe, if she was quick and bribed them with ice cream, she could convince them one turn each was good enough for the day.

"Right." Thomas pulled a fresh package of cigarettes from his pocket and tore open the cellophane covering. "Evan's next, ya?"

"Then me, again!" Noah enthused, while Jake helped him out of the kart.

Claire's shoulders slumped. Damn. Too late.

* * * *

"Nice that the rain cleared up." Jessica glanced up at the sky from her place on the curb.

Claire, seated next to the pile of discarded rain gear, agreed. "Uh-huh," she said, watching Sophia sail down the block in the go-kart. *She* stayed on course, every time. It seemed only Evan and Noah found it amusing to aim for Jessica's neighbor's trash cans on every run they took.

"So, what's the deal with Thomas and your Mom?" Jessica leaned in closer, so as not to be overheard.

Claire grimaced. Her mother had been staging such an overt flirtation towards Thomas no one could miss it.

"Is there some sort of *thing* going on between them?" An amused smile played at Jessica's lips. "'Cause, if so, she may have to watch her back with Rosa."

"I honestly have no bloody idea if there's any sort of *thing* going on." Claire shuddered at the thought. "But, it would be so like my mother if there is."

Jessica giggled. "Well, for what it's worth," she said, pointing at Thomas while he kept an eye on the boys and Sophia. "He doesn't exactly look like he's ready to drop to one knee and propose."

"Oh, God." Claire blanched. "Don't even say it. As far as I'm concerned, Rosa can have him."

Jessica sniggered. "Oh, come on. He's not *that* bad."

"Easy for you to say." Claire gave her shoulder a soft shove.

"I don't know," she said, smiling as she watched how much fun Thomas seemed to be having with Josephine. The two of them were chatting and laughing while Rosa, on the other hand, looked like she'd bitten into a rotten tomato.

"Remind me of this conversation when your mother comes to visit," Claire commented, teasingly, before calling out to Jake. "Hey, Jake. How about this is the last turn?"

"Awww." Evan and Noah's voices whined in perfect unison while Jake lifted Sophia out of the kart.

"It's almost time to get lunch," she wheedled. "I'm making burgers."

His stomach growled and Jake backed her up. "Mom's right. This is the last turn and we can make plans for next time."

"Okay," Noah relented and scrambled into the vacated seat. He looked up at Evan. "Ready?"

Evan nodded, all business. "Ready."

Claire watched them take off, half her thoughts already on lunch preparations. She mentally added up her numbers. Jake and her and the boys made four. Add in her mother, that made five…. She glanced over at Thomas, still chatting with Josephine, and wondered if she'd have to invite him as well. It seemed only polite, considering. And it evened up the number.

"Oh, crap," Jake said.

Claire dropped her tallying and returned her full attention to the street. "What? What is it?"

"Bullocks." Thomas' face twisted into a grimace when Corkscrew darted out at the top of the crescent, seemingly from nowhere, and went streaking across the road.

Claire followed his gaze and *scared Mommy* began to shriek in her head. She wanted to shout out at Noah, but knew it was useless. He'd never be able to pull the brake in time. And so, like some sort of statue game they played as children, they all froze.

* * * *

It was like watching a slow motion movie. Corkscrew ran full tilt into Noah's path, he caught the movement out of the corner of his eye and instead of swerving left as usual, he spun the wheel to the right to avoid the grey cat - sending the kart directly into the brown trash cans they'd been skirting all morning.

The sound was thunderous.

The go-kart charged into the first container, sent it domino-style directly into the second, and scattered them apart with surprising force. In a split second they went from sitting tidily curbside, to being launched into the street, their contents spilling messily across the pavement.

Noah, meanwhile, finally came to a stop; one wheel of the kart up on the sidewalk. In the next instant, while Claire struggled to catch her breath, Jake was sprinting down the length of the street as though he was the one with wheels strapped to his feet.

* * * *

"NOAH! EVAN!"

Noah twisted around in his seat, none the worse for wear. "I'm okay, Daddy."

"Me, too," Evan said, a few paces away, having had the swift reflexes to jump clear of the collision.

Jake crouched down and ran his hands over Noah, making sure he really was okay. Claire, her heart racing so hard she felt dizzy, staggered over to Evan to do the same.

"Are you sure you're alright?" She didn't wait for his reply before grabbing him and clutching him against her in a fierce hug.

"I'm sure, Mommy." His voice came out a mumble as he attempted to answer with his face pressed into her chest.

"Are they okay?" Jessica called out, having kept out of the way with Josephine and the rest.

Thomas nodded, a large grin on his face. "Aye. Right as rain."

It was the last thing he said, before all hell really broke loose.

* * * *

"Oh, my, GOD!"

Alarm jumped in her chest and Claire's eyes widened. She released Evan and spun around in the direction of the outraged voice. Oh, dear. It was the neighbor, and owner of the recently abused trash cans, Deborah.

"THOMAS!" Deborah charged down her walk, her face a picture of untempered fury. "Thomas McLeod! We had an understanding! An UNDERSTANDING!"

"Whoa." Jessica took a step closer to Josephine. "She's not kidding around."

Josephine shook her head. "Nope. That's one pissed off woman." She grinned and added, "Wonder how he's going to get out of it."

* * * *

Claire yawned while she brewed a strong pot of coffee. The fresh air, never mind her nerves and adrenaline, had wiped her out. She left the coffee maker to do its work and walked into the family room.

"And then the neighbor came barreling out, looking for blood." Jake's voice was laced with mirth as he brought his parents up to speed on the events of the morning.

"Goodness!" Peggy, sitting primly on the beige sofa, pressed a hand to her chest. "It sounds terribly dangerous. It's a good thing everyone was okay. Can you imagine what *could* have happened?"

Claire frowned and leaned against the door frame. First they arrived without invitation, then Peggy starts mixing it up.

"Anything *could* have happen." Josephine, lounging on the love seat, opened her arms wide. "My God, that's life."

Thomas shifted in the large, easy chair beside the fireplace. "The kart is as sturdy as they come. Nay harm could'ave come ta the lads."

Yay, Thomas! Claire inwardly cheered him on, while Peggy went prune faced and raised an eyebrow at Earl.

"Sounds like a great kart," Earl offered, nodding at Thomas. "I'll have to get a look at it."

If possible, Peggy's face stiffened further.

"But, that lady wasn't okay." Oblivious to the adult tension in the room, Noah shook his head, his eyes wide.

Evan nodded in agreement. "She was very angry, that lady."

Josephine stood up and sashayed through the room, all smiles. "It wasn't any of our hides she was after," she trilled over her shoulder, heading for the kitchen. "It was a certain *Scotsman* she wanted to flay."

"Well, if you asked me, I'd say she had just cause."

The haughty comment from Peggy made Josephine roll her eyes. "Of *course* you would," she stage whispered as she passed by Claire.

Claire followed her into the kitchen. "Leave it," she instructed, between clenched teeth. "We've only just managed to get peace again."

Josephine stuck her tongue out then sang, happily, "Coffee's up! Come and get it!"

Claire couldn't help herself and grinned. Her mother turned everything into an event. She picked up the pot and began pouring the fresh brew into the first mug. "How many do we need?"

"I'm in." Jake strode into the kitchen and planted a kiss on Claire's cheek. "Thomas? Can I bring you a cup?"

"Aye." Thomas ambled into the room. "Just going to step out a moment." He tapped his shirt pocket and Josephine, if possible, perked up even further.

"I'll keep you company." She stepped lightly, the orange nail polish on her toes sparkling in the overhead lights as she danced behind him toward the back door.

He gave her a wry smile and held the door.

"Thank you, kindly." She curtsied slightly and stepped out ahead of him, moving slowly enough that when he brought up the rear, he was almost right up against her.

Claire inwardly groaned. Subtle, her mother wasn't.

"I suppose I could dare a cup." Peggy's tight lipped words cut through the room.

"Of course." Claire turned her attention back to pouring more coffee and stepped back to allow Jake to give the cup to his mother. "Earl?"

Jake's father moseyed into the kitchen and nodded. "Sure. Might even have it outside. It's turned into a decent afternoon."

"Good idea." Jake reached out and opened the back door. He stopped short when he came face to face with his mother-in-law, wrapped firmly in the strong arms of the Scotsman she'd been so fervently pursuing.

"Oh, my!" Peggy slapped a hand on her chest, over her heart.

"Mother!" Claire wanted to tear out her hair.

"Oopsy!" Josephine giggled as she leaned slightly away from Thomas, her eyes sparkling with mischief.

* * * *

CHAPTER 20

Josephine reclined on a bamboo lounger in her backyard and reveled in the star filled skies above. What a day, she mused, while Bear nestled himself comfortably beside her on the chair.

She tucked a multicolored fleece blanket securely around them and snorted quietly with mirth when her daughter's aghast face drifted into her thoughts. Poor Claire. She'd been so very upset at discovering her in Thomas' arms, the two of them snogging like teenagers.

Peggy had been no better. Jake's mother had practically swooned right there in the kitchen. Josephine rolled her eyes. Please. Had the woman forgotten what it meant to be a sexual being?

She grinned into the darkness. Despite the momentary mayhem, it had been worth it. It had been quite some time since she'd been delivered such a passionate kiss and, if she had her druthers, she was going to find out just how deep that well of passion ran. It would be criminal not to.

* * * *

CHAPTER 21

Thomas sat in the shaded darkness of his front porch, only the red tip of his cigarette a visual indicator of his presence. It was a perfect night; still and clear. A full moon shone brightly above and he wondered if it might have been the reason for his sudden, unexpected behavior. He'd heard such things; people acting out of the ordinary during a full moon.

"Would be a fine thing, were it true," he said, exhaling a stream of smoke as he spoke to Corkscrew sitting companionably beside him on the stoop. "Otherwise, I might juist be in a wee spot of trouble thare, CS."

Josephine's sparkling eyes and inviting mouth danced brazenly into his thoughts, making him sigh. She'd have him *haivering* in no time if he wasn't careful. He took a last drag off his cigarette, the ash from the tip loosening and floating toward his lap. Against his better judgement, he grinned.

* * * *

CHAPTER 22

"Eggs," Claire muttered to herself as she pushed her over-loaded grocery cart into the cooler aisle of the supermarket. She had to remember to get three dozen, so she could bake the muffins she'd promised the boys. One more thing to add to her ever growing list.

She paused in front of the rows of orange juice and took a breath. The past couple of weeks had been a challenge. A challenge she felt she was losing. Peggy had been continuing her *proper mother etiquette* campaign and it was starting to rattle her. Add in the boys play school schedule and she felt she was slipping further and further away from herself.

"Oh, my!" Jessica came sailing around the corner, just as Claire pushed her cart forward, causing them to barely dodge a head-on collision. "Claire! God, sorry."

Claire held her cart steady and waved her hand in the air. "No worries! All good. Everything is still intact and I didn't even get the eggs yet."

Jessica laughed. "Well, thank goodness for that." She eyed Claire's densely packed cart and raised her eyebrows. "Looks like you're going to feed an army."

Claire exhaled a harried breath. "Sometimes it feels like it, trust me. I let things go too long between shopping trips and now the cupboards are almost bare." She took a deep breath. "And, of course, I went ahead and promised I'd bake muffins for the boys for school." She swallowed and pushed her hair away from her forehead. "But, did I have enough eggs? No." She wiped her upper lip, where a thin film of moisture had begun to bead. "So, not only do I have the usual, but I have muffin ingredients as well." She shifted from one foot to another. Her heart seemed to be beating unnaturally fast. And was it getting a bit stuffy in the cooler aisle?

"Are you okay?" Jessica looked at her closely. Her pupils seemed dilated and her chest was rising and falling too quickly.

Claire tried to nod, but it only made her light headed. She gripped the handle of her cart.

"Claire?" Jessica reached out a hand to grasp her forearm. "Seriously? Are you okay? You look a bit—"

Claire let out a huge gasp when her stomach turned. She thought she might throw up, right there on the tile floor. The handle of the cart felt slick under her suddenly sweaty palm and she looked at Jessica imploringly. "Oh, God. Jessica, please…." She needed to sit down.

Jessica threw her arm around Claire's shoulders and helped ease her to the floor. "It's okay," she said, while watching for someone, anyone, to come into the aisle. "I'm here."

A man came around the corner, carrying a hand basket. "You!" Jessica pointed and shouted at him. "Get help! Quickly!"

The man nodded, dropped his basket and took off at a run.

"It's okay, Claire," she told her again as her friend gasped beside her and shook under her protective arm. "It's going to be okay."

* * * *

Jessica paced the hallway in the emergency room, clenching and unclenching her fists to try and release the tension she was feeling. She'd been so scared! Claire had turned on a dime in the grocery store, going from smiling to gasping for breath. She pressed her hands to her own chest, sympathy and fear for her friend making it difficult for her to keep her emotions in check.

"Jessica!"

She whipped around, relief flooding her when she saw both Jake and Kevin sprinting toward her. "Thank God," she exhaled.

"Where is she?" Jake looked around, his face panicked, and Jessica wanted to reach out a hand to steady him.

"She's in with the doctor." She pointed further down the hallway, in the direction of where they'd taken Claire.

Kevin wrapped an arm around her shoulders and she felt her knees weaken slightly from gratitude. She suddenly felt very tired. "How are you?" he asked, warmth and concern lacing his words.

"I'm fine."

"*God.*" Jake uttered the single word like a plea and Jessica went with her initial impulse this time, reaching out to squeeze his arm.

"It's going to be okay," she stated. "Claire's a strong woman. She just had a moment, that's all."

Jake raked his fingers through his dark hair. "Yeah, but you said on the phone she couldn't stand." He inhaled deeply through his nose, his jaw locked in his attempt to control his emotions. "What if...."

"Forget that." Jessica stood up straight, determined to exude strength for her friend's husband. "There is no *what if.*"

Jake looked like he wanted to believe her. In the place of words, he nodded.

"Mrs. Coombs?"

Jessica turned at the sound of the doctor's voice. "Yes." She nodded vigorously. "Yes, that's me." She pointed to Jake. "And this is Claire's husband. Jake, this is Claire's doctor."

Jake shook the hand the doctor offered. "Is she okay? Can I see her?"

The doctor nodded. "Of course."

"What happened?" Jessica couldn't stop herself. She had to know.

The doctor smiled and Jake exhaled a shaky breath. A smile. That had to be a good thing, right? Doctors didn't smile if the news was bad.

"I'm about to speak with her now. But, rest assured, she's going to be fine." She addressed Jake. "Would you like to join me while I explain what happened, to her?"

Jake followed her down the hallway.

* * * *

"Pardon me? A *panic attack*?" Claire sat stiffly on the emergency room bed, surrounded by the white curtains that created her 'room'. "That's your diagnosis?" She didn't care how loud or skeptical she sounded. She was slightly outraged.

"Yes, Mrs. Jamieson. A panic attack. They're quite common—"

"Not for me, they're not!"

"Claire." Jake reached out to gently rub her shoulder. "It's okay."

"No, it's not!" She frowned and shrugged him off. "I do yoga, for God's sake! It's all about relaxation!"

The doctor smiled and nodded in an infuriating manner. Claire wanted to reach out and slap her.

"As I was saying, we see this quite often." When Claire opened her mouth again, she quickly added, "Even in people who do yoga."

"And I have four year old twins!"

"Oh, *well then*." The doctor made a note on her chart.

"Exactly! I'm a marathon runner in handling stress…." Claire stopped talking when she realized both Jake and the doctor were staring at her.

"Oh, forget it," she said, slumping against her pillow. Clearly, 'oh, well then' hadn't been offered in the way she'd thought it was.

"So, what now?" Jake asked. "I've taken some rudimentary psych classes in my past—"

"He's a dentist," Claire offered, by way of explanation.

The doctor nodded.

"Do you believe, based on the evidence, it's likely to happen again?"

"It could. Or, not." The doctor spoke to Jake directly and Claire pursed her lips in annoyance. Great, now that his background had been established, she was the patient that needed a spokesperson.

"Meaning?" Jake leaned forward, focused.

"For some, this sort of thing can be a one-off experience. A sort of wake up call, if you may, that a life change is needed."

"I have had a few other times recently where my heart was beating pretty fast," Claire admitted.

"What?" Jake looked at her, incredulous. "Why haven't you said anything?"

Claire shrugged and the doctor nodded. "It's also common for a person to not mention it, until a full blown episode occurs," she explained, supporting Claire's silence.

"Okay." Jake rubbed the stubble on his chin, processing the information. "So, the conclusion is, this could be the first and last time this happens unless—"

"Unless your wife does some evaluation to make some changes. Not just in lifestyle, but also in her emotional state."

Claire watched them, her head going back and forth like she was at a tennis match.

"Right." Jake nodded, all business. "And if she does that, it could mean she'll be fine."

"Absolutely."

"Did you hear that, Sweetie?" Jake reached for her hand. "You can get this in check and be just fine."

Claire suppressed the desire to roll her eyes and, instead, smiled at her husband. He was just trying to help, or fix it, after all. It was what he did.

"I'll help," he added, nodding at the doctor for approval. "Whatever I have to do to take off some of the stress, I'll do."

The doctor smiled and extended a hand for Jake to shake. "I think you're in good hands," she told Claire, before exiting the 'room'.

* * * *

(HAPTER 23

"Knock, knock!" Josephine peeked her head around Claire's bedroom door, a perky smile on her face.

Claire was laying on the bed, breathing. "Come on in, Mom." She shifted over, giving Josephine room to launch herself onto the mattress.

"So, a panic attack, huh?" Josephine lay back beside her, wiggling herself into the soft duvet. "This is a lovely cover. Where did you get it?"

Claire sighed. Leave it to her mother to both get down to brass tacks and trivialize things at the same time. "Yes. It was terrifying."

"Oh, I know." She nodded, her chin bobbing up and down in Claire's peripheral vision.

She turned her head sharply to stare at her mother. "Pardon me?"

"Been there, done that."

"*You*?"

"Yes, *me*." Josephine raised an eyebrow, her face indignant. "Why not me?"

Claire couldn't help herself and laughed.

Josephine laughed, too.

"Gee, I don't know," Claire said, sarcastically. "Maybe because you are the least stressed person I've ever met!"

"Oh, well, *that*." Josephine waved a hand in the air above her head. "I wasn't always."

Claire waited. Her mother waved her other hand, then began to alternate the two, and she broke. "You weren't always? When were you not, because *I* certainly don't remember."

Josephine dropped her hands back down and shifted herself up on to one elbow. "Well, of course you don't. It was nearly thirty five years ago."

"What happened?"

"The usual." She ran her fingers over the duvet cover as she talked. "I worried about every little thing. What to feed you. When to feed you. Was the food I was feeding you healthy enough. Was I reading to you enough. Was I being too strict, or not enough. Was I cleaning the house enough. Was I being supportive enough." She exhaled. "God, it was exhausting. Finally, I hit my limit and had a meltdown. Hard core. I couldn't breathe, felt faint, nauseous, the works. I thought I was going to die and leave you an orphan."

"My Dad was still alive."

"Pah! He was as good as gone at that point. More away than around."

Claire sat up and considered her words.

"Believe me, what you went through is more common than you realize. You're not the first mother to break down and you won't be the last." She looked up at Claire. "This parenting business is tough. Not for the faint of heart."

"So, what did you do?"

"I changed." She frowned and added, "Or, rather, I realized I was making myself crazy, so I gave up worrying about every damned thing and went back to being me."

Claire rubbed her temples. "Yes, but that means you were…." She paused and searched for the words. "Already easy going, in the first place. Whereas I've never been—"

"Bullshit!"

"Mother!"

"Well, it is." Josephine sat up and reached for Claire's hand. "You were one of the most carefree little kids I could have ever hoped to meet, Claire Rose. You were giggly and silly and smart, just a delight."

For some reason, that brought tears to Claire's eyes. The very idea of herself as carefree. She sniffled against the emotions churning in her chest.

"And I know for certain that that free-spirited girl is still inside of you, waiting patiently." She cocked an eyebrow. "Well, judging by what's happened, it's *possible* her patience has finally run out."

Claire laughed and tears spilled down her cheeks.

Josephine looked at her with adoration and sighed. "I think she's waiting for you to let her out of her room."

The damn burst. Claire crumpled and cried harder. The very idea of a little version of herself, trapped in a room of fear and no fun, was too much.

Josephine pulled her into her embrace and began to rock her back and forth, just as she'd done when she was a little girl. Claire wept, tearing streaming down her face and onto her mother's blouse, her breath ragged as she let loose the fear and worry she'd been keeping trapped inside for more years than she could remember.

"It's going to be okay." Josephine spoke softly into Claire's hair, speaking the very same words Jessica had in the grocery store. "I'm here and it's all going to be okay."

Claire, amidst her tears, believed her.

* * * *

CHAPTER 24

"I think we're going to have fun, today." Josephine smiled winningly from the passenger seat of Claire's van. She'd heeded her daughter's call and was eager to get the ball rolling.

Claire smiled weakly. After her meltdown, she'd realized she couldn't change things - mainly her knee-jerk stress reaction to pretty much everything - without help. And whether she liked it or not, the truth was, the best person she could turn to for such help was Josephine. Her mother had taken the idea of flowing with life and turned it into an art form. Who better to hold her hand as she relearned to ride the metaphorical bike of life with ease; instead of stress? No one. That's who.

Josephine sighed contently as the town passed by the van's windows. She loved Boxwood Hills. "I think it's a lovely, kind idea that you're going to get Jessica flowers. She's such a dear girl, I'm sure she'll be thrilled."

Claire smiled a genuine smile. "I don't know what I would have done if she hadn't been there in the grocery store. She was a rock for me and I want her to know how much I appreciate it."

Josephine nodded. "Funny how friendships can develop, isn't it?"

"What do you mean?" Claire turned the van into the parking lot of the local flower shop and pulled into an empty space.

Josephine unclipped her seatbelt and shrugged. "Well, just think, if you hadn't been returning that cat after the boys picked it up, you wouldn't have met Jessica."

Claire released her own seatbelt and nodded. "True." She laughed, wryly. "Who knew their antics would give such a great payoff."

"Exactly." Josephine twisted in her seat. "And it's just that sort of realization and attitude we're going to work on cultivating." She placed a slim hand on Claire's forearm. "The more you can adopt the idea that possibility exists in everything you encounter, the easier and more stress free you're going to get."

Claire looked into her mother's bright eyes. If she could harness even half of her *joie de vivre*, she'd be golden. "Flowers?"

"Yes!" Josephine turned smartly in her seat, opened her door and hopped out of the van.

* * * *

CHAPTER 25

"Are you sure about this? Because, if not, you can change your mind."

Josephine rolled her eyes at Claire. "Yes, yes. I said I was. Quite making such a big deal of it. Worst case scenario, it looks like crap and we paint over it."

"Oooh, Gramma, you said a bad word!" Noah's eyes were wide and he was trying not to giggle from behind the hand he had pressed against his mouth.

Josephine laughed out loud, freeing him to do the same. Evan willingly joined in and the three of them chortled merrily.

Claire, paint brush in hand, shook her head at them. They were cut from the same cloth, that was certain. She turned her attention back to the wall in her mother's spare bedroom and wondered, not for the first time, if the woman had finally taken leave of her senses. Asking her grandsons to help paint, then offering them not one, not two, but *four* color choices was a recipe for certain disaster.

"Think of this as an exercise in your rehab." Josephine's eyes sparkled with mischief as she started pulling lids from paint cans.

Claire released a puff of air. "And how do you see that, exactly?"

"Well," Josephine said, pausing to reaffix the clips holding her hair up on top of her head. "I'm no counsellor, but it does seem to me you have a hard time when things aren't in order. So, if you can take anything from this experience, I hope it will be to revel in the moment, allow it to be fun and release the need to control where it goes."

Claire raised an eyebrow. The woman had a point. In the past couple of weeks since her episode, she'd become aware that many of her stress triggers were of her own making. She'd trained herself to be so damned reliable and problem solving, she'd caused herself more grief than she probably even knew. Or wanted to acknowledge.

"So?"

"Okay." She reached out to pull the lid off the final paint can.

"Wonderful." Josephine clapped her hands happily.

* * * *

Claire's stomach hurt. Or, more accurately, her stomach muscles were sore. From laughing. She couldn't remember the last time she'd spent so much time giggling, snickering and full-on belly laughing. She was happy and relaxed and it was glorious.

"Well, despite some initial misgivings," Josephine said, waggling her eyebrows. "I think we've created a masterpiece."

"Aye. Hear, hear." Thomas raised his hand up in agreement. He'd shown up at the door in the middle of their painting and was nearly bodily dragged into the house to see the aforementioned 'masterpiece' in progress.

Claire drank in the joy on her sons' faces. They were radiant and she was grateful.

"Do you really like it, Mister Thomas?" Evan nearly tap danced as he waited for his reply.

"Aye." Thomas gazed upon the wall that now looked as though Van Gogh and Pollack had joined forces. "'Tis a creation of unique inspiration."

"I like the green," Noah offered, moving his arm in a wide, circular arc as he gestured at the wall.

Evan agreed with his brother and added, "Me, too. And the blue."

Noah cocked his head, making Claire giggle. He looked like a miniature art critic.

"Well, I think it's brilliant and I couldn't be more pleased." Josephine stood with her hands on her hips, her clothes splattered with green, blue, yellow and orange paint - much like the rest of them - and admired the wall. She turned to Claire. "Did you have fun?"

Claire hadn't been expecting the question, so she paused a moment to collect her thoughts.

"I did!" Noah jumped up and down. "We should do a wall in our house!"

"Oooh!" Evan clapped his hands.

"Whoa." Claire raised a hand, stopping them in their tracks. "Hold up on that. We don't know how Daddy would feel about it."

Josephine crossed her arms loosely over her chest and smiled warmly at her daughter. "Really?"

Claire met her eye, then shrugged. "Point taken."

Thomas stood up from where he'd been sitting on the floor. "I'm stepping out for a moment."

"Good idea. We could all use some fresh air, I think."

Claire let her mother usher she and the twins out of the room, behind Thomas. The question, did she have fun, still hung unanswered, waiting for her reply. She stepped over Bear, waiting patiently outside the room, and turned around in the hallway to meet Josephine's eye.

"Yes," she said, while the boys trailed Thomas toward the backyard. "I did. More fun that I'd expected, in fact. It was liberating."

Josephine gave her a hug. "Wonderful. Baby steps."

* * * *

CHAPTER 26

C laire clenched her teeth as she tried to sew a felt patch the color of egg yolk on a piece of cloth cut to look like egg white that was supposed to end up a Halloween costume for Noah.

"Oh, man," she said, her shoulders slumped in defeat. "How the hell did I get talked into this?"

It had been Jake's idea for the costumes. He'd suggested the boys dress up as breakfast foods: bacon and eggs for Noah and pancakes and butter for Evan. Naturally, they'd loved the theme and the rest was left to Claire to figure out. Okay, in all fairness, Jake did sketch out the plans.

Noah was going to don a hat that looked like a pile of bacon and the body of his costume would be the fried egg. Evan's hat would be a bright yellow pat of butter and the body a beige pancake with a dark splash of syrup sewn onto the middle. They'd drape them placard-style over their shoulders, allowing their hands to remain free to carry their loot bags.

Claire had thought the idea a delightful way to give them original costumes. However, with just five days left until Halloween and so much left to be done, she was having serious second thoughts. And mean spirited thoughts, too.

The doorbell rang and Claire stopped sewing, thrilled to have a reason to quit. She threw down the fabric, jabbed the needle and thread back into her pin cushion and stood up from her chair with a groan.

"Doorbell!" Noah came charging into the family room from the kitchen and headed straight for the front door.

"Slow down!" Claire braced herself in case he didn't stop in time and rammed the door instead of opening it. It had happened before and she hoped he'd learned from the experience, as opposed to being doomed to repeat it.

Noah came to a halt just shy of the door, twisted the handle and flung it open. Jessica stood on the other side and his face lit up when he saw her there. "Jessica!"

She laughed when he launched himself at her and hugged her around her upper thighs. "Hey, buddy. How are you, today?"

Noah released her legs and grinned up at her. "Great! Evan and I are going to rake leaves in the backyard, then jump in them."

She nodded her approval. "Nice. I'll have to come out and see you guys in a bit, after I talk to your Mom."

"Okay!" He spun on his heel and darted back toward the kitchen, calling out to Evan even before he got there. "Jessica is here and she's going to watch us in the leaves in a bit."

Claire grinned as she listened to their excited chatter, then turned to Jessica. "Come in." She waved her into the house and asked, "What brings you to this loony bin?"

Jessica closed the front door and slipped off her shoes and jacket. "There's a rumor going around that you're finding some Halloween costumes a bit of a challenge, so I thought I'd stop by and see if you wanted any help."

Her mother. Claire would have bet money it was Josephine who had shared the information because it had been only yesterday she'd been on the phone to her, bitching about how much more work the costumes were than she had expected them to be.

She folded her arms across her chest and grinned. "I see. And, by any chance, would the source of this rumor have riotous red hair, a near constant mischievous smirk on her face and usually be seen wearing some sort of flowing skirt that looks like it was pulled out of the wardrobe of an aging hippie?"

"Nailed it in one!"

Claire laughed and Jessica joined her.

"So," Jessica said, while taking in the fabric and felt strewn across the couch, chair and floor of the family room. "Should I dare to assume she was correct?"

"God, yes." Claire unfolded her arms and she shook her head. "I should have run from the idea when Jake suggested it, but I didn't. I don't know why the heck I agreed. I suck at sewing."

Jessica grinned and rubbed her hands together. "Well then, my friend, you're in luck. Because I do not suck at sewing. In fact, I'd even go so far as to say I'm rather good at it."

"Seriously?"

"Seriously."

"Boys!" Claire called out to Evan and Noah, still finishing their snack in the kitchen. "Halloween has been saved!"

Jessica laughed as they poked their heads around the corner.

"We still have to wash our hands, Mommy," Evan reported.

"Okay, that's fine. Do it quick and come back to hear the good news."

Jessica moved some fabric on the sofa aside and sat down. Judging by the state of things, she had some work to do.

* * * *

CHAPTER 27

"Oh, my!" Josephine clapped her hands and broke into a loud whoop of laughter when she saw Noah and Evan in their Halloween costumes. "They're fantastic! Just brilliant!"

The twins grinned and giggled, pointing at each other while Bear sniffed tentatively at their garb.

"You have a bacon head," Evan said.

"You have a butter head," Noah replied.

"We're bacon and butter heads!" They sang in unison, then fell all over themselves laughing.

"Jessica is a genius," Claire stated as she handed them their candy bags; one was made to look like a syrup bottle for Noah and the other a ketchup bottle for Evan. "She went above and beyond the call of duty and even made their bags match!"

Jake grinned at his sons and pulled out his phone. "Smile for me guys!" He snapped a few photos while Noah and Evan mugged for the camera.

"So, does that mean I'm forgiven for spreading rumors?" Josephine pressed her palms together in a feeble imitation of begging.

Claire rolled her eyes. Her mother never begged for anything, she just threw caution to the wind and blazed ahead. She looked at the eager expressions on her sons' faces and nodded. "Yes. In this instance, you are one hundred percent forgiven."

Josephine threw her arms around her in a tight hug, then stepped back. "Wonderful. I'll be able to sleep tonight."

"Ha!" Claire shook her head. Please. Like her mother ever lost a wink over anything.

"Trick or treat!" Peggy's voice rang out from behind the front door.

Bear barked and Jake stopped taking photos to intercept him.

"Bear, come away," Josephine called, while Jake held open the door for his mother.

"Hey, Mom," he said, stepping around the dog. "What are you doing here? Don't you have to hand out candy at your house?"

"Only four blocks away?" Josephine muttered, under her breath, before picking Bear up into her arms.

Claire shot her a warning look.

"I told your father I wanted to stop in for a moment to make sure you were all set for your first Halloween in Boxwood Hills and…. Oh, my goodness! Look at the two of you!"

Evan and Noah grinned proudly at Peggy as she gasped over their costumes.

"They turned out well, huh?" Jake matched their smiles with his own.

"They're just adorable!" Peggy reached out to touch the fabric of the costumes. "Just so cute I could eat them up!"

Noah and Evan's smiles drooped a little.

"They're more like cool, Grandma Peggy," Noah informed her.

Evan nodded. "Or, brilliant, like Gramma said."

Josephine's eyes widened, but she kept her mouth shut.

"Well, of course they are!" Peggy said, slightly flustered. "I was getting to that, too."

"So, is that why you stopped by?" Jake asked. "Because you didn't have to leave Dad at the helm. We were planning to stop at your place."

Peggy waved her hand dismissively. "Oh, I know that. I just wanted to pop over in case there was anything else you needed help with." She smiled pleasantly at Claire. "Maybe some extra candy, if you didn't have time to get enough? Or a break from answering the door, if you needed it?"

Claire narrowed her eyes and took a deep, steadying breath. The lack of sincerity was staggering. "Thanks, Peggy. I'm sure I'll be just fine."

"And," Josephine cut in, her eyes glittering dangerously. "If she runs out of candy she can always hand out those small, single serving liquor bottles. The kids might not appreciate them, but their parents would!"

Peggy's eyebrows shot up on her forehead as Josephine threw her head back and laughed raucously. Jake laughed, too, which made the boys' laugh despite not understanding the joke.

"Okay, then." Claire moved things along. "I think it's time to send these breakfast foods out into the neighborhood, don't you?"

"I'll walk out with you," Peggy said, tightly, her face set in a frown as she turned to leave.

Claire couldn't be bothered to pat her down. She'd been doing it for too many years. All that mattered right then were her sons. "Okay, you guys." She pulled them into a gentle embrace so as not to disturb their costumes. "You have fun and remember to pick up Sophia."

"We will!" Noah gave her a kiss on the cheek before he stepped out of her embrace.

Evan imitated Noah, then reached out for Jake's hand. "Ready, Daddy."

Claire waved them off into the night, closed the door, then turned to her mother. "You are a terrible person, do you know that? Terrible. Did you see Peggy's face?"

Josephine widened her eyes and placed Bear on a blanket on the sofa. "I don't know what you're talking about."

Claire shook her head and tried to keep the amusement in her voice hidden as she began to tear open bags of candy to pour into a bowl by the door. "Terrible."

Josephine giggled and shrugged, then reached out to steal a fun-sized chocolate bar.

* * * *

Peggy outwardly smiled at Noah and Evan's running commentary as she walked down the block with them and Jake. What she was doing inwardly was another story. That Josephine! What was wrong with the woman that she seemed compelled to always say the most bothersome things, especially when the little ones were around? Did she not realize the influence she was exerting by her off-hand remarks? What if the boys turned into drinkers, just because she'd made it seem funny? And, why didn't Claire temper her mother? Did she only have time now for picking out new outfits?

"Okay, this is our turn." Jake pointed at the street into the neighboring crescent.

"We're going to pick up Sophia," Noah offered, helpfully.

Peggy nodded. "I look forward to seeing you at our house in a little while."

"Bye, Grandma Peggy." Evan waved and started off down the street, Noah at his side.

Jake grinned at the two of them, bacon and eggs and pancakes and syrup moseying along, not a care in the world except for loading up on candy. "I'd better keep up with them," he said. "Don't want to chance them running into a knife and fork."

Peggy tittered. Jake was so funny. So appropriately funny. Why Josephine couldn't take a page from his book, she'd never know.

"You'll be okay on your own from here?" He looked around at the streets, already starting to fill up with kids and their parents.

Peggy patted his arm. "I'll be just fine, dear. I'll scoot home and hope your father hasn't already eaten all of the treats."

Jake gave her a hug, then set off quickly to catch up with his sons.

Now, that's the example a mother should be setting, Peggy thought smartly, before straightening her shoulders and marching determinedly ahead into the evening.

* * * *

"Merrily, merrily, merrily, merrily, life is but a dream!" Josephine clapped her hands in time to the rhythm as she finished singing along with the group of children at Claire's front door. She tossed candy treats into their outstretched bags and waved them off as they left the stoop.

Claire, lounging on her overstuffed armchair, silently marveled at her energy. Granted, it could have been the numerous snack sized candy bars she'd been 'sneaking', but Claire knew better. For as long as she could remember, her mother had always had bucket loads of energy.

"Weren't they great?" Josephine grinned from ear to ear as she flopped down on the couch beside Bear. He wagged his tail, sighed and went back to sleep.

"Fabulous," Claire agreed. "And you weren't so bad yourself."

Josephine chuckled. "Next time you'll have to join in on the harmony. You have a lovely voice."

"Wine?" Claire pulled herself out of her chair and went over to their makeshift wine cabinet beside the entertainment unit. "We have a lovely merlot."

"You had me at wine." Josephine fluffed her hair, then reached over to run a loving hand over Bear's soft head.

Claire pulled out two glasses hanging from a rack on the wall above the wine cabinet, grabbed the merlot and brought them over to the coffee table. "Things are quieting down," she began, before being interrupted by the text sound on her phone.

"Here, let me." Josephine took the wine and glasses from her grasp.

"Thanks."

"Is it Jake?" Josephine swiftly opened the wine bottle and began to pour.

"Uh-huh." Claire picked up her phone and read the words on the screen. "He and the boys have dropped off Sophia and Rosa and are on their way home."

"Ahh, yes. Rosa." Josephine placed the bottle on the table and picked up one of the glasses.

Claire sent a quick reply, then put down her phone and returned to the armchair. She watched her mother smelling the wine in her glass and sighed. She might as well ask. "What does that mean, 'ahh, Rosa'?"

Josephine took a sip of wine and smiled. "Oh, nothing. I just think the lovely woman might be wise to set her sights in a direction that doesn't point toward Thomas."

"Oh, God." Claire picked up her glass and took a large swallow.

"What?" Josephine raised her eyebrows. "What's that for?"

"You didn't even know the man existed until we moved into the neighborhood—"

"Or, did I?" Josephine cut in, coyly.

Claire pointed her index finger at her, "No, you didn't. And now you're making waves all over the place."

Josephine rolled her eyes.

"Don't roll your eyes at me." Claire settled back into her chair, a self-righteous expression on her face. "You know I'm right."

"She didn't own him." Josephine took a swallow of wine, then placed her glass back on the coffee table. "It's not like I stole him away, or something."

Claire shot her a withering look.

"It's not! He's a grown man and whatever his decisions, I'm certainly not swaying them."

"So, you're telling me you haven't done anything at all to try and take his focus away from Rosa?"

"Absolutely not." Josephine tucked her feet underneath herself on the cushion and added, "Besides, don't you think that, if he'd been interested, he would have done something already?"

Claire shrugged. "I suppose."

"No, whatever he does, or doesn't do, are his choices." She reached out for her wine glass and lifted it in a toast. "I'm just enjoying the *ride*."

Claire closed her eyes and groaned.

* * * *

CHAPTER 28

Peggy flipped the pages in her cookbook, agitation making them snap with each turn. She was trying to concentrate upon the recipes, but was having a difficult time of it. It was almost Thanksgiving, for goodness sake, and she and Earl had barely set eyes on Jake and his family since Halloween.

Alright, she'd admit, perhaps she was exaggerating ever so slightly. They had had dinner at their house twice in the past month, but *still*. Claire was going to have to accept, once and for all, that things were different. Now that they lived in Boxwood Hills, things had changed for good. They were a family that lived near each other and that meant more get togethers. Period.

She didn't like what was happening with Claire. Not one bit. Since their return home, she was acting... unglued. Instead of the patient, dedicated mother she had finally become in the city - it had been so *trying* to watch her learn how to do things correctly - her daughter-in-law had been steadily reverting back to the person she'd been when Jake had first met her. It was grotesque.

Peggy blamed the mother. That woman was a bad influence. It was no wonder Claire was doing things like getting hairstyles and new clothes, going to yoga and parties, when Josephine kept praising her actions. What was next? Was she going to ditch her children all together and start doing something really foolish, like that glass thing she used to do?

And that whole *episode* nonsense, Peggy thought as she got up from the table to fetch her tea steeping on the kitchen counter. Why, any sane person could see it was the stress of letting things slide and not being an attentive mother that had caused Claire to snap.

She carried her cup to the table and settled back into her chair. Enough was enough. Once she had finished her tea, she was going to march over to Jake's and set things straight.

* * * *

CHAPTER 29

Claire scooped coffee beans from a canister on her counter and enjoyed the quiet. It was a rare treat for her to be solo in the kitchen and she was looking forward to nothing but the sound of the coffee pot working its magic.

A sharp rap on the backdoor made her jump and she managed to call out, "Just a sec," before the knob turned and Peggy strode purposefully into the room.

Nuts, she thought. She knew she should have parked in the garage.

"You're here." Peggy's voice was heavily accusing, instead of pleased.

Claire blinked and wracked her brain for a reply that wasn't the obvious. "Yes," was all she could find.

"I saw your van on the driveway, so I figured I'd try my luck and here you are." Peggy tugged on the bottom of her sensible, white blouse; straightening it. "I've called. A lot. Maybe you haven't had time to check your messages, being so busy with *other* things and all, but I just want to state for the record that I've been trying to get ahold of you so that I can have a visit with my grandsons. *If* that's not too much to ask, I might add."

Claire sighed. She knew very well Peggy had called. Numerous times. She just hadn't felt up to dealing with the woman, so she'd been avoiding calling her back.

"Are they here?"

Claire shook her head. "No, sorry. They're playing with Sophia today."

Peggy's face wrinkled, as though she'd smelled something unpleasant. "Figures."

"Pardon me?" Claire cocked her head.

Peggy shrugged her shoulders. "It's just that it seems I have to constantly badger you people just to interact with my own family."

"Now wait a minute." Claire held up her hand, her heart beating faster. She had to stop this in its tracks.

"I mean, are you and Jake really so busy you can't take the time for a simple phone call? Maybe offer an invitation to dinner? Or, are you too busy with your *life*, to be a part of your family."

Claire took a breath. "Peggy," she said, gritting her teeth. "We have you and Earl over plenty."

"Oh, I don't know." Peggy sniffed. "I have friends who have nothing to talk about except how much time they spend at their kid's houses. In fact—"

"Peggy!"

Peggy shut up, her eyes wide. Her daughter-in-law had never raised her voice to her. Never. She wasn't sure what to do, or say.

"Now, listen up." Claire walked over to the table, pulled out a chair and sat down. "Ever since my... *episode*, I've been working on reducing the things that bring me stress and relearning how to handle the things I can't get rid of."

Peggy frowned.

"So, if that means I'm not throwing out dinner invitations left right and center, it's only because—"

"Are you trying to say Earl and I cause stress?" Peggy folded her arms across her chest and glared. "Because I'd like to be the first to remind you—"

"Stop it!"

Peggy's eyes widened for a second time and her mouth nearly fell open.

"You don't seem to listen, Peggy." Claire reached out to grasp the edge of the table to steady herself. "You are stressful, yes." When Peggy looked about to offer her opinion, Claire blazed forward. "And, up until now, I haven't said anything."

"Well, I don't think—"

"It doesn't matter what you think, only what *I* think." Claire's voice grew stronger as she spoke. "You have always had an opinion, or comment, about more or less every darn thing in our lives and I've held my tongue. Well, no more. I'm not like you. After four years of pushing myself to be perfect, whatever that is, I've finally realized it isn't serving me. I have more to offer than... clean laundry! I'm done with hearing about trivial things like how I could spend more time presoaking the boys' clothes to brighten them. They're not even fully five and couldn't care less."

"I wasn't thinking of *them*." Peggy sniffed and refolded her tightly crossed arms.

"I'm also done with your running commentary about how I keep the house. The boys have toys, often they don't get put away, deal with it." Claire stood up and strode back across the kitchen to retrieve her coffee beans. "*And* I'm really tired of hearing cracks about how I make coffee and at what time of day I chose to drink it."

Peggy blanched.

"Basically, Peggy, things have to change. They *have to*. Otherwise, you're going to find we're not available to you and Earl very often anymore." Claire stood solidly on her feet, heart beating rapidly, but not panicking. It felt good.

Peggy was at a loss for words. A first, as far as Claire could remember.

"Now, if you don't mind, I'm busy." Claire walked over to the backdoor and placed a hand on the handle.

Peggy released her tightly wrapped arms and straightened the hem of her blouse with a sharp jerk. She gave Claire a curt nod and walked over to the door. When Claire twisted the knob and held it open, she stepped through the doorway and said, "Fine. Goodbye."

Claire closed the door gently behind her, slumped against the frame and exhaled a breath she'd been holding.

From around the corner, Josephine appeared, smiling in admiration. She clapped lightly. "Congratulations and welcome back."

* * * *

CHAPTER 30

The telephone rang in the family room while Claire shoved yet another load of clothes into her washing machine. It seemed like all she did was feed the damned thing and, yet, the pile didn't appear to get any smaller.

"I'm coming, I'm coming," she called out, just before she heard Evan answering.

"Hello?" went his high pitched voice. "Oh, hi, Grandma Peggy."

Claire cringed while she poured liquid detergent into the washer. It had been four days since she and Peggy's altercation and she'd been wondering if she'd finally break the silence.

"Yes, he is," Evan said.

Claire cocked an ear as she closed the detergent dispenser and pressed the buttons to set her cycle.

"Okay. I'll find him."

Oh, boy. Claire braced herself for what she knew was to come next.

"Daddyyyyy! Telephone for youuuu! It's Grandma Peggy!"

The water began to rush into the machine and, despite her nerves, Claire grinned. The idea of Peggy holding the phone at arm's length when Evan's ear splitting bellow came through the receiver was amusing.

Footsteps from upstairs, then on the stairs, signaled Jake's arrival. "Hello?"

Claire stood stock still. What to do? Did she leave the laundry room and venture into the family room? Sneak into the kitchen? Stay put?

"Hey, Mom."

She chose to stay put. The other options held the possibility she'd be interrupted in her eavesdropping.

"Uh-huh. Sure."

Claire could see Jake in her mind's eye, nodding and possibly running his fingers through his dark hair as he listened to Peggy.

"Right. Okay."

Claire rolled her eyes. So far, the conversation was anything but riveting.

"Alright, sounds good. I'll talk to Claire and we'll call you back."

Uh-oh. Her name. That couldn't be good. She suddenly felt trapped by the walls of the laundry room and quickly shot into the kitchen. She pulled open the door of the fridge, hiding behind its wide expanse, as Jake walked into the room.

"Hey, Hon?"

She took a bracing breath, affixed a pleasant smile to her face and closed the fridge door. "Hmm?"

"That was my Mom on the phone." He reached out and grabbed an apple from a bowl on the table.

"Oh? Did the phone ring? I was doing laundry, so...."

"Yeah, Evan picked it up." He grinned. "He must have nearly blast her ear off when he yelled for me to come to the phone."

Claire snickered, glad for the opportunity to do so out loud. "We're still working on that part of phone etiquette."

"Did something happen between you two?" He took a large bite of his apple.

Claire stopped giggling and clearly her throat. "Me and Evan? No, not that I can think of."

"No." He swallowed and laughed. "You and my Mom."

"Umm…." Claire broke eye contact and fidgeted with her silver, butterfly necklace.

"She said she'd had a conversation with you a few days ago and I gotta be honest, she seemed really pleased about it. I don't remember the last time she sounded so chipper."

Claire's eyes widened. Okaaay, that wasn't what she'd been expecting to hear.

"She said you guys had a great talk and cleared the air and she realizes you've had too much on your plate." He took a breath, while Claire just stared in shock. "And then she said she and my Dad *would love* to host Thanksgiving, if you're okay with that."

"Wow." Claire blinked and digested what he'd said.

"That's an understatement." He put down his apple and pulled her into a hug. "Whatever you two talked about, I'm sayin' hallelujah. And if you need to talk about it again, go for it."

Inhaling the fresh, crisp scent of apple on his breath, Claire hugged him back.

* * * *

CHAPTER 31

"Oh, I see them!" Josephine waved her hands excitedly at the group gathered around her. "Jake's parking the car."

"What are we going to do, again?" Travis cuddled Bear to his chest and frowned, trying to remember.

Jessica and Kevin laughed quietly, while Gerry grinned and gave his shoulder a gentle shove. "We'll say surprise and let Jake explain the rest."

"Shhh!" Josephine said, and they all fell silent as the door opened.

"What is this place?" Claire asked, before stopping in shock in the doorway.

"SURPRISE!"

* * * *

Claire looked at the faces of her friends and family, speechless. They were all staring at her, huge grins on their faces.

"Mommy, Mommy!"

Claire laughed as Noah and Evan barreled through the sea of legs to arrive before her, slightly out of breath.

"What is this place?" she repeated, looking around with confusion at the cavernous space. "And why are you all yelling surprise?"

The group laughed and Jake took her hand. "This *place*, is yours."

"Pardon?" Claire blinked, not understanding. "Mine? Why is it mine?"

Jake gestured to Travis and Gerry as he spoke. "Our brilliant real estate friends did the deal and you're now the proud owner of this soon-to-be glassworks studio."

"It's all yours, Mommy!" Noah hugged Claire around her thighs as she tried to wrap her head around what Jake was telling her.

"And, it's big!" Evan's eyes were wide with excitement as he tugged on Noah to follow him. They took off, running around the concrete floor in large laps like excited puppies.

"We have great plans drawn up to separate the space into two areas, one for selling and one for working," Travis told her. He set Bear down and the dog ran off after Noah and Evan.

Gerry nodded. "And, all it will take is some input from you to make sure it's done exactly how you want."

"Are you serious?" Claire looked Jake in the eye.

"As a panic attack," he told her, a small grin curling his lips.

Josephine broke ranks and came forward to hug her daughter. "It's time, Claire. You have a lot to offer and it's time you did."

Claire hugged her back, then asked, "How on Earth—"

"It was Jessica's idea." Josephine reached out and pulled Jessica forward.

She twinkled. "I'm a huge fan of your work."

Claire laughed and hugged her. "This is too much for words," she said, softly, into her ear. "Thank you."

Jessica gave her another quick squeeze, before she pulled back. "Oh, don't thank me. Your husband is the real mastermind behind all of this. I just gave the suggestion and he ran with it."

"I had help," Jake said, determined to give credit where it was due. "Travis and Gerry are a serious force to be reckoned with."

Claire beamed at them. She never would have thought, when she'd first met them at Jessica's hair salon, she'd be so lucky as to one day call them friends.

"And I'll happily watch the boys anytime you need to work." Peggy clasped her hands together, looking slightly nervous and hopeful at the same time. "You just say the word and I'm there."

Warmth ran through Claire. Since their no-holds-barred conversation, Peggy had been trying so hard to get things back on track. She smiled kindly at her mother-in-law. "Thank you. The boys are lucky to have you."

Peggy brightened and Josephine patted Claire on the arm. "Good for you," she whispered, before turning back to the group. "Okay, let's get this celebration started! Thomas, my good man, you brought the sound system. Music please!"

Claire reached for Jake's hand, holding him back as the rest went over to a long banquet table offering all sorts of goodies. She looked up into his eyes as music began playing and said, "How can I thank you? I don't know where to start."

He pulled her into his arms, kissed her gently, and a slow lascivious grin spread across his face as he remembered her glass blowing days. "We'll think of something."

THE END

ABOUT THE AUTHOR

Kathleen began storytelling in grade school. She has many fond memories of passing summer afternoons out on the swing-set in her childhood backyard, creating tales to entertain her neighborhood friends. Many years later, too many talk about without seeming rude/nosy, Kathleen has traveled to a new backyard with a breathtaking mountain view and channeled her imagination to the pages of her novels.

She spends her free time with her beloved husband, adored son and sweet dog. Often she tells them stories and they always laugh in all of the correct places. She's lucky and she knows it.

Connect with Kathleen

Website: kathleenkole.com

Facebook: facebook.com/KathleenKoleAuthor

Twitter: @kathleenkole